THE EXPLOITS OF

Edna & Gertie

ENDORSEMENTS

The Exploits of Edna and Gertie

Readers will cheer for Edna from page one. Her energetic personality radiates from every paragraph. Sparks fly between these two senior girlfriends as the characters jump off the page in living color. Keep turning pages to find out what Edna *didn't* tell Gertie.

—Tracie Heskett, author of inspirational fiction, curriculum, and Bible studies

Remember Lucy and Ethel? Janet Evanovich's Grandma Mazur? Those feisty ladies have nothing on Edna and Gertie. You'll laugh, shake your head, wipe tears away, and sigh audibly over these Golden Girls' antics. Life is short—laughter is good. Get to know Edna and Gertie—but hang on tight!

—Dawn Shipman, award-winning author of *Kingdom Lost*, Book 1 in The Lost Stones of Argonia series.

Edna and Gertie are fascinating characters with contrasting personalities, who somehow became best friends. The ladies careen from one mishap to another, but somehow find a way to make the best of things. The book is a humorous romp with a solid and touching friendship at its core.

—Susan Maas, author of middle grade novels, *Picture Imperfect* and *Abbie's Woods*: *Defending the Nest*.

I laughed out loud while reading Jan Pierce's *The Exploits of Edna and Gertie*. The leading characters are a refreshing odd couple whose adventures are both entertaining and inspiring. Jan's writing is fast-paced, humorous, and full of surprises! Kudos for a boisterous-yet-endearing take on the senior years. You'll love following the fun—and the mishaps—of these two spry, spunky, and golden-aged best friends!

—Leslie Gould, #1 best-selling and Christy Award-winning author

THE EXPLOITS OF
Edna & Gertie

JAN PIERCE

ELK LAKE PUBLISHING INC
PUBLISHING THE POSITIVE
Plymouth, Massachusetts

COPYRIGHT NOTICE

Cover and Interior Design: Kelly Artieri, Derinda Babcock

Editor(s): Jeannie Leach, Cristel Phelps, Deb Haggerty

PUBLISHED BY: Elk Lake Publishing, Inc., 35 Dogwood Drive, Plymouth, MA 02360, 2022

Library Cataloging Data

Names: Pierce, Jan (Jan Pierce)

The Adventures of Edna & Gertie / Jan Pierce

298 p. 23cm × 15cm (9in × 6 in.)

ISBN-13: 978-1-64949-593-8 (paperback) | 978-1-64949-594-5 (trade paperback) | 978-1-64949-595-2 (e-book)

Key Words: humor; senior citizens; friendship; adventures; cruises; Las Vegas; dude ranch

Library of Congress Control Number: 2022941255 Fiction

DEDICATION

Dedicated to my husband, Roger.
We're keeping the promise.

ACKNOWLEDGMENTS

Soon after I retired from a long career in teaching, I attended a seminar on "The Power of Story." Several attendees encouraged me to follow up on my interest in writing by attending an Oregon Christian Writers Conference. The minute I walked in, I knew I'd found my people.

So, thank you to everyone who works hard for OCW to make all the conferences burst with information. Thanks also to LeAnn Beebe who recommended I read *On Writing Well* by William Zinnser and to Barclay Press for publishing my first submission, a set of devotionals for *Fruit of the Vine*. A special thank you to my critique groups over the years. I learn something new every time we work together.

And thanks to my family who show an interest in my writing and sometimes even read it.

Jan Pierce

EDNA & GERTIE DO VEGAS

CHAPTER ONE

Edna Gratzer retrieved another pink, scoop-necked T-shirt from her closet and tossed it on the growing pile of things to pack. "Can't have too much pink," she muttered and flattened the T-shirt on the bed to admire it.

Sassy Senior Citizen, scripted in glitzy rhinestones, sparkled up at her. Edna grinned. The infomercial hadn't lied. These T's screamed sexy. "Hot daaang." She dragged out the word. "Las Vegas, here I come." Being old enough to remember hula hoops was no reason to skimp on her wardrobe. She'd ordered five T's, all the same model, in a bevy of rainbow pastels—light pink, dark pink, lavender, aqua, and mint green to go with her black polyester slacks. They looked good enough to eat.

She grabbed the cosmetic case from her dresser and, as she did, glanced at the photos of Fred and Sam, two bookends to her love life. She'd lost Fred to a heart attack and Sam to a blonde twenty years his junior. Well, no time to fret. She'd loved them both. Now she was filed under "available."

Back to business. She had to finish packing and drop off her kitty at the pet hotel. The Pet-o-Rama had agreed to make an exception and keep Big Bertha for the entire weekend *if* they could keep her kenneled. The last time BB had stayed for an overnighter there had been ... incidents. When it came to other cats, BB was rather territorial. Edna had paid for the vet expenses, but Rose, the proud owner of the Pet-o-Rama, was understandably leery.

Edna glanced at her Timex. "Holy cow, I gotta get a move on." She grabbed a T, folded it in thirds, and rolled it. Her ma, rest her soul, may not have done everything right, but rolling clothes into tight wiener-like bundles was hands-down the best way to cram a closetful of clothes into one piece of luggage.

The whole pile lay rolled and stashed in ten minutes flat. She poked in the edges of the fabrics and zipped up the bag with a satisfied, "There."

Big Bertha hated enclosed spaces, so to avoid hissing and scratching, Edna crept up behind her and wrapped her in a fluffy towel to soften the blow then stuffed her into the pet carrier. As she reached for the doorknob, her phone rang. It could go to voice mail—people never got tired of her message that began with George Strait's "All My Exes Live in Texas," and ended with Edna's rendition of the song. She was, after all, a born and bred Amarillo, Texas, gal.

Wait, that might be Gertie. She plopped BB's carrier down and checked her phone. Sure enough. She speed-dialed her BFF.

"Gertie? You ready?"

"Just about." Her voice sounded faraway.

"Me too. Are you as excited as I am? I'm taking Big Bertha to Rose's and then I'll meet you at the Walmart. They said they'll pick us up right by the Garden Center doors."

"I still think this trip sounds too good to be true. And you know what they say ... "

Edna paused and clenched her jaw. "Don't pour any rain on my parade, Gertie Larsen. I found this deal, and I couldn't pass it up. Two nights and three sun-soaked days at the MGM with all our meals covered. The whole trip is free to seniors. What's not to like? All we pay is seventy-nine bucks for a round-trip bus ride. They've got those plush reclinable seats, cupholders, a john at the back—the whole nine yards. Trust me, you won't miss your Hallmark shows. We're going to Vegas, baby!"

Edna parked at the back of the lot where overnight campers and long-distance truckers hung out. She dragged her suitcase along behind her with one hand and carried a bulging Fiesta Foods grocery bag with the other, struggling past row after row of parked cars. But at least no one would tow her while she was gone.

She looked around for Gertie and spied her a few lanes over. She walked straight and prim toward the Garden Center and pulled a small postage-stamp suitcase along behind her.

Edna sighed. She hadn't told Gertie everything about this trip. She had some explaining to do, and Gertie wasn't going to like it. Her bosom buddy preferred things straightforward and safe. Boring. *But I like a little edge to life—something to keep the old heart pumping.* Edna shifted the grocery bag, trying not to squish the banana bread, then grabbed the handle of her suitcase again and marched along toward trouble.

As she neared the sidewalk, she sidestepped a teen-aged couple who had exited the Garden Center door, he with the bright blue Mohawk and her in her jammie bottoms. The girls arrived at the pick-up point at the same time.

She heaved a big "Whew" and set her suitcase and the bulging bag on the sidewalk. "Hey, girlfriend. Won't this be fun?" Edna put a chirp in her voice and smiled her brightest, toothy smile.

"Edna, I don't know how I let you talk me into these things. I had a garden club luncheon tomorrow and a potluck dinner after church on Sunday and ... My word! What did you do to your hair?"

"Nothing. It's grown a mite long, is all. I'd made an appointment at the Clip Joint to get it cut, but when this special deal came up, I canceled it. Maybe I should try to tame it down until I can get a trim."

"A trim! You'll need a combine to get that mess in shape. You look like you stuck your finger in a light socket." Gertie's agitation showed itself in her usually calm face. A muscle twitched in her jaw, and her mouth pursed up in a tight bunch.

"So, what if my spiky do has grown a little long? I'm not going to let you ruin this trip. When the nice, young man phoned, he told me the whole story. We get a luxurious ride in a top-of-the-line Greyhound, and two nights at the MGM Hotel with all our meals included. It's a Senior Special to encourage more of us to visit Las Vegas. I jumped at the chance. You should be thankful I thought of my best friend and got you included in the deal. Don't worry if you get a few phone calls later. The young man was only doing his job, and you can always say no to whatever they offer."

Gertie froze, her eyes burned hot and bright. She reminded Edna of a cartoon character about to shoot steam out of her ears, but the words came brittle as ice. "You gave him my phone number?"

"Sure, it's not like it's a secret. It's right there in the phone book anyway." Edna raised her chin in a show of bravado.

"I don't believe you. Don't you read the AARP bulletins? Don't you know about phone scams? Oh, Edna, this sounds like a disaster in the making. Do you realize how many hours it is from here to Vegas? We're going to ride all night and arrive exhausted."

"The bus should be here any minute. They said four o'clock sharp. We can pretend we're on a luxury airliner on an overnight flight. *Sit back and enjoy.* We'll get there bright and early in the morning, check in, eat a gourmet breakfast, and hit the slots. Oh, girlfriend, I feel lucky."

"You'll be lucky if I don't snatch you baldheaded," Gertie muttered.

"Now, Gertie—"

The roar of a gigantic engine and the whoosh of the door folding open drowned out any more argument. A uniformed driver, middle-aged with a sizable paunch, climbed down the steps. With his wrinkled shirt and his hat at an angle, he looked harried. He never made eye contact or spoke a word as he helped them stow their luggage in the hold. They were the only two to board at this stop, but when they climbed the stairs, they found themselves looking into dim, sleepy eyes—lots of them.

"How long have you folks been on the bus?" Gertie asked an especially disheveled woman.

"Seems like forever, but just since this morning." The woman held a basket on her lap with one hand stroking the fur of a shaky, rheumy-eyed chihuahua. "Little Pepe is about tuckered out. We'll get there sometime tomorrow morning. Can't be soon enough for me. Pepe isn't getting enough potty breaks either. I hope this trip doesn't back things up for him."

Edna gave Gertie a shove to hasten her trip down the aisle. "There's two seats together back there on the right. Grab 'em."

"I'll sit by the window. You can sit in that aisle for umpteen hours. See how luxurious that seems." Gertie's face was flushed as she flopped down by the window.

"No problem. And don't be so huffy. Before this trip is over, you're going to have the time of your life. You'll see."

Gertie rested her head against the seat and closed her eyes. "Oh, Lord, what have I done?" She took several deep breaths.

"Calm down, my friend," Edna said and flashed a smile. "Listen. They're playing my favorite ... George Strait." She tapped her big foot in time to "The Fireman."

Gertie let out a small moan.

Edna lay back in her reclined seat and closed her eyes. A flutter of excitement shot through her. *Can't wait to see the lights of Vegas.* She opened her eyes and ventured a peek in Gertie's direction. There she sat, body rigid, with a tight, scrunched-up face.

"Come on, Gertie, don't be mad. Relax and have some fun for a change. You haven't done anything exciting since we got home from the Tuscany Tour."

"That's because I haven't recovered from it yet. I still get the shivers when I think of that Ramon guy you took up with. You're lucky he wasn't an ax murderer."

Edna waggled her eyebrows. "I get the shivers when I think of him too. Hey, want some banana bread? I wasn't sure about meals on the trip, so I brought a lot of snacks. I got Big Hunks, cheesy puffs, and canned potato chips too."

"I'll take a slice of banana bread, I guess."

"That's the ticket. Let's have a little picnic, and then, maybe we can get some sleep. Doesn't this bus ride nice? Exactly like the young man said."

"The bus is fine—it's the young man I'd like to throttle."

"What about *free* don't you appreciate, Gertie?"

Gertie sighed, turned in her seat, and rested her head against the window. "Nothing is free these days. There's a catch somewhere and probably a great big fat one. But now that I'm here, we might as well try to have fun."

"That's the spirit."

"All I can say is Donald would be fit to be tied if he could see the escapades I get into with you. You're a terrible influence on me." Gertie nibbled her banana bread.

Edna chomped a large bite out of her slice. "Well, Donald—may he rest in peace—is not here. We are. More cheese puffs?"

Edna strained her eyes trying to read the hands on her Timex. Only ten-thirty. Gertie was all sprawled out, coat thrown over her chest to act as a blanket. The peaceful countenance on her face as she slept touched Edna's heart, rendering it soft and motherly toward her best friend who still missed her Donald. She pulled the coat up to better cover Gertie's shoulder. *You need to loosen up and have some fun, my friend.* Gertie might be a stick-in-the-mud, but she meant the world to Edna. *I swear, that woman can sleep anywhere. Wish I could. I'm too keyed up to nod off.*

She leaned back and closed her eyes again. The whole bus had quieted around eight-thirty. *Bunch of duds. I'll bet not a one of 'em is ready for a good time.* She counted backward from one hundred but was still wide awake at zero. "Maybe another little snack would help." She rifled through the grocery bag and found a Big Hunk, remembering to chew on the right side. *These babies can pull the molars right out of your head.*

With the rattle of the bag, Gertie shifted and sank lower into the seat. Her head rested on Edna's shoulder. Edna managed to unwrap the big rectangle of rock-hard candy and sank her front teeth in slow and steady. She pulled the bar away from her mouth and watched it stretch like taffy. "Umm. Good." She finished the bar and settled back carefully so as not to waken Gertie.

Maybe now she could get some shut-eye. *I wonder when I should tell her about the Elvis contest.*

CHAPTER TWO

Edna awoke to the screeching of brakes and the smell of burning rubber. Several of the other passengers stood in the aisle with their hands to their hearts. Little Pepe was barking like crazy.

"Nothing to worry about, folks." The driver's voice blared over the intercom. "We had a little aggressive driving situation. Someone must have been in a hurry to get into those casinos." He laughed a deep, throaty laugh.

"My goodness, Edna. That scared the life out of me." Gertie's usually perfect coiffure was flat on the right side of her head. Her hands were tightly clamped to both arm rests in a death grip.

"Good morning to you too." Edna settled back in her chair and caught her breath. "Whew, what a way to wake up."

"Are we there?"

"You can see as much as I can. We're in a city—that's for sure. Looks like the industrial part of town. I can't wait to see all the glitz and glamour. The Strip, with all the lights." Edna glanced at her watch. "It's nearly six a.m., so this must be the outskirts of the city. Did you sleep well?"

Gertie ran her fingers through the matted part of her hair and stretched. "I guess I must have. Don't remember a thing. My stomach is rumbling though. Banana bread isn't much of a dinner."

"I hear ya. I'm starving too. The nice, young man on the phone said the buffets here are amazing—all you can eat and one tempting treat after another." Edna took a quick and discreet sniff beneath her armpit. "We have to check in first though. I need to put on a fresh T. I expect they'll have room service if we want it, and maybe I can send these clothes out to the laundry."

The bus slowed and came to a halt. The gears ground and innards whined as if the entire vehicle were as tired as its occupants. Edna half-stood and leaned over Gertie to get a look out the window. "Must be making a stop before we get into town. Maybe Pepe needs a bathroom break."

They were parked at the back of a parking lot with a used car lot on one side of them and a Quik Stop grocery on the other. Edna eyed a pawn shop sign past the used cars.

At the front of the lot was a long row of parking spaces, empty except for three older-model vehicles.

"Hey, Mister," a male passenger called out. "Where the heck are we?"

The driver hauled himself out of his seat, stretched, and turned to face the passengers. "Welcome to Las Vegas, folks. Hope you enjoyed the ride. We've got a nice, sunny day ahead—plenty of time to enjoy the city and all its sights. I'll pick you up right here at this same location on Sunday afternoon—four sharp. Don't be late. It's a long walk home." He offered another tentative laugh.

The passengers sat in stunned silence. The questions popped up like kernels of popcorn.

"What?"

"Where's the MGM?"

"Is this some kind of joke?"

One woman gave a wail and said, "My daughter said this was a hoax. I'll never live it down."

Edna stood to her full five foot nine and belted out her words. "Okay, mister," she growled. "Give us the straight scoop. Where the heck are we, and where is the Las Vegas Strip?"

"Listen, folks. I don't have anything to do with the arrangements for this trip. I do my job and drive the bus. I can tell you from experience that some of the folks are a teensy bit disappointed when they first get here, but by the end of the weekend, they've enjoyed themselves and look forward to the ride home.

"I'll *bet* they're ready to go home," Gertie hissed.

A general stir of disgruntled voices rumbled through the bus. The driver spoke again with more oomph to his voice. "Now, folks. This here's your hotel. It's called the MGM Too. Like in also, not the number. You'll roll your bags to the front of the lot, go on around the side of the hotel building and enter on the other side. Your manager will meet you and assign your rooms. So, have a great time, and I'll see you Sunday at four.

Edna sat back down. "Well, this is a fine kettle of fish. Gertie, you were right, I'd like to strangle that young man with my own hands. Here I was all ready for the MGM and a nice luxurious weekend. And I hadn't even had time to tell you about the Elvis Impersonator contest."

Gertie's face crumpled. She looked as if she might break down and cry right there on the bus.

Edna patted her shoulder. "Hey, Gertie, it's all right. Let's get our bags and find out how bad it is. Maybe it looks better from the front."

Gertie sniffled. "It sure couldn't look much worse." She gathered her purse and jacket while Edna scrambled to organize the grocery bag so she could manage it with one hand. "Cheese puffs don't look so appetizing at six in the morning, do they?"

Gertie glared at her friend but didn't answer. Edna pushed out into the aisle, eager to escape the confines of the narrow, dark bus. A bit of fresh air would be welcome. She stood on tiptoes. "Hey, let's get a move on up there."

The passengers shuffled down the aisle, a few giving the driver a final piece of their minds as they passed him.

He stood, head down, and scuffed his feet back and forth. He finally turned and made his descent to the pavement.

Edna stepped carefully as they reached the stairs. Wouldn't do to turn her ankle again as she had on the Tuscany trip. They followed the straggling group of seniors and took their place in the luggage line. "Shoot, Gertie. I almost feel sorry for the guy. He's only trying to make a living. It's not his fault that we're at the MGM Too instead of the real one."

"Let's look at the rooms before we get all peace, love, dove." Gertie had seen the Woodstock movie and sometimes surprised her friends with a smattering of hippie rhetoric.

The air was cool and dry and promised a scorcher later in the day. The driver pulled out each suitcase and lined them up in a row. Edna spied the pink bow on the handle of her bag and pounced on it. Gertie found her mini-bag as well, and they joined the bedraggled line of MGM Too guests. Every head was down, every shoulder drooped.

"We've only been in Vegas ten minutes and we're already losers," Edna groused.

As they rounded the corner of the MGM Too, the line of seniors came to an abrupt halt. Luggage pieces clanked together in a series of collisions.

"What now?" Edna used her considerable height to report to the seniors in proximity. "Looks like the guy up front can't get the door open. There. It took two of them to pull it open and move their suitcases out of the way. Now we're moving."

One by one the passengers made their way through the double doors, wrangling their luggage as they went.

Gertie took a deep breath. "At least we don't have to walk through one of those automated circle-door things like at the airport. I got my suitcase stuck in one of those last time I went to see the kids. I was on one side of the door and my bag was on the other. Put the whole thing out of commission. By the time they called a maintenance man to rescue my bag, I missed my flight and had to wait two hours—"

"Can it, Gertie. What's holding up the show?"

"Well, excuse me. We might as well have polite conversation while we wait." Gertie clammed up and stood, tapping her toe.

They finally passed through the door and into a dark, cramped, smoke-filled lobby. Two limp, potted plants sat on either side of the doorway. A faux-gold-framed mirror sat askew on one wall and a wire rack of Las Vegas excursions, and nightlife brochures graced the other. "Here we go. Looks like there's two floors. Do we want first or second?"

Gertie wrinkled her nose. "Ew. Look at this carpet. That's thirty years of yuck if it's a day. Are we sure we want to stay here? It smells like a barn."

"A barn would be more refreshing. But hey, this is just the lobby. Let's take a look at our room."

The couple in front of them seemed to be having words with the woman at the desk. "We gotta have a non-smoking room." The man's voice held a note of hysteria. "The missus has asthma. What?"

Edna strained to hear the clerk's reply. No luck.

The man snatched a key from the desktop, and the couple waddled off. He threw a parting remark over his shoulder. "This place stinks."

Edna moved up to the counter, let go of her suitcase, and plunked down the grocery bag. "Whew, that thing weighs a ton." She stood face to face with the source of the screen of smoke.

The pudgy, middle-aged woman before them wore a blue-flowered blouse with coffee stains down the front. Her permed hair frizzed on top and sported orange chrysanthemum hair clips on either side. A cigarette dangled from the corner of her mouth and smoke spiraled around her head. Her face held deep wrinkles and one largish mole on the end of her chin.

Edna tried hard not to look at the mole. "Gertie and I will share a room. We'd like the second floor, please. All the senior pamphlets say a second floor is safer."

"Yer in luck, cupcake," she said, her smoker's voice deep and rumbly. "Got a nice corner room fer ya. Room 223. Here's yer key—don't lose it or ya gotta pay to replace it. Breakfast in the community room down the hall until 8:30. All ya can eat." She shoved a key toward Edna.

Edna paused. She needed answers. "So, is the MGM Too sort of a sister hotel to the real one? We thought we were going to stay on the strip."

The woman gave a deep, raspy laugh. "No, not a sister hotel. More like a distant cousin." Her laugh turned into a coughing fit. She hacked a final time and turned back to Edna. "Don't worry, you'll get a piece of the action. Shuttle runs every two hours, twenty-four seven. Schedule's posted in every room. Back of the door."   .

"May we have a duplicate key? There's two of us."

"One room, one key. Deal with it." She moved her gaze to the next in line. "Move it, cupcake."

Edna stomped across the lobby toward the elevator sign. "Can you believe the nerve of that woman? I should have punched her right on that ugly mole." They entered the rickety, dark elevator, and Edna pushed the number two.

"Calm down, Edna. Let's get our luggage stowed and get on down to that buffet. I'm starving."

The elevator door creaked open. Edna peered left and right. "Okay. Let's see—she said a corner room and the numbers go down to the left. There it is, 223. We're gonna have to stick together for sure with only one key. What a witch."

She stuck the key in the lock and turned it. The door squeaked as it opened, and stale, smoky air quickly enveloped them. "P-U." Edna stepped in first, dragged her suitcase inside, and set the grocery bag on the nearest bed. "I could just cry. Here I had a picture of a luxury suite in my mind. Fancy bedding and lots of fluffy towels. Maybe even a hot tub to soak in. This isn't even a *Motel 6*. More like a Motel 2."

They stood for a minute taking in the sad, grungy, little room. Dark-green shag carpet, shiny orange wallpaper darkened from years of smoke, brown bedspreads with snags and questionable spots.

Gertie reacted first. "Let's look on the bright side, Edna. We'll eat breakfast and maybe clean up a little and then grab the shuttle. You'll feel better when you see the lights on the strip. Let's see … the shuttle schedule is right here on the door. Next one leaves at eight o'clock. We can make it if we hurry, or maybe we'll want to wait until ten."

Edna's shoulders slumped. "Thanks for being a good sport, Gertie. I'm sorry, I guess I let that young man take advantage of me and fill my head with nonsense. I should've known better. I've stayed in worse places, but I don't remember when."

Gertie wheeled her suitcase beside the twin bed nearest the window. She pulled the tattered, forest-green curtains open wide. Sunlight streamed through dusty, streaked windows. Edna walked over to take in the view. "Holy cow," she whispered and pulled them closed again. They'd pass on viewing the row of garbage cans next to the chain-link fence topped with razor wire.

CHAPTER THREE

Only a few of the seniors from the bus sat in the community room, eating in silence. They kept their eyes on their food as if embarrassed to be alive. Four round tables covered with peeling, wood-grained, contact paper sat crowded into the small space. Six molded, orange-plastic chairs graced each table. A built-in Formica bar ran along the right side of the room.

"Uh, oh. This doesn't look good," Gertie said.

Edna led the way, and they grabbed paper plates, plastic utensils, and some Kleenex tissue-thin napkins. Her eyes grew wide as she surveyed the offerings. She made a trip down the counter and back again. "All you can eat, my foot. I could eat everything here and still go away hungry."

In the first plastic container sat boxes of dry cereal. A thermos of milk with drips running down the side came next. Then three warming trays with Sterno cans underneath contained a pint-sized pile of rubbery-looking scrambled eggs, exactly six little pig sausages, and some limp, undercooked hash browns. The final tray held Danish pastries, four lemons and three mystery berries. They stuck together in a clump.

Gertie took a box of Rice Krispies and a lemon Danish. Edna chose some eggs, three little pigs, and pried loose two of the mystery berry rolls. She sniffed to hold back the tears. "Dang, Gertie. It keeps getting worse and worse. Let's eat and get out of here."

The shuttle roared up to the entrance of the MGM Too. The little bus handled about twenty passengers, and the driver was so young Edna wondered if she should ask to see his ID. Skinny and jumpy, he wiped his nose with the back of his hand. "All aboard, ladies. Are you ready to hit the big city?"

"We're ready, all right." Edna threw the handle of her all-purpose handbag over her shoulder, grabbed the railing, and hurried up the steps. "Come on, Gertie, let's go see some lights."

"Do they light them up in broad daylight? We should've gone when we first got here if we wanted to get the full effect."

The shuttle was half-full, and Edna recognized five or six of their cohorts from the MGM Too. She sighed and fingered her new slacks. She'd chosen the dark pink T for her debut appearance in Las Vegas. "Guess if I want to wash any of my duds, I'll have to rinse them out in the sink."

"We're only here for three days. You won't even be able to wear all the stuff you brought." Gertie had chosen a simple outfit—gray tunic top over darker gray slacks and sensible SAS shoes. "You're going to be sorry you wore those pointy flats. Your feet will kill you by tonight."

"I don't care if they fall right off my legs. I'm not going to show up for my first visit to the Strip in old-lady loafers."

They settled back for the ride. Dust and palm trees, everything flat. Nothing new to hardy women of the Texas panhandle. "Looks like we're getting into a busier part of town." Edna craned her neck as they passed taller buildings and several fast-food restaurants. After twenty minutes she couldn't restrain herself any longer. "Hey, Driver! How long until we get to the MGM?"

Several of the other riders perked up and waited for the response.

"Depends on the traffic. The drive is usually about thirty, thirty-five minutes. Don't worry, we'll hit the strip before you know it. I'll drop you off right in front of the MGM. That's where you can catch the shuttle every two hours, day or night."

Edna clutched her handbag to her chest and jiggled her foot. "How can you just sit there, Gertie? Aren't you even a tiny bit excited?"

Gertie remained her usual, calm, controlled self. "What's to get so excited about? There will be very big buildings and thousands of slot machines in each one. We could've bought lotto tickets at the Elks, lost, and been done with it. Would have been cheaper than seventy-nine dollars too."

Edna's raised her eyebrows, kept them high and lofty, and then dropped them again. "Gertie, you have no imagination."

A collective "Oooooh" arose from the shuttle riders.

Edna followed the line of interest and snapped her head in that direction. Her mouth formed the same round "O" shape of its own volition. "Would you take a look at that! Oh, my stars. That's about the prettiest thing I've ever seen."

The huge structure, lit from stem to stern in brilliant green, rose above surrounding buildings. Stairstep-shaped on one side, the structure rose majestically some twenty stories high. Two large wings crossed the ascending one at right angles, giving the impression of a giant insect awaiting them. A golden lion a story tall sat at the entrance to a smooth, circular driveway large enough to house a football field. The driveway held limos, buses, and other vehicles of all shapes and sizes.

"Impressive, isn't it?" The young driver turned to his entourage with a mischievous grin on his face.

Edna bolted up from her seat. "Come on, Gertie. This is the most exciting thing I've done since I cozied up with Ramon in that wine cellar."

Gertie, ever the faithful friend, chose not to address that topic. "I'm coming."

They moved toward the steps, all the while admiring the real, live MGM. Edna waxed poetic. "You know, things haven't gone so well so far, but now, I really do feel a surge of pure luck. Can you feel it? Maybe we'll go home with a pile of money. How much did you bring to gamble with? I've got two, crisp, hundred-dollar bills. Woo hoo! Las Vegas MGM, let's see what you've got."

They hurried off the shuttle, noted their whereabouts for the return trip later, and waved farewell to the driver who sped off, one hand on the wheel, the other raking across his nose.

Edna set a brisk pace as they made their way toward the lobby entrance. They passed a large Greyhound bus and found themselves surrounded by a sea of Japanese tourists. Edna towered over the men and women who followed their tour guide, chattering and laughing as they went.

"See, Gertie? *That* is what a visit to Las Vegas should look like. Every one of those people is thrilled to be here."

"Humph."

They hustled on with the group and entered through the oversized doors. Another session of oohs and aah ensued, this time in Japanese, as everyone took in the glamorous MGM lobby.

Cream-and-gold marble floors shone beneath their feet, and crystal chandeliers winked and glistened overhead. The room formed a gigantic circle, with another gold lion smack dab in the middle. He sat, shining and imperious, four feet above floor level, surrounded by a riot of begonias, and potted mums.

The girls looked in all directions as they took in the sumptuous space. All around the edge of the room sat information desks with fancy-clad young people ready to sell package deals for every show and restaurant.

The tour guide, face stern and imposing, gathered his group with hand motions and spoke in quick, staccato words.

"Must be giving them instructions," Gertie whispered.

Edna craned her neck back as far back as it would go to take in the expanse of the huge ceiling. "Look at that main chandelier. Can you imagine having to keep the cobwebs off that thing?" She swayed, and in an effort to catch her balance, she bumped into a Japanese gentleman at the edge of the group. "I'm so sorry," Edna said. "I must have been gawking around. Hope I didn't hurt you." The gentleman bowed and spoke a few words in Japanese, bowed again, and turned to rejoin his group as it made its way through the lobby and followed its guide down a side hallway.

Gertie stooped to retrieve something from the sleek, beautiful flooring. "Hey, I think that guy might have been wearing this." She held up a plastic-coated card with a metal clip attached. "Looks like some sort of ID card. Let me see if I can catch him."

She took a few steps in the direction the group had traveled but stopped short. A sea of heads bobbed up and down. "Shoot, I can't tell where they went."

"Don't worry about it. You'll never find them now. We can track down a lost and found after I've located the loo. I need one right now. Follow me." Edna took off toward a carpeted area adjacent to the lobby, Gertie at her heels.

Edna squirted luxurious, foamy soap into her hands and took her time washing. "Even the bathrooms in this place are spectacular." She reached for a hand towel. "Look at that sofa. I could use one like that in my living room. I'm gonna sit down for a minute. I'm pooped."

She plopped down and sighed a deep sigh. "You were right, Gertie. My feet are already killing me." Wiggling her feet out of the pointy flats, she put both hands behind her head and stretched out her legs. "Aah, that's better. I could get used to fancy digs like this."

"I think we should try to find the lost and found and get this ID tag back to that nice Japanese man." Gertie's pretty face, wrinkled with concern, appeared yellowed by the artificial light.

"You worry too much. We don't even know for sure if it belonged to him. Let me see it."

Gertie handed over the card. "Yup. *Mr. Yakimoto's Tours—experience the wonders of Las Vegas*" She stared at a blurry thumbnail photo that might have been the man she'd bumped into. Or maybe any other person in that group. "Can't tell. I wonder if he really needs it."

Gertie spoke in what Edna referred to as her *stuffy librarian* voice. "It doesn't matter. It's our civic duty to turn it in. Now, get up, and let's find an information desk."

Edna slid back into her tight shoes, hauled her long body upright, and they reentered the massive lobby.

Gertie hurried to the first desk she saw. "Miss, can you please tell me where to find the lost and found?"

"Yes, ma'am. There's one on the seventh floor and another near the Amethyst Lounge."

Gertie looked at the young woman as if she'd been speaking Hindustani. "Well, maybe you can handle this for me. I found this badge on the floor and thought the person who lost it might need it back."

"How thoughtful of you. Well, yes, the person might need the card to enter the restaurants booked with his tour. But most likely the tour guide has extras and will give him a replacement. Don't worry. Would you like me to take it for you?"

Edna threw her body against the desk and reached in front of Gertie to grab the card. "No thanks, maybe we'll keep it for a souvenir."

"Okay, suit yourself. Have a wonderful day at the MGM and good luck!" The words rolled out of her mouth as if repeated for the millionth time.

They stepped away from the desk.

"What in the world do you want with that card? Edna, answer me, you're making me nervous."

"Didn't you hear what she said? This card gets people into restaurants. Now I don't know about you, but I don't want to waste my gambling money on food. We were promised an all-expense trip, and this is the Good Lord's way of keeping that promise."

Gertie bristled. "Don't you dare bring the Lord into this. And maybe you haven't noticed, but you are a great big, silver-haired white woman, not a petite Japanese man."

"Stop worrying. We'll save it for later when we get hungry. Come on, let's find some slots, this money is burning a hole in my pocket."

The Silver Dollar Lounge sported hundreds of clanging, gaudy slot machines of all sizes. Some of them looked like miniature spaceships with towers rising into the air, and others rolled sevens and aces and dolphins and other tawdry faces and shapes in endless circles. They all made a lot of noise.

Gertie held her hands to her ears and complained, "My word, this is worse than the bowling alley back home. Are they all this noisy?"

"I'm gonna play this one with the Chinese food on it. I love Chinese symbols. They're so intriguing." Edna sat down, settled her bag on her lap, and fished inside for her money.

"Don't you think you should break that hundred? It's going to be too easy to play it all in one whack."

Edna sat up straight and pointed her chin in Gertie's direction. "I'm a woman of self-restraint, my friend. I can stop and get my change ticket anytime I choose. Here goes." Lights blinked and little bowls of rice and golden medallions spun. Tinny music accompanied each push of the play button. "Whoopee, I won fifteen credits."

"Yes, and you played thirty-five."

Edna's eyes stayed glued to the screen. "Find yourself a machine and have some fun." She checked the time. "Let's meet up by that Jimmy Buffet poster over there at eleven o'clock. We'll be hungry by then, and we'll beat the rest of the lunch crowd."

Gertie sighed. She searched around the gonging, roaring room. "I'm going to try to find a quieter spot and maybe a poker machine. At least I can understand those."

Edna didn't answer. She sat absorbed in her game, had entered the "Bonus Dragon Round" and was raking in credits by the hundreds.

CHAPTER FOUR

Gertie paced back and forth in front of the Jimmy Buffet poster. She checked her watch again. 11:24. She'd been waiting for nearly a half-hour. Could she be by the wrong poster? No, Mr. Sand and Sun still smiled and held up a margarita. Edna was merely late. Again.

Her stomach growled.

"Gertie! There you are. Sorry, I'm late, but I found a machine with old I Love Lucy videos and, wow, what a hoot. I lost my last ten bucks on it, but worth every penny."

"You lost two hundred dollars already?"

"Of course not." Edna raised her head and stretched to a regal stance. "I am a woman in complete control of my finances. I only allow myself to wager one hundred dollars per day. We have all of tomorrow yet, so I had to save the other hundred. How'd you do?"

"I played the poker machine for a while, but I wasn't winning, so I wandered around and then waited for you. I've been waiting since eleven."

"I know. I kept hoping the Fred and Ethel reel would come up again and that I'd get into the 'Lucy Works at the Chocolate Shop' video. No luck. Oh well, I had fun."

Gertie eyed her tall, 'Sexy Senior' friend. No way to talk sense into her. The only way to co-exist was to take her as is. "What now?"

"I don't know about you, but I'm starving. Those little pigs and Danish went down a long time ago. I saw a map of the layout of this place, and there's a buffet down this hallway and to the right. Let's go check it out."

"Now, Edna, before you get us into a big fat lot of trouble ..."

But Edna had lit out at a gallop, and Gertie had to stretch to catch up to her.

"Yup, there it is. Let me get the lay of the land. Gertie, you go and sit down in that dining area. Find us a nice table for two. You can gather up our utensils and napkins and get us some of that free coffee. Okay? Don't worry about a thing."

"But ..."

Edna headed for the buffet line, little plastic doodad clipped to her sexy, dark-pink tee. It made a bunch-up that would probably leave a wrinkle, but that would have to be the price of two free meals. A hostess stood behind a desk at the far entrance, but Edna walked straight into the serving area looking casual and confident.

She grabbed a tray and eyed the nearly endless line of steaming hot comfort food. Chicken, pulled pork, salmon, shrimp, prime rib. And that was just the meat section. Salads, pasta, mashed potatoes, and gravy. Edna's mouth watered as she looked down the span of the buffet tables. A swarm of people grabbed plates from a warming tray and dove in. She joined them. No one would notice if she took enough food for two. *I'll come back for a second plate after I get the grub.*

She grazed down the aisles, heaping the generous-sized plate to a mountain. An assortment of rolls with butter on tiny paper plates dotted the tray. Tiny squares of cake and wedges of pie filled every other available space. Edna kept her head down as she neared the end of the line. No one had noticed her. So far, so good.

"Excuse me, ma'am." A burly man in a wrinkled suit touched her arm. Edna froze. "I think you may have dropped this."

She rested her tray on the edge of the dessert table and reached out her hand. The man placed the plastic ID card in it. "You might need this later. I know they check them when you enter the shows. Don't want to miss the Elvis Review, do we?" He cackled out a hoarse laugh and leered at Edna's shirt. "Sexy, huh? Maybe I'll see you later." He sauntered off toward the pizza bar, turning once to offer Edna a broad wink.

"Jerk." Edna let go of the breath she'd held for the last minute and swayed a bit with dizzy relief. Sure enough, a wide wrinkle marred her shirt, but no ID tag. No wonder that little Japanese man had lost it. The clip was bent. She'd have to be more careful.

Now, where was Gertie?

She found her faithful friend sitting in the darkest corner of the dining area, her back to the wall. Poor Gertie. She'd massaged a little wad of napkins, shredding them into a pile of fluff on the table. Two cups of steaming coffee and a couple of sets of silverware awaited.

"Good work, Gertie. Oh, rats. I forgot to get the second plate. Be right back." Edna placed the tray on the table and disappeared into the buffet. She appeared seconds later, empty plate in hand.

"Put that plate down. Stop waving it around; you're attracting attention." Gertie's voice was high and squeaky with near hysteria.

"Relax. No one cares if we eat ten trays of food. Man, that was some spread. Let's dig in." Edna proceeded to fill the empty plate with hearty servings of everything.

Gertie sighed and resolutely picked up her knife and fork. The food did look and smell delicious, and she was hungry. Maybe Edna was right. In the grand scale of casino life, who cared if two old ladies ate a free meal?

"Hey, hey, hey. I see you have a friend. Is she a sexy senior too?" The disgusting man must have lurked his way through the buffet and followed her.

Edna didn't mince her words. "Get lost, buster, we're trying to eat a nice, quiet meal here."

"Don't get all huffy. If you advertise sexy, you'd better be ready for some comments. No harm intended. See you two ladies tonight?"

"In your dreams." Edna waved the intruder away with her free hand and took a large bite of prime rib dipped in horseradish sauce.

Gertie's eyes registered as big as the cake plates. "Who was that?"

"Just a guy. But he did remind me of something important."

"Don't you dare go chasing off after some man and leave me all alone here."

"What a thing to say. I'd never do that." Edna casually buttered a roll.

"You did it in Tuscany. Old Ramon winked his eye, and you left me in the dust."

"That was a one-time event. Besides, this guy is a creep. Not my type."

"Well, thank God for small favors." Gertie made a fussy face. "All this food is mixed together. I got horseradish on my Jell-o salad."

"Would you be happier if you'd gone through the buffet to the tune of $15.99?"

"Point taken."

"Now, about this Elvis Review."

Gertie's face dropped from scrunched up to blank. "What Elvis Review?"

"Where have you been? I told you on the bus there's a special Elvis Tribute Review here this weekend. It's an annual event—part of our package deal. At least that's what the young man said. Not sure what to think of him now, but—"

"Get to the point. What does an Elvis Tribute Review have to do with us?"

Edna leaned back and slapped one hand on the table. "Gertie, I don't believe what I'm hearing. Elvis was the King, for Pete's sake. He was the greatest. He made every little girl pee her pants. Now we get to be part of a tribute to him. And if we play our cards right, we'll get to be on the team of senior delegates to elect the best impersonator. That guy gets $5,000. After all, Elvis was from our generation. We know him best."

"People win money for dressing up like Elvis?"

Edna's eyes went soft, and she rested her hand on Gertie's arm. She spoke with quiet reverence in each word. "It's not just dressing up. They study for years to perfect all his mannerisms. They perform his songs exactly the way he did. They *immerse themselves*. They become Elvis and do him great honor." At this phrase, she raised her arms in a grand flourish.

Gertie's response came after a long pause. "How about doing *me* a great honor and leaving me out of this one? I'm about worn out, and we've only been here one morning."

Edna snapped out of her reverie. "Oh, Gertie, I'm sorry. Okay, I'm a little tired too. Must have been the bus ride. I'm usually rarin' to go. We don't need to line up for the event until around three. I figure two hours of standing in line will get us on the list. They're taking the first twenty-five seniors who show up." Edna stopped talking and took a good look at her friend. She did appear a mite spent. "Cheer up, Gertie. I know just the thing to perk you up. Let's go."

They bussed their tray and dishes, and Edna led the way out of the buffet, down a long hallway, and out a heavy side door. They found themselves outdoors in brilliant sunshine in the middle of a gigantic pool complex. The sun beat down white and hot.

Edna squinted and put her hand to her forehead to act as a sunscreen. "Holy guacamole." She took another step onto the paved deck and did a 360-degree turn. Palm trees, lounge chairs, pools, fountains … had someone moved the entire island of Maui and attached it to the side of the hotel?

Gertie laid one hand on her chest. "Mercy, I never expected this. Too bad we didn't bring our bathing suits along. I was so disgusted by the hotel room I didn't even think to unpack and get organized."

"Me neither. But there's always tomorrow. Let's walk through. It looks like it goes forever."

They followed a stone walkway that took them along a narrow "river" of water and stopped when it dumped into a large lap pool. Bathers lounged in the water on floating devices and in lovely, padded lounge chairs near the pools. Tiny poolside tables held pastel-colored drinks with paper umbrellas and flowers attached to the stemware. Sheer heaven.

Edna noticed a large bed-like contraption with an overhead gazebo canopy for shade and plopped down on it. She tossed off her flats and wiggled her toes.

"Edna, get off that thing. Can't you read? It's reserved. Someone must have paid hard cash to save that spot."

Edna looked from side to side in exaggerated motions. "Don't see anyone coming this way. Or that way. Seems like I can rest here a bit if I like." She put both hands behind her head and stretched out with yawns and satisfied grunts.

Gertie fidgeted with her handbag and looked over her shoulder from time to time. "I'm going to see what's in this little area back behind the tall palm trees. It says *Palm Garden Room*." She disappeared through a cave-like opening in a rock wall.

Edna relaxed further into the bed. Mere seconds had passed when Gertie shot back out through the entrance, face red as a tomato.

"Edna, this is your fault."

"Gertie, are you all right? You look like you're about to explode."

"Palm Garden," she sputtered. "More like the Garden of Eden, and I mean *before* Adam and Eve ate that apple. Those people don't have a stitch on—they could use some fig leaves. Why didn't you warn me?"

Edna stood to comfort her friend and struggled to stifle her giggles. She failed and laughed heartily. "You should see your face. Come on, girlfriend. What happens in Vegas, stays in Vegas. I'll scooch over and you can join me." Edna lay back down, resumed her relaxed position, and patted the spot next to her.

Gertie collapsed on the bed. "My hands are shaking. My blood pressure must be two hundred. I don't think I've ever moved so fast in my life. I sure hope I don't run into any of those people the rest of the weekend."

"If you do, you probably won't recognize them, you know, with all their clothes on." Edna chortled again. "We're gonna have stories to tell, my friend."

"I think I need one of those little umbrella drinks ... to steady my nerves."

Edna motioned to one of the pool boys and placed an order. "Two strawberry margaritas, please. One for me and one for Miss Palm Garden Room here."

Gertie squeaked and covered her face with her hands.

CHAPTER FIVE

"Gertie, wake up. It's three-fifteen. We should already be in line."

Gertie roused up on one elbow and squinted against the hot afternoon sun. "What?"

"I said, wake up. Let's get going. We fell asleep, and it's way past time to get in line for the show."

"I don't want to go to the show."

"Yes, you do. We want to be two of the twenty-five senior citizens who vote on the Elvis Tribute winner. If we don't get a move on, we're going to miss out. Let's go."

Edna stood and straightened her clothing. In the heat of the day, her black pants stuck to the sides of her legs, and her dark-pink tee looked mussed and frowsy. "Boy, I hope they don't judge us by our appearance. We both look a bit … discombobulated."

"Speak for yourself." Gertie miraculously had come out of her nap with a minimum of wrinkles. "I actually feel better than I have all day. I needed that little rest."

"Good. Follow me." Edna lit out toward a doorway leading back into the casino and practically ran down hallways until they entered a door marked *The Ruby Room*. They stood in a foyer punctuated with dozens of Elvis memorabilia stalls. Clusters of senior citizens browsed their way through black velvet paintings, mugs, pen and pencil sets, and a whole host of everything Elvis. "Oh, look.

Elvis stuff. Let's get our places in line and then take turns coming back to shop."

Gertie's eyes darted from one stall to another. "Shop? I don't want any of that stuff."

"Well, I do. We can't attend an Elvis tribute and go away empty-handed. We're going to want to remember this for the rest of our lives."

"You're right. I probably will remember this till the day I die." Gertie's voice dripped with anti-Elvis acid.

"Don't go getting all high and mighty on me, girlfriend. There! The line is forming down by the stage. Let's go." Edna pointed through another set of doors toward a medium-sized theater with rows of upholstered seats and a maroon velvet curtain with gold fringes across the stage.

A small entourage of theater types bustled around, everyone kowtowing to a tall, thin, middle-aged man who called out orders in a whiny, high-pitched voice. He held a microphone that buzzed and squawked. "Can't you guys get the sound working?"

Edna made a beeline for the aisle.

A final shriek from the sound system and the man's voice morphed into bass, theatrical tones. "Ladies and gentlemen, please take your places behind the stanchion rope. Thank you for being part of our annual Elvis Tribute Extravaganza. We're so glad you're here. Be ready to show your identification and please be patient. We like to interview our participants, and we base our decisions on the results of a short survey. All decisions of our judges are final. We'll take the first twenty-five qualified voters."

The skinny man of the hour reminded Edna of a circus barker without the top hat. His spare body, encased in a shiny-black suit cut one size too small, stood in a rigid pose, one arm lifted high in the air. He kept fingering his dark mustache and pointy goatee.

An involuntary shudder passed through Gertie's body as she caught up with Edna at the end of the line. "He looks a little bit like the devil."

"Hush, Gertie. Did you hear what he said? We have to go through an interview and take a survey. Do you think that means a test? I thought we just lined up and joined the team."

"Life is full of surprises."

"Now, Gertie, that is a mean thing to say. You know how much I've looked forward to this."

A chubby woman wearing a caftan and fifties' eyeglasses opened the velvet stanchion and allowed five seniors through. They followed the woman's gestures to take seats in the front row. Once in the plush chairs, another woman greeted them with a smile and issued each a clipboard and pencil.

A hush fell over the room as the five seniors bent over the clipboards and marked their answers.

Edna's neck hurt from stretching it high to see the action up front. "If they only take five at a time, we'll be in the fourth group. Now I'm nervous. I never thought I'd have to take a test."

Gertie yawned. "I'm going to find a cold drink. I think I saw some vending machines out in the hallway. Do you want a coke or something?"

"Sure, that sounds good, but don't take too long. We don't want to miss our turn."

The five original seniors finished one by one, turned in their clipboards, and were directed to a door to the left of the stage. They disappeared, and the next five candidates made their way through the stanchion and into the hot seats.

Man, I hope Gertie gets back here quickly. What in the world will they ask us? I better run through some Elvis songs and lyrics. Edna hummed and snapped her fingers through *Blue Suede Shoes* and *You Ain't Nothin' But a Hound Dog.* The woman in front of her turned to comment, but Edna placed one hand on her hip and glared until the woman turned back around.

"Here you go. I had to get Pepsi instead of Coke."

Edna grabbed her drink and took a long swig. "Whew, thanks. This whole thing is making me jumpy."

Gertie left the line to sit in one of the end-row seats. She leaned back and crossed her ankles.

"How can you stay so calm and cool?" Edna jittered around in line, shuffling her feet. "I'm a wreck."

"Oh, for goodness' sake. Come sit down."

The third batch of candidates went through the stanchion leaving Edna third in line. "Get back up here. If you're lounging around when our turn comes, they might disqualify you."

"I should be so lucky." Gertie sighed and joined the line again. "I don't know why you're so hot and bothered. There can't be more than thirty or forty people here. Maybe they'll take everyone." Gertie took Edna's empty cup, popped it inside hers, and disposed of both in a nearby trash container. Another four or five people wandered into line.

"Here we go. Gads, my hands are all sweaty." Edna wiped her hands down her black slacks.

The eyeglass woman pointed at them, and Edna and Gertie took their places in the front row. The smiley lady handed each of them a clipboard and pencil. "Write your name at the top and mark your answers. Be sure to fill in each circle completely. When you're finished, please return your clipboard."

"I haven't had to take a test since I flunked my driver's test fifty years ago," Edna said.

The smiley lady's face turned grim. "No talking, please."

Edna took a deep breath and hunched over the clipboard and read the first question.

1. The years known as Elvis's Jumpsuit Years were:
   a. 1958-60
   b. 1969-1977

  c. 1963-67
  d. 1966-75

"What?" She read the next question.

  2. The winner of the 2014 Elvis Impersonator Tribute
     contest was:
     a. Donny Edwards
     b. Shawn Klush
     c. David Lee Elvis
     d. Dwight Icenhower

Holy cow! I'm in trouble! Edna sat tensed and tight. She didn't know one answer, she'd have to guess. She glanced over toward Gertie and saw she'd already finished the ten questions and handed in her clipboard. *Impossible.*

"One minute left, ladies and gentlemen."

Edna wildly filled in circles and had barely finished question ten as the smiley lady raked in the clipboards. She stood and moved with the little group of five toward the stage door. "How in the world did you finish that test so fast?"

"I alternated my answers, a, b, c, d, to the end. I didn't know any of that stuff."

"Me neither. And I consider myself an Elvis aficionado."

Gertie lifted her eyes toward heaven. "What next? This place is giving me the creeps."

"Come right on in, folks," the circus ringmaster called, "and take a seat in one of the booths. Our interview is brief. Answer the questions as clearly as possible, and you'll find the list of winners' names posted in the foyer at five p.m. Good luck, and thank you for taking part in our Elvis Impersonator Tribute weekend. Please accept a bona fide Elvis cape as your parting gift."

Edna stood from her mini-interview and spied Gertie's back as she left the theater and reentered the foyer. She hurried to her side. "Hey, what's my annual income and my life insurance policy got to do with this thing? What did they ask you?"

"Well, first they asked me the last grade I finished in school and then they asked me the same two things—life insurance and annual income."

Edna shook her head. "Something is rotten in Denmark. Those questions don't have a thing to do with Elvis. I'll bet that "nice young man" had something to do with this. When we get home, we'll have to remember to get back on the "no-call list" right away."

"Edna, you do beat all. I should hit you over the head with this thing."

Gertie took the plastic-wrapped parting gift, shook it in Edna's face, and stuffed it in her handbag. Edna removed hers from the plastic sleeve, shook it out, and watched it unroll to the floor. It smelled of cheap plastic. The off-white expanse was trimmed in gold ribbon, the stitching missing the mark in several places.

"Hey, a bona fide Elvis cape. This is kinda jazzy. I think I might wear it tonight to the show."

"Are you kidding me? It reeks. Looks like a Halloween costume."

Edna carefully rolled up the cape and slid it back in its plastic baggie. "Let's see. We can't see the list of winners until five. Good, let's browse a bit through these stalls. I always wanted one of those Elvis bobbleheads. Maybe the whole body." Edna cackled.

Gertie slumped. "I'll wait for you outside. There's a couch out there and several magazines."

"Suit yourself. But I bet you're gonna wish you'd bought something when we get back home to our boring daily lives."

"Boring sounds exquisite right about now."

At five o'clock sharp, Edna bellied up to the bulletin board. The woman with the pointy fifties' glasses had just marched through the lobby doors and posted the list for all to see. At least those up front could see. The rest of the mob craned their necks and complained.

"Hurry up, there are other folks who want to see too," a grumpy-looking woman at the back of the group said as she elbowed her way toward the front.

"Oh, can it, I can't seem to find my name." Edna scanned the list again. Twenty-five names in alphabetical order. "There you are, Gertie—Gertrude Hansen. I should be above you—Edna Gratzer, Gratzer." She traced her finger down the list. "Huh."

She stepped over to the pointy glasses lady and reported the error. "Excuse me, but I know I made the list. There must be some mistake. I've been counting on being part of this for weeks."

"No mistake, ma'am, and as we informed everyone earlier, our judges' decisions are final."

"What judges? Can I see my test score? And why do you care about my life insurance?"

"I'd appreciate a softer voice, ma'am. Let's see if we can resolve this problem. Our judges are officials of the Southern Local Life Insurance Company, our sponsors for this event." The woman's voice quavered as she spoke, her eyes cutting to the nearby exit. "I'm sorry for your disappointment. However, our decision is final, and, of course, you're welcome to attend the show tonight and the grand finale show tomorrow evening as well."

Gertie spoke up. "Can I bequeath my spot to another person? I have a sick headache coming on."

"I'll have to check on that, I believe there are several alternate names in case of illness or other untoward events. Excuse me for a moment." The woman disappeared through the foyer doors.

"Gertie, I don't want you to give up your spot. We need to do this together."

"Doesn't sound like that is going to be an option."

"Maybe if I slipped that woman a twenty, she'd change her mind or maybe add another slot."

Gertie opened her mouth to speak, a look of horror on her face.

The lady returned, smiling. "Ma'am, you're in luck. One of our executives from Southern Local was touched by your sincere interest in the event. But, please, for the sake of everyone who didn't make the list, let's keep our voices down. Edna Gratzer? Of Amarillo? You are lucky voter number twenty-six."

.

CHAPTER SIX

Edna lifted her double-bacon burger to her mouth and sank her teeth in deep. "Wow, I was hungry. All that waiting and worrying gave me an appetite."

Gertie forked in a bite of her chicken Caesar and delicately chewed. "You know this whole voting thing is a big farce. They only wanted more information so they can sell us life insurance when we get home. By the way, thank you for allowing me to pay for this meal to keep us out of the hoosegow."

"You're welcome." Edna dipped a French fry in a secret sauce and ate it in two bites. "I'm choosing to take the high road. I'm going to ignore anything negative in my aura. Tonight, there will be thirty men paying tribute to the King, and you and I get to be part of a historical event. Tomorrow night, there will be a winner, and you and I will help elect him. We're almost like political figures assisting in making a landmark decision."

Gertie delicately wiped her mouth with her napkin. "Whatever. What are we going to do for the next three hours?"

"It's only two and a half before the show starts at eight, plus we're supposed to be there and get seated a half-hour early. And that nice lady gave me a list of the Elvis challengers with a bio and picture for each one. We need to do our homework—become familiar with them.

We also need to go over the score sheet. It's an awesome responsibility."

"Humph." Gertie chewed some more salad.

Edna studied the glossy, three-page brochure. "Look. Some of these guys are as old as the hills. And a couple of them look like teenagers. Ooh, look at this one, Elvis Aaron Snodgrass. He's like Baby Bear. He's just right." She tapped her finger by his photo. "I guess he must be portraying the jumpsuit era. He's got it going on right down to those shiny-white shoes."

"Pardon me while I vomit." Gertie gathered her plate and utensils and stood to dispose of them.

"I wonder if those are their real names. Like maybe their moms were Elvis fans and decided to name their sons after the King."

"Suddenly, I have a yearning for the poker machine I tried earlier. I haven't used up my quota for the day, and anything sounds better than drooling over those pictures. I'll meet you at the theater at seven-thirty."

Edna's eyes widened. "Really? You're going to desert me at this important moment? You're going to go into the show with no background information? Where's your respect for the system?"

But Gertie was headed toward the cafeteria exit. Edna watched her disappear through the door, tossed her wadded-up napkin on the table, and sighed.

Edna idly jiggled her new, full-body, bobblehead Elvis and watched his head and hips swivel and sway. Gertie was nowhere in sight, and her watch showed 7:42. Some of the other voters were already seated in a special, cordoned-off zone delineated by another red-velvet rope. Edna had counted the seats. Exactly twenty-six. She stood beside the doorway leading into the theater so she could keep an eye on both the foyer and the goings-on up front.

Gertie huffed and puffed her way into the foyer. "I made it. I got lucky on that poker machine and came away with thirty dollars."

"Okay, well you're here now. Let's get inside and take our seats. I'll try to catch you up on the study material. I'm leaning toward Elvis Aaron Snodgrass, and not only because he's hot. His bio says he loved Elvis even when he was a kid."

Edna led the way, reported both of their names to the security guard down in front, and hurried through the stanchion into the VIP voter section. The theater was beginning to fill up, and Elvis love songs permeated the air above dimly-lit rows of seats.

"There's something magical about theaters, isn't there?" Edna scooted forward in her chair and turned around to take in the full ambiance of the room. "I mean, the curtain is still closed, but you know that soon wonderful things will happen. It gives me goose bumps just being here."

"Yeah, it makes my skin crawl too."

"Gertie, I get so disgusted with you sometimes—"

"Ladies and Gentlemen." The skinny guy in the bad suit said in true showmanship manner. In the dim light, he looked bright and perky and maybe even handsome in a greasy kind of way. "Welcome to our nineteenth annual Elvis Tribute Show!" He threw out his arm, and with that, the curtain was hauled back to reveal a glitzy cover band playing a wild version of "That's All Right, Mama," featuring Dwight Icenhower as Elvis.

Edna let out a whoop and stood to her feet. The electricity in the room was contagious, and soon the entire voting group led the audience in foot stomping and hand clapping to set the stage for a night to remember.

Gertie stayed seated until peer pressure forced her to stand up, but that was the best she had to offer. No clapping or whooping for her.

The band segued into "All Shook Up" and ended the mini-medley with another upbeat version of "A Little Less Conversation (A Little More Action)." Dwight's face ran rivers of sweat by the time they finished. The crowd clapped and cheered. Edna let out one of her two-fingered whistles a bit late, and it hung in the air like a bad smell. Everyone sat down.

"Did you have to do that?" Gertie wrinkled her nose in disgust.

Edna's enthusiasm knew no bounds. "Isn't this great? That band can really play. No wonder Dwight won the contest a few years back. Oh, boy, this is gonna be fun."

Pointy-glasses lady came around with a new clipboard for each voter. A copy of the scoring sheet lay on top, along with the brochure containing the bio and picture of each impersonator plus two pencils in case one broke.

Mr. Black Suit returned to the stage. "Ladies and gentlemen, my name is Skip Diamond, and I'll be your emcee for the evening. Allow me to introduce our panel of judges. He directed his gaze to the first two rows of the audience. "Each one of these fine senior citizens has agreed to be our eyes and ears tonight." He swooped an arm toward the judges and said, "Friends, please stand and take a bow."

Edna and Gertie rose along with their voting cohorts, turned to the audience, and received appreciative applause. Edna did a sort of curtsy, and Gertie elbowed her. "Sit down," she hissed out of the side of her mouth.

"I never got to bow in front of an audience before. I might as well take advantage of the opportunity."

"For your information, the Queen skipped this event. It's just us peons here."

The judges took their seats, and Skip Diamond continued. "Our senior team has prepared carefully for the right to select our new Elvis. And the grand prize, five thousand dollars, will be awarded to the winner at the end of tomorrow night's show. You won't want to miss it."

"Skip Diamond? Don't any of these people live in the real world? I suppose the woman who handed out the pencils is Hope Diamond." Gertie printed her name at the top of the ballot sheet and sat, grim and resigned, to mark down scores.

"Is everyone ready?" Skip asked. A smattering of applause and a few 'ready's' emanated from the crowd. "I said, is everyone ready?" Edna whistled again, and the crowd ramped up the applause. "Well then, I present to you all thirty of tonight's hopefuls."

At a hand signal from Skip, a second curtain lifted from the back of the stage, and thirty big-haired, white shoed, side-burned, shirts-open-to-the-navel, Elvis wannabes gyrated forward.

The crowd hooted and cheered.

Rhinestones flashed as each impersonator channeled the King. Every contestant wore a number on a cord around his neck.

Edna was overcome. "Mercy, I can't take it all in. Look at number eleven. That's Elvis Aaron Snodgrass. Oh, I could eat him with a spoon."

"Mercy is right. Lord help me. I'm not sure I can do this."

"Don't be nervous, Gertie, I'm right here to help you if you get stuck on anything. Remember, the most points go for the ones who can really *be* Elvis—the ones who truly look and sound like him. Don't be fooled by a nice voice or a tiny sneer. They have to ooze with Elvis-ness."

Skip continued. "Gentlemen, remember the rules—no more than three, forty-second portions of Elvis hits in your medley, only one scarf given out per performance, and no lewd or profane behavior at any time. Okay? Let the show begin!"

Pointy-glasses lady had been put in charge of background CDs. Elvis hopeful number one swaggered out to a lone microphone in the center of the stage, nodded his head, and she pressed a button.

Edna leaned forward in her seat, eyes riveted on the first contestant, and her pencil poised over her clipboard.

They were an hour into the show and had seen ten acts. These included Fat Elvis, Skinny Elvis, older-than-dirt Elvis, and one kid who couldn't hide his acne with the fake sideburns.

Edna had given several decent marks on appearance and mannerisms. The performance scores were another matter. Most lacked any semblance of choreography and relied on a few sneers and a whole lot of hip wiggles.

Gertie spoke into Edna's ear. "I only give them a two if they can't come up with more charisma than a few wiggles. And If I have to hear "Love Me Tender" one more time, I think I'll need another little umbrella drink."

"I told you to spend some time on the score sheet. Think A-P-V from now on—appearance, performance, and vocals. And if they really look or sound like Elvis, they get bonus points."

"I can't see how sounding more like someone else makes them any better. I like that cute little number three. He sang like a dream."

"Yeah, he sounded like he was singing the aria from Madame Butterfly. This ain't no opera, girlfriend. They have to sound like Elvis."

"I'm getting sleepy. I don't think I can go through twenty more acts."

"You have to. Tonight, they'll put all our scores together and eliminate all but ten of them. Tomorrow night will be easier. We got a ten-minute intermission now. I'm gonna hit the bathroom. Hang in there. Don't forget we're making Elvis history."

Ten minutes flew by. Edna took her seat, and Gertie yawned as Skip Diamond reappeared on the stage. "First intermission is over, folks. Haven't the performers been superb? Now, on to impersonators eleven through twenty. Give it up for Mr. Elvis Aaron Snodgrass."

Edna perked up and leaned into Gertie's shoulder. "Here he comes—Mr. Cutie Patootie. All his numbers are going to be sky high."

Contestant eleven walked to the center of the stage, grabbed the mic off the stand, and slid his lip into a true Elvis sneer. He greeted the audience. "How y'all doin' tonight?" He sang a heartrending version of "I Want You, I Need You, I Love You." Elvis Aaron stepped as far forward as he could without falling off the stage, crooned to the front row of voters, and let his eyes rest on each face for a full five seconds.

"We should've sat in the front row." Edna leaned forward, minimizing the distance from her to Elvis Aaron.

He finished his first song clip and moved on to a jerky and convincing rendition of "Heartbreak Hotel." He threw the audience a curve, and instead of finishing with a hand-clapping upbeat song, he got down on one knee as if to tell a story to a child and sang a heart-wrenching version of "Old Shep." When he sang about how the dog expired, there wasn't a dry eye in the house. And then Elvis Aaron slowly removed the red scarf from his neck, carefully wiped his teary eyes and his brow, and gently tossed the scarf to Edna in the second row.

A collective gasp arose from the audience, and the voters burned lead filling in their score circles.

Edna sat frozen in place, red scarf hanging limp in her outstretched hand.

"Edna, are you all right?"

"I feel a little woozy." She sat back in her chair and held the scarf out to examine it. She draped the scarf around her neck. "I guess it's kind of like attending the Oscars or the Emmys. All the glitz and glamour is more than I'm used to. Did you see the way he looked at me?"

"Honey, he looked at everyone the same way, including all the men."

Edna's eyes were as dreamy as a schoolgirl on prom night. "I swear he's the best-looking Elvis I've ever seen. And that last song was genius. He's gonna win for sure."

"Well, no rest for the wicked. Here comes Elvis number twelve." Gertie grabbed her scoresheet and tightened her grip on her pencil.

"I'd sure like to meet Elvis Aaron in person. Do you think they've planned a meet and greet for us voters?"

Gertie's words came through clenched teeth. "I sincerely hope not."

CHAPTER SEVEN

Edna's gritty eyes burned, and Gertie looked as if she might drop if someone touched her with a feather. Thirty performances at approximately five minutes each, from the time each Elvis wannabe came on stage to his final bows. The work had been grueling.

"Okay, Gertie, let's turn in our clipboards. I say it's a job well done. Maybe there's time for a drinkie poo before we catch the shuttle."

"I sure don't like thinking about that nasty hotel room we got."

"I know, but we'll only be there long enough to sleep and grab a shower. We'll be back here tomorrow morning. We'll skip the all-you-can-eat breakfast buffet if you want. I saw a coffee pot in the room. Let's grab some muffins or something in one of the cafés before we go."

"Good thinking. Best idea you've had all day." Gertie took Edna's clipboard and handed both of them to Miss Glasses.

They trudged up the theater aisle, Edna limping in her tight shoes, and entered the foyer. The crowd had mostly dispersed except for a few stragglers who dotted the Elvis memorabilia stalls.

Edna came to an abrupt halt. "Gertie! Look there ... at that stall in the corner. That's Elvis Aaron Snodgrass. He still has his hair and sideburns on—no costume, but I'm positive that's him."

"Are you sure? There were thirty guys, and they all have pretty much the same hair."

"No, that's him. I'm going to go and get his autograph."

Gertie sighed and looked for an escape route. "I'll be waiting on that couch outside. I can finish that article in Las Vegas Today on the Miracle Mile. Not that I can afford any of their 'sales.'"

Edna strode within handshake range of Elvis Aaron where he was talking to the woman behind the counter of the stall. Edna took a step nearer. *My heart is beating a mile a minute.*

"Don't look like you sold much tonight, Ma." Elvis Aaron spoke in a deep bass voice but kept his words soft. "I think I did all right. You were right—"Old Shep" was a winner. You shoulda seen them old folks tear up."

"Excuse me, Mr. Snodgrass?"

Elvis Aaron turned around and faced Edna. Her heart clenched up in her chest. Her right knee began to wobble out of control. "I wondered if you might sign the base of my Elvis bobble doll?"

"Yes, ma'am, be glad to. Ma, you got a pen that'll work on this plastic?"

Elvis Aaron's mother provided a permanent marker, and he did the honors. 'E.A. Snodgrass'. He finished with a flourish of curlicues.

Edna couldn't think of anything to say, but then she went on autopilot. "You did good tonight. I'm one of the judges, and I gave you only top marks. You're sure to get into the finals tomorrow night. When you got to the end of "Old Shep," I thought I'd bawl my eyes out. That was a good choice and a smart one too. Now, do you and your mother travel together to enter these things? My friend and I won an all-expense trip here although they tricked us about the hotel we're stuck in. But we're having a great time anyway and—"

"Much obliged, ma'am." Elvis Aaron had taken several steps back from Edna and was almost sitting on the counter of the memorabilia stall. "Guess it's about time for me to retire for the night."

Edna clucked her tongue. "I understand. I bet you have to practice all the time and get your beauty sleep and keep fit for all the performances, huh? Well, you run along. I got to find my friend, and we have to pick up muffins for breakfast because the all-you-can-eat at the MGM Too is just plain pitiful, and then, we have to catch the shuttle. We need our beauty sleep too," she finished with a nervous chuckle.

By this time Elvis Aaron had retreated behind the counter and stood behind his mother. He ducked around the curtain at the back of the stall and disappeared.

"I guess he's a bit shy," Edna said to Mrs. Snodgrass.

"Yeah, it's past his bedtime." Her voice was low and gritty, and she chuckled as she straightened up the posters, wallets, cups, and other Elvis products. "Bet he's already out in the bus and getting himself ready for bed. He's an early bird, that one." She laughed again, deep and growly.

Edna thought she detected a hint of ugly behind the laugh. "You all travel in one of those big fancy tour buses?"

"Sure, honey. It's big and fancy. Gets us where we need to go. Elvis Aaron's daddy left it to us when he passed on. It's a living."

"Oh, my. I always wondered how the big stars liked those buses they travel in. Seems like they could be a mite confining at times. And all that driving time."

"When you're in the Elvis game, you gotta go where the action is."

"I guess so. Well, tell Elvis Aaron that I'll cheer him on tomorrow night."

"I'll do that." Mrs. Snodgrass closed down the stall, covering all the merchandise with a black velvet cloth. She left the same way Elvis Aaron had.

Edna moved away slowly, overcome by her proximity to greatness. *I shoulda asked for a picture—one of those selfie things. Maybe tomorrow.* She gathered herself and walked out the foyer door to find Gertie.

Gertie sat on the bench outside the theater. She leafed through a *Las Vegas Today* magazine. Glossy photos of beautiful people shone out from each page.

Edna returned from the Elvis memorabilia stalls. "I'm still shaking. I got the autograph. He was real polite too, like the real King, and you'll never guess."

"What?"

"His mother runs one of the memorabilia booths. Remember how Elvis loved his mother? He was always hugging and kissing her even though I always thought she looked kinda dumpy. He was sweet that way."

"His mother? Are you sure? That seems strange."

"Well, that's how it is. He and his mother travel on a big tour bus and they enter Elvis contests. And they sell Elvis memorabilia. I think it's wonderful how some people find a way to use their God-given creativity."

Gertie closed her magazine, placed it carefully on an end table, and took a deep breath. "Are you ready to find something for tomorrow's breakfast and head for the shuttle? It's late, and I'm tired."

"Sure, we can stop at the little quickie bar near the main entrance, grab some goodies, and catch the midnight shuttle."

They made their way back through the maze of hallways, slot lounges, and restaurants toward the main lobby. Gertie led the way this time because Edna limped with each step. "I gotta wear my tennis shoes tomorrow. I hate to do it, but these dogs won't take another day of high fashion."

Gertie slowed in front of a shop window. "Let's get a couple of those bran muffins. All this traveling and cavorting around has messed up my regularity."

"You go ahead. I'm going for the chocolate with chocolate chip muffins. I'll need the caffeine boost in the morning to be at my best."

"I'll bet you two gals are always at your best." Mr. Sleazy came up behind Edna and rested a hand on her shoulder.

"Beat it." Edna shook off the hand and turned to face him.

"Hey, I saw you all at the show tonight when you stood to take a bow. You must be real Elvis fans to spend your vacation time voting. Some of those guys are total losers."

Gertie sucked in a breath and stood stock still, her hands clutching her handbag to her chest.

Edna put one hand to her hip and tipped her head from side to side. "Losers? I'll show you a loser. I'm looking at him right now."

Edna's voice boomed through the hallway and reverberated off the walls. It caught the attention of a uniformed security guard who moved toward them. "Any trouble here, ladies?"

Gertie spoke up fast. "No trouble, officer. We're on our way to catch our shuttle back to our hotel. This gentleman asked for directions to the main lobby."

The officer eyed the man whose gaze shifted to inspect his shoes. "Through this hallway and to the right."

Mr. Sleazy grinned as if caught with his hand in the cookie jar. "Thanks, officer, I'll head that way right now." He turned and walked away at a fast clip. The officer tipped his hat to the women and returned to his rounds.

Edna watched both men leave, and her shoulders lowered on her big body. "Let's get our muffins and head out to the shuttle.

Gertie shivered. "We're going to have to watch out for that guy. He gives me the creeps."

"You and me both. Guess it's my Sexy Senior tee. Well, tough. They're all I've got, and I'm going to wear another one tomorrow."

"I think it's your hair." Gertie paid for the muffins, and they made for the shuttle stop.

The room at the MGM Too was indeed as horrible as they'd remembered. The air hung heavy with odors—dust, smoke, and decay. Deep-down grime in the greens, browns, and dingy oranges evoked misery. Edna surveyed their little world for the night and opened her suitcase. "Good thing I brought flannel pj's—they must not pay for heat in this place. It's all so icky I'm not sure I'll be able to sleep."

Gertie grabbed a limp, white towel off the rack. "I'm taking a shower. At least I'll feel clean before I get into that bed. Even horrible hotels have to launder the sheets and pillowcases. I'll just close my eyes and pretend I'm at home."

"Okay. I'm gonna go back over the evening in my mind. I never thought I'd actually be able to speak up close and personal with a celebrity. And especially one as handsome as Elvis Aaron." She sighed.

Gertie retreated into the bathroom. Edna heard the squeak of the faucet and the rumble in the walls as water ran through the pipes. She lay back on her bed, glad for the relief that came from bare feet, free of pinchy shoes. She bent one leg, rested her foot on her knee, and rubbed her aching foot, then switched and rubbed the other.

A shriek came from the bathroom, and she stood up fast enough to make her head spin.

"There's no hot water." Gertie appeared seconds later, wrapped in the flimsy towel, and dripping on the green-shag carpet. "It started out lukewarm, and I thought I'd hurry through a quick shower, but then it went ice cold."

"Let me try the sink." Edna turned the H knob on all the way. No dice. "Sorry, Gertie, I guess there's nothing we can do. This place is falling apart, and I don't think Ms.

Tact from downstairs will call a repairman at one in the morning."

"No, you're right. Brrr. I'd better get my pajamas on before I freeze to death. We'll report this in the morning."

Edna muttered something under her breath.

"What?"

"I said, sure, we'll report it first thing." She peeked under the covers to check for anything untoward inside them then crawled under them.

Gertie emerged from the bathroom, her exposed skin pink and blue and goose-bumped. "Edna, one of these days I'm going to forget that you're my best friend, and I'm going to absolutely beat the tar out of you."

"Look on the bright side, Gertie. We're in Vegas; we're on the select voting team for the annual Elvis Impersonator Extravaganza; we might get to see the guys at the after-party tomorrow night; and there's another whole day to play the slots. Plus, we got the ID card for another big old buffet at tomorrow's lunch. We have a lot to look forward to."

"What after-party?"

"Good night, Gertie."

CHAPTER EIGHT

"Wake up, Gertie, we overslept."

Gertie opened one eye. "What's your hurry? We aren't on a schedule here."

"It's already nine o'clock. By the time we get dressed and eat something and catch the shuttle, the day will be half gone. I want to take my suit and get a dip in some of those pools this afternoon."

"I don't think we actually have access to all that. We're not even staying there."

"We were promised an all-expense trip with all the benefits and—"

"I know. The Good Lord will make that possible." Gertie stretched and groaned and sat up in the bed.

"Let's wear our suits under our clothes and see what happens. Pack your undies. They sure don't seem to watch the doors trying to catch people. We waltzed in there yesterday." Edna raised her hands high in the air and did five toe-touches in quick succession.

"Maybe they rely on honest people and good judgment. Maybe they don't think people will use a fake ID and take advantage."

Edna moved her feet apart to shoulder width and touched her right hand to her left foot and then repeated the motion on the other side. "I say maybe they want folks to have a good time and spend their money. I fully intend to do that. I'm gonna take one of these hotel towels and stuff it inside my handbag. They aren't very big, and I found a plastic bag in the closet. We can stash our suits in it when we're done."

Edna completed her morning exercises with an energetic set of three jumping jacks. The windows shook, and the beds shifted. "I'm religious about my morning exercises. They help keep me so trim." She took Gertie's silence for approval and went into the tiny bathroom where she huffed and puffed her way into her knock-off Rolph Lorenzo one-piece bathing suit. She hollered out, "This skirt is going to bulge a little inside my pants. Guess I'll pull my T down to cover it."

Gertie sighed, put her bathing suit on under her pretty teal pantsuit, and geared up for another day of hair-raising uncertainty.

They ate their muffins with cups of tepid instant coffee and hurried to catch the ten o'clock shuttle. They hopped off by the giant golden lion and made their way to the gargantuan green building.

"What if we took our dip in the pool right now before the hottest part of the day? I bet it's pretty empty in there, and it's plenty warm enough."

"How are we going to change if we can't go in through the dressing rooms?" Gertie hurried to keep up with Edna who trotted along at a brisk clip now that she had her tennis shoes on.

They made their way through the MGM lobby and, seasoned guests that they were, entered into the pool and spa area undetected.

"I want to go down one of those tube things. They didn't have stuff like that when I was a kid."

"Are you nuts? I heard just last week that a guy went down one of those and spilled out over the side. He's still in intensive care."

"That's probably one of those urban myths young people talk about. Whoever heard of getting hurt going down a kiddie slide? 'Course, I have my hairdo to think of."

They walked past a row of cabanas and into a heavily palm-treed section where two mini-pools adjoined a children's area. "Here, this is perfect. There's lots of cover. You relax, and I'll hop over to the slide and go down once. It'll be fun." Edna proceeded to strip down to her suit and tossed her clothes on a lounge chair. "Hold this little towel for me. I'll be right back. Ooh, I can't wait." She pulled off her tennis shoes and white anklets and padded off through the palm fronds toward the kiddy slide.

As Edna headed off to the children's pool, a young man with a whistle and an MGM insignia on his shirt approached. Gertie opened her mouth to call out to Edna but managed a mere peep.

"Good morning, ma'am. May I see your MGM tags please?"

Gertie smiled to buy some time. "I don't exactly know where the tag is right now. My friend over there had it last time we used it."

"MGM policy, ma'am. Each guest must carry his or her own tags and keep them pinned to their person when using the pool complex."

"Yes, sir. I'll make sure to tell my friend."

"Fine. Have a wonderful day at the MGM." He tipped his MGM ball cap and moved on down the line of cabanas.

Gertie collapsed in her lounge chair. Her heart raced and her head thumped. She willed her body to relax.

A shriek pierced the hot morning air, followed in short order by a gigantic splash. Gertie sat upright and covered her eyes with one hand. Moments later, Edna barged through the palm branches, dripping as she came. Her hair lay plastered to her head, and her smile stretched from ear to ear. "You gotta try it, Gertie. That was fun with a capital F."

"Listen, Miss 'Capital F,' I got busted by a security guy. We're supposed to have our IDs clipped to our clothing at all times."

"What did you tell him?" Edna mopped her face and arms.

"I said the last time I saw the ID, you had it." Gertie refused to look Edna in the eye.

"Really? Miss Perfect lied to a security guard?"

"I did not lie. That's the truth. You did have the ID, just not your own."

"Where is he?"

Gertie pointed in the direction he'd walked.

Edna stretched to look for him. "The coast is clear. Let's take a quick dip and then we'll hightail it out of here."

"How are we going to leave? Where are we going to change?"

"Do you want to cool off or not?"

Gertie removed her outer clothing, folded it, and neatly set it on the lounge chair. She tiptoed to the nearest kidney-bean-shaped pool. She waded in from the shallow side and step by step immersed her body. "It does feel good."

"That's the spirit. I'm gonna come in too." Edna entered the pool her way—a full-body cannonball at the deep end.

A shrill whistle cut through the air, and Mr. Security loomed over the kidney-shaped pool. "Ladies?"

"That's okay, officer, we're cooling off, and then, we'll go right to our rooms and get our ID tags." Edna moved toward the shallow edge of the pool and climbed up the ladder, dripping and trying to look sincere.

"See that you do." He scowled and waited while they gathered up their clothing and handbags and headed toward the dressing room doors.

Edna stopped and turned. "Thank you for doing such a good job of policing the area, officer. There are so many deadbeats around these days that you can't trust anyone." She kept her voice soft and respectful.

"Good day, ladies. If I see you again without tags—"

"Oh, you won't. We're on our way right now."

They scampered away between palm trees and behind cabanas until they'd lost the officer.

Gertie's voice wobbled. "Oh, my word. Look, my hands are shaking. How can you act so nonchalant when the police are about to arrest us?"

"You worry too much, Gertie. He's just a college kid with a part-time job. Come on, let's make a break for it and find a bathroom where we can change."

They half-trotted, peering frequently over their shoulders until they found their exit. Then they hustled the short hop from there to a ladies' room.

"Ma always said there's a first time for everything. I've never dried my hair under one of these hand dryers before." Gertie pushed the button for Edna who stooped over, her head taking the full force of the hot air.

"I'm not sure you're going to like the result. It looks awfully ... fluffy. Did you bring any gel?"

"It'll be fine. The guys back home at the Elks' dances seem to like my hairdo just fine. I think I'm going to junk this wet towel. It isn't much anyway, and I don't want to get stuff soggy in my purse." Edna tossed the wet, flimsy, MGM Too towel into the trash.

"I managed to keep my hair dry, but I'm still a bit damp. Don't you dare tell anyone I dried off with paper toilet-seat covers. I'd never live that one down with my garden club ladies."

"Never fear. I keep my distance from that group. A bunch of snobs if you ask me."

"No one asked."

Edna stepped back to get the full effect of her image in the mirror. "I'm glad I wore the mint green tee today. I think the color sets off my eyes, don't you? Ready to hit the slots? I'm gonna try the jungle animals first and then that cute bunch of machines on the back wall where those smiley faces pop up in the middle of your game. You never know when they'll appear. Makes it so exciting."

"I might as well go back to my poker machine. I won thirty dollars yesterday. I feel comfortable there. Here, take my suit. I wrung it out the best I could."

Edna plopped Gertie's suit into the plastic bag alongside hers. "Don't you know anything about gambling? You'll never win on the same machine twice. They have those things rigged to go off at certain times. You want to find yourself a nice used one where no one has won for a while."

"I suppose you're right. Maybe I'll move one seat over."

"That's right, you take a walk on the wild side, girlfriend." Edna smiled, but her voice had a nasty edge to it.

Gertie stared at her best friend, a hint of hurt clouding her eyes. "It's not kind to make fun of people. Don't forget, I gave up several social events to come on this crazy trip with you. I wouldn't trust you here alone."

"Oh, relax, Gertie. You know I love to tease you."

They exited the ladies' room and walked down the hall toward the slots. Edna chattered as they went. "It's so strange how we've only been here two days, and this place is starting to feel like home."

"Perish the thought. What time shall we meet? I'm kind of hungry already."

"Duck!" Edna shoved down hard on Gertie's shoulder and pushed her toward the wall where they both ended up squatting behind an ATM.

"Ouch, what in the world are you doing?"

"Shh. It's that awful guy who keeps showing up—the one from the buffet yesterday. I don't want to talk to him again. Stay down for a sec. There, he went around the corner."

"Was it worth half-killing me to avoid him?" Gertie stood and ran her hands over her pant legs and then her sleeves.

"There's something about him. It's not natural the way he keeps showing up wherever we are. I get the willies when he talks to me. Sorry if I bumped you into the wall. I didn't mean to ... Gertie?"

But Gertie had left the scene of the accident. Edna caught a glimpse of her best friend rounding the corner and heading out an exit into the hot Las Vegas sunshine.

CHAPTER NINE

Edna hurried after Gertie, swimming against the current of guests entering the MGM on a sunny Saturday. She puffed from the exertion. "Gertie!" Edna called out in hopes of bringing her back.

She stopped and craned her neck in all directions, trying to get a glimpse of Gertie's head in the sea of noggins. There she was, stomping her way toward the big lion and the shuttle stop.

"Gertie, wait!"

Edna elbowed her way through a steady rush of bodies and reached her friend as she sat down on the shuttle-stop bench.

"Don't try and stop me, Edna, I'm going back to the hotel."

Edna sat down next to her and spoke in a soft, comforting voice. "You don't want to do that, Gertie. That room stinks. There's nothing to do there. I'm sorry I shoved you—didn't mean to hurt your feelings."

"It's not my feelings you shoved into the wall. I bet I'll have bruises tomorrow." Gertie massaged her right shoulder and gestured toward her hip. She sniffed and turned her head away.

Edna reached out and gently patted Gertie's uninjured shoulder. "I'm sorry. I get carried away sometimes. Next time we see that guy, I'll ignore him. I didn't mean to hurt you."

Gertie stretched the silence out a good, long time. "Well, okay. I really don't want to go back to that hotel. But everything here makes me a nervous wreck. Is there somewhere we can sit for a while and maybe have a rest?"

"How about this? You said you're hungry. It's full-on lunchtime in there. Let's go back to the buffet. You find a nice, quiet place to wait again, and I'll get us a super-snazzy lunch. What's your favorite? Prime rib? Shrimp? You name it, and I'll get it for you. I'll keep the food separate. And then we'll play some slots, and before you know it, it'll be time for tonight's show. Oh, man, I can't wait."

Gertie turned on the bench and stared. "You haven't heard a word I said, have you? You never cease to amaze me." She threw her hands in the air. "Why not? We haven't been incarcerated yet. We can always plead insanity." She turned her face upward, a gleam of crazy in her eyes. "I'm sorry, Donald, things go to pot when I spend time with Edna."

"Let's do our best to think positive. My ma always said to look for the silver lining, and you'd probably get rained on. That was her little joke. Let's make the most of the time we have left."

"Yes, I remember your ma. She scared me to death." Gertie stood and faced the huge, green building as if she were walking to the gallows.

They ambled back toward the hotel. Edna guided Gertie by the elbow and whispered encouraging words into her ear. "There you go, we'll go back inside and have a yummy lunch. You'll feel better with some food in your stomach." Gertie moved robotically, her eyes blank.

They covered familiar territory. Edna deposited Gertie into the same back booth as the day before, and Gertie collapsed and leaned her head back against the upholstered seat.

"You rest. I'll be back in a jiffy with all your favorites. I'll see if I can find a place to get a drink to go with the meal. It'll help relax you. You'll be fine."

Edna darted off.

Mere seconds later, Edna exploded into the dining area. "The nerve of that guy." Her gritty words startled Gertie into a full-upright position. "I'm so mad I could spit nails." Edna stood beside the table with both hands on her hips, her head tossing and causing her hair to sway back and forth like an underwater scene from The Little Mermaid.

"Mercy, you scared me. What happened?"

"Mr. *You don't have the proper identification, madam.* That's what happened."

"You had a false ID."

"That's not the point. It wasn't *what* he said that made me so mad, but the way he said it. He practically threatened me. He grabbed my arm and tossed me out the door. He kept the ID too. They don't teach young people any respect for the elderly anymore."

"I doubt if they've ever lavished respect on people trying to mooch a buffet lunch." Gertie visibly relaxed, even managing a weak smile. She leaned forward and rested her elbows on the table. They'd escaped the long arm of the law again. "Let's get out of here before something worse happens. Let's go find somewhere we can get a sandwich and that drink you mentioned earlier."

Edna steadied herself. She pulled back her shoulders and tugged the sides of her sassy tee down into place. "You're right, girlfriend. I'm not going to let a little bad luck ruin my day. Let's eat and get back to the slots. Your poker machine awaits, and my jungle animals are ready to roar." Edna beamed at her friend. "You're the best, Gertie. Couldn't ask for a better friend in times of trouble."

Gertie scooted out of the booth. "Thanks, I guess. Let's try to have a normal lunch and then kill some time until the show. Lord, I'll be glad when this whole thing is over."

"I'll bet all the contestants are busy rehearsing, don't you think? They said the ten finalists' names will be posted by five p.m. Let's get there early so we can go over the score sheets again. I know Elvis Aaron is going to win. Someday that man's name will be up in neon lights."

Gertie sighed. "The only neon light I want to see is one with a cocktail logo on it."

Edna hustled down the hallway. *Here I come, Elvis Aaron, I'm gonna be your biggest fan tonight.* She spied Gertie sitting on the same couch outside The Ruby Room lobby that she'd used the evening before. "How long have you been waiting here?"

"Oh, I don't know—maybe forty-five minutes. I lost the thirty dollars I won yesterday on that second poker machine and decided to quit. What time is it?"

Edna gawked at her Timex. "It's four forty-five. We should be able to see the finalists' list in a few minutes. I'll die if Elvis Aaron isn't on it."

Gertie rolled her eyes but held her tongue. "Why are you hopping around like that?"

"I gotta visit the little girls' room. Stay here, I'll be right back."

Edna was no sooner gone than Mr. Sleazy sidled up beside Gertie's couch. He stepped into her personal space.

"Hello, again. Where's your friend? She dump you and leave you all alone for some wolf to gobble up?"

Gertie slid to the far end of the couch.

"Cat got your tongue? Hey, are you two coming to the after-party? There's gonna be good eats and all the Elvis guys who haven't blown town will be there. Lotsa fun."

"I—"

Edna reappeared, wiping her hands on the sides of her pants. She stood toe-to-toe with Mr. Sleazy. "Get lost."

"Can't do that, beautiful. I got work to do. See you girls later." He turned and walked through the door into the lobby of The Ruby Room.

"I wonder who that guy is, anyway. He keeps turning up like a bad penny. He and I are gonna come to blows one of these times."

Gertie got up off the couch and peered into the lobby. She stretched to watch Mr. Sleazy enter the theater. "Looks like he's going right backstage."

"He better keep his distance from me. I'm ready to punch his fat face."

"Don't you dare. You've gotten into enough trouble for one day. Where's all your paperwork on these guys? Come on, let's go see if your Mr. Wonderful made the cut."

The girls made their way into the lobby and past the memorabilia stalls to the bulletin board by the theater entrance. Sure enough, the finalist list, printed in bright red letters, announced full names and bios for each of the ten winners.

"Look, Elvis Aaron is number five. I'm gonna go say hello to his mama. Hmm. Looks like her booth is all packed up and gone. Bet she wants a front-row seat for the finals. I hope they perform in that order, being in the middle is a lucky slot. People will forget the first guys and be tired by the tenth."

Gertie wrinkled her nose. "Get a load of those names. Roger Vallee, Gypsy Mose Lee, Shawn E. Rivers. Oh, my word. I can't remember what any of them did last night. Can hardly tell them apart."

"Now, Gertie. I've been thinking. We're making light of some of these boys, and we need to stop. After all, they've dedicated lots of time and energy learning all those songs, buying their costumes, and honing their skills. Some of them even grow their own sideburns. These men are Tribute Artists, not pretenders. Let's show some respect."

"I stand corrected, Madam Elvis Voter. I hope the time flies by so we can get this over with. What are you doing?"

Edna rummaged through her ample handbag past the bag of damp bathing suits and pulled out the parting gift from the night before. She slid it carefully out of the plastic bag, unrolled it, and held it up against the wall to press out the wrinkles with her other hand. "I've made up my mind. If the organizers of this event cared enough to give us a parting gift, it would be downright ungrateful of us not to wear it. Here, tie the strings for me."

Gertie's eyes grew large, and she took a step backward. "I will not. You're going to look like a darn fool in that thing."

"An Elvis cape is not foolish. Besides, I feel a mite underdressed for the after-party in slacks and a tee. This is more elegant." Edna draped the cape around her shoulders and searched for the strings.

"It's white plastic, and it smells."

"It's creamy-colored, and it looks exactly like the capes Elvis wore toward the last of his career. And when he knelt to take a bow and spread out both arms, he was," her voice became soft and reverent, "magnificent."

Gertie stood, eyes agog, grasping for words. "I ... Oh, what's the use. Go ahead and wear that ridiculous plastic cape. You go on down there in those front row voter seats and do your homework. I hear another margarita calling my name."

"What, again? You expect me to do all the studying while you drink?"

"Yes, Edna, I do. And I plan on copying your paper. Better yet, I'm going to give Elvis Aaron the lowest marks on every A, P, and V. I hope he loses and that cute little guy with the high voice wins."

"You wouldn't."

Gertie's eyes narrowed. "You just watch me." And she flounced down the hallway leaving her plastic-caped, sputtering friend behind.

CHAPTER TEN

Edna sat hunched over her papers. Gertie's "cute little guy with the high voice" hadn't made the cut. That would fix her. *Wait. I'm better than this. I need to keep an open mind here. Can't just give the win to Elvis Aaron, no matter how much I'd like to.*

Edna turned around in her seat to search the crowd for Elvis Aaron's mama and to see if Gertie was coming. No luck on either count. The clock read seven-fifteen, and she fidgeted. Was her best friend mad enough to skip the entire show? No, Gertie was too conscientious for that.

She caught sight of Gertie rounding the corner from the lobby into the theater and breathed a sigh of relief.

Gertie stopped at the top of the aisle, swaying slightly. "Gertie?"

Gertie placed one foot carefully in front of another and made her way down to the voting section. The upholstered seats gave her something to hold on to as she went. She stepped sideways over other senior voters. "S'cuse me, shorry," she said and plopped down in her seat. She put one elbow on the armrest of her chair and offered Edna a lopsided grin as her elbow slipped off the armrest.

Edna took stock of her BFF, torn between clapping her on the back and scolding her like a five-year-old. "Gertrude Ann Larsen, you're drunk." Edna drew back to get a good look at her staid, usually straight-as-an-arrow friend. Then the enormity of the moment struck at Edna's heart. The show was about to begin. "How could you?"

Gertie hiccupped. "I am *not* drunk. I had a couple of margaritas to get me through the show. I am perfectly fine. Now, where is that list? I want to find my cute little guy."

"Your cute little guy is probably on a bus back to wherever he came from. He's out. Now get hold of yourself. The show is about to begin."

A microphone let out a high-pitched squeal, and the entire audience covered their ears. Then out strode Mr. Skip Diamond, his skinny, shiny black suit reflecting under the lights, and they were off to the races.

"Ladies and Gentlemen, welcome to our nineteenth annual Elvis Tribute Artist Finale. Let's hear it for our ten finalists."

Skip gestured with his hand, and the curtain flew open. Ten finalists attacked the stage, each with a microphone in hand. The cover band jived in full force as the contestants gyrated their hips and wailed out an energetic version of "Blue Suede Shoes."

"Look, Gertie. They're all wearing blue shoes. Isn't that great? So authentic."

Gertie stood and tried one of Edna's two-fingered whistles, but failed, only managing to spray spit on the bald head of the man in front of her.

"Sit down, Gertie." Edna refocused her attention on the ten Elvises who were introduced in order of performance. She caught Elvis Aaron's eye and winked. He winked back, and her heart did a cartwheel. But he kept winking. Did he have a nervous twitch? *Well, no wonder he's twitching. This is a big deal, and there's a lot at stake.*

Skip Diamond took center stage and calmed the crowd. "Okay, ladies and gents, save your energy for the rest of the show. Allow me to introduce our esteemed panel of voting seniors once again. Please stand and take a bow."

Gertie jumped up and pivoted around, taking a full bow from the waist. Edna found it difficult to manage her cape which had stuck to her behind. She pulled it loose with a graceful flourish of her arm and did a quick curtsy. Gertie still faced the audience and was about to lean into another bow.

"Gertie, sit down." Edna grabbed her arm and pulled.

"Ouch. Le'go. You wanted me here, and you got me." Gertie sat. "Now where's my number two pencil and my score sheet?" Senior heads turned to stare from all corners of the voting section.

"Shh, they're coming to pass them out right now. Hold your horses."

Soon the seniors sat with pencils in hand, ready to seal the fate of one, fortunate, Elvis tribute singer. What would they do to top last night's performances?

"Okay, Gertie, it's show time. Here comes contestant number one, Roger Vallee. His sideburns don't look like they match, and his chest is too hairy for me. I'm gonna give him a two on appearance. How 'bout you?"

But Gertie's head lay snuggled on her chest, eyes closed with an innocent countenance curving her lips into a Mona Lisa smile. She snored softly.

"Holy cow. What a time to spread your wings and feel your oats. I'm going to have to fill in your scoresheet too."

Edna returned to the task at hand, giving fair and honest scores to each contestant except for Elvis Aaron who scored solid fives from her. *Who am I trying to kid? He's as close to perfect as a man can get. He deserves to win.*

At the end of number eight's performance and Shawn E. Rivers' rendition of "Burning Love" echoing in her head, Edna gave Gertie a poke. "Hey, girlfriend, it's almost over. You better wake up and smell the roses."

Gertie roused, quivered, and grabbed both armrests on her chair. "Oh my goodness, you startled me."

"Startled you, my foot. You were sound asleep. I'm trying to save you from embarrassment when they come to get our score sheets. Here, you score the last two guys."

"What? You did the scores for me? You better not have—"

"Relax, I put threes on everything. You can change them if you want."

"But I don't remember any of the performances."

"Well, Elvis Aaron outdid himself. He did a full gospel medley and ended up with "Peace in the Valley." I'll bet his mama burst her buttons with pride."

"Humph."

"You better watch your p's and q's, Miss Humph. I've got something to tell the ladies of the garden club back home. Miss Larsen of the genteel set of Amarillo, Texas, got a snoot full in Las Vegas."

Gertie put her hand to her forehead. "Oh, my head."

"Shh, here comes number nine."

Skip Diamond stretched out the drama until every member of the audience was on the edge of his or her seat. Edna's heart hammered in her chest. Elvis Aaron had to win. "Ladies and Gentlemen, the moment you've all been waiting for. Drumroll, please."

The drummer from the cover band began the roll. All ten tribute artists stood in line, hands behind their backs, sweat running from every pore.

Gertie tipped her head toward Edna. "I'll bet those leather suits are the reasons they sweat so much. Those things probably have to be hung out to dry after these performances." She wrinkled her nose in disgust.

"Shh, he's about to announce the winner."

A spotlight from the balcony flooded each contestant in turn, and the audience cheered for their favorites as they lit up. Then the spotlight roamed in a random pattern until it finally exploded with extra glare on contestant number five.

"Ladies and gentlemen, your Elvis Tribute King of the year, Elvis Aaron Snodgrass!"

Elvis Aaron beamed and took a step forward. The light pulsed on him while the other nine contestants receded into oblivion.

Skip Diamond shook his hand then motioned for the audience to quiet. "It is my distinct honor and pleasure to introduce to you the CEO of our esteemed sponsor, the Southern Local Life Insurance Company. Mr. Theodore M. Lawson. Mr. Lawson is here to present the winner's check for $5,000. Mr. Lawson?"

Skip Diamond held out his arm in a theatrical welcome, and who should peacock his way onto the stage but Mr. Sleazy himself.

"Gertie, Look! That's our guy—he's the CEO of the insurance company. Maybe we should change our phone numbers when we get home."

"Ooh, that guy gives me the creeps from way up there. Let's keep our heads down so he doesn't see us." Gertie ducked her head and closed her eyes.

The presentations continued. Elvis Aaron took possession of a sturdy, oversized check, received a kiss on the cheek from a skinny girl in a low-cut gown, and Mr. Sleazy finished up with a hearty handshake. Skip Diamond continued calling out his name until the spotlight died, the curtain closed, the theater lights came up, and the audience stood and shuffled their way out of the room.

Gertie remained seated with her head down and eyes closed. "Hey, are you asleep again?"

"Not really, but I sure am tired. That second margarita might have been a mistake. Let's get back to the shuttle."

"Not on your life. I'm gonna find the after-party and give my regards to Elvis Aaron and his mama. This is a once-in-a-lifetime opportunity for me, and I'm gonna soak up all the star power I can."

"How will you even know where to go? Looks like everyone is going out the door and heading home."

"That's what happens for peons, but you and I are special guests of this whole shebang. All the senior voters are invited—says so right here in tonight's packet of information which you would know if you hadn't gone on a toot."

"I did *not* go on a toot. I simply had one too many margaritas. There's a difference."

"Yeah, tell that to your garden party ladies."

"Edna, if you tell anyone back home, I'll—."

"Don't get your panties in a twist. I'm kidding." Edna crinkled her way down the row and out into the aisle, pulling the cape free of her warm body.

"Phew, that thing smells worse when it's warmed up." Gertie moved a step away.

"I'm gonna go to the stage door and ask someone where the after-party is."

Gertie sat back down to wait it out. Edna returned in a jiffy with a smile the size of Texas on her face. "Conference room 7-A. Woo hoo, let's go."

The nearest elevator was a bit of a hike. Gertie struggled to keep up with her near-ecstatic friend. "Slow down a little. I still don't feel so good."

Edna slowed her pace, all the time singing the praises of the Tribute King. "I knew he could do it. I'm so proud of him. I can't wait to hug his mama. And bless my soul if I don't intend to plant a kiss right on the side of his sideburns."

Gertie stopped in her tracks. "I think you could get arrested for that. You'd better be careful."

"Girlfriend, there has never been an arrest for a simple

kiss on the cheek. It's not like I plan to attack him or anything."

They reached the elevator, entered, and found themselves alongside several of their senior voting cohorts. Edna jiggled with excitement, her cape alternately expanding and deflating. Edna pushed the button for the seventh floor. "Didn't any of the rest of you all try on your cape?"

No one answered.

The elevator swooshed them to their floor in seconds. Directly in front of the elevator door lay Conference room 7-A, double doors open wide. Elvis tunes wafted out into the hallway.

"Oh, boy, I bet this will be like a trip into the Jungle Room at Graceland. Elvis Aaron, here I come."

CHAPTER ELEVEN

Conference room 7-A had been set up with red-linen-covered tables around the edges of the largeish room. A bar ran along the wall to the right where two bartenders wore white aprons and did a brisk business. To the left, several tables sported trays of hors d'oeuvres prepared for the after-party guests. Elvis aficionados, senior voters, and Elvis tribute artists along with their retinues mingled in small groups. An instrumental version of "Love Me Tender" created a calm ambiance.

"Wowee, look at all those horsey doovers. I hope they have those little smokie wieners. I love those." Edna blew through the door of the room, cape billowing behind.

"It's not horsey doovers, It's hors—"

"I know, I know. It's just that Ma always called them that, and it's stuck in my brain. Now, where are Elvis Aaron and his mama?"

Edna scanned through the groups of party-goers looking for her hero. "He has to be here. This is his big moment. It's his time to bask in the glory of being the winner. I'm gonna go get some food and ask the waitresses if they've seen him."

Edna hoofed it over to the food tables, filled a plate, and fell into conversation with one of the pretty, young women outfitted in French maid uniforms.

Gertie arrived at the tables as one of them said, "I saw him go through that door a minute ago."

Edna jerked to attention, a plate of meatballs, wieners, and mini cheese balls in one hand, nose attuned to the opposite door like a hound dog after a raccoon. "Here, Gertie, hold this for me. I'm gonna plant a big one on Elvis Aaron's cheek."

Edna galloped out the door leaving Gertie with a plate full of protein and a look of bewilderment on her face. Gertie sidled over to a quiet corner of the room and sank into a folding chair.

Edna caught a glimpse of white pants and blue shoes down a side hallway. *There he is.* The figure turned a corner and disappeared, and Edna redoubled her efforts to catch up to him.

Now I gotta get a hold of myself. Don't want to come on too strong. His mama might think I'm one of those hangers-on. I only want to show my appreciation of his stardom. Edna was deep into self-talk as she approached the corner and heard a scuffling noise. A "thunk" landed against a wall, and she came to an abrupt halt.

"Five hundred was the agreement, and that's what you're gettin'," someone said in a surly voice with an ugly edge. "Me and Ma know how to deal with creeps who try to throw their weight around."

"Don't you threaten me. I could ruin your whole pathetic career if I let people know you make deals to win these little contests."

More thumps and bumps. Edna backed up a few steps until her curiosity pulled her forward to take a peek around the corner.

There stood Mr. Sleazy and Elvis Aaron nose to nose. Elvis Aaron's right fist threatened the Insurance CEO's jaw while his left hand held the smaller man's white shirt in a twisted bunch. "Take the five and get out of here before I change my mind and keep all of it. Your grimy little insurance company Board of Directors wouldn't be too happy to hear their boss takes kickbacks, now, would they?"

Edna gasped. She rounded the corner and stopped in front of the two men, hands on her hips. "Elvis Aaron Snodgrass, what would your mama think? Shame on you. All of us voters gave you the highest marks. Why'd you sink to making a deal with this awful man? The very idea! Where is your mama, anyway? I'd like to have a word with her."

The two men stood frozen in time. Slowly Elvis Aaron removed his fist from in front of Mr. Sleazy's face and dropped his left hand from his shirt.

Mr. Sleazy took a deep breath and retreated a step. "Now, lady." He twisted his flushed face into a conciliatory smile. "This isn't what you think. Merely a misunderstanding between two friends. You go on back to the party and have a good time."

"I'll say it's a misunderstanding." Edna shook her head and pointed her finger. "You hoodwinked this poor, young man into making a deal he didn't entirely think through." Edna took on a motherly tone as she turned to address Elvis Aaron. "You would have won this contest hands down without agreeing to any deal. Tsk, tsk. It's a shame is what it is. Where *is* your mama?"

Elvis Aaron looked as if he were torn between returning to the task of throttling Mr. Sleazy and escaping his admiring fan. "Ma's in the bus, and I'd best get down there too. We have a lot of miles to cover tonight." He gave Mr. Sleazy one last squinty-eyed look, turned, and marched down the hallway toward the elevator.

Edna held her ground. "Look at you, you big bully. My friend and I better not get any insurance solicitation calls when we get home. You mark Edna Gratzer and Gertie Hansen off your list of victims. And I'll be writing a long letter to your Board of Directors."

"Aww, write your heart out. They'll just think you're another Elvis nut. Who listens to them?"

Edna opened her mouth to answer with a stinging retort when it dawned on her that Elvis Aaron was getting away. Unkissed.

She hustled down the hall and into room 7-A. She grabbed Gertie just as she made to pop a little smokie into her mouth. "Get up. Hurry. Come on, we're gonna miss him."

"Miss who?"

Edna ran to the elevator, dragging Gertie by the hand. She pushed the down arrow and tracked the progress of the numbers as they counted down from seven to one and then "G." The parking garage.

"Elvis Aaron must be meeting his Ma at their bus down on the ground floor. Come on, elevator, get back up here." Edna huffed in a big breath and banged on the down arrow again. After interminable moments the door slid open, the two women leaped inside, and Edna pushed the "G" for all she was worth.

Gertie pulled her hand loose. "What in the world are we doing? I didn't even get a chance to finish eating."

"There's trouble, with a capital "T." Elvis Aaron's done something he never should have done, and we need to get down there and talk some sense into him before he gets away." Edna paused. "And, besides, I want to tell him goodbye."

"You want to attack him is what you mean."

"I want to tell him how wonderful he was on that stage. Every eye was on him—he's a true artist."

Gertie wiped some crumbs from the front of her blouse. "What's all the fuss? What'd he do?"

"It's just a little mistake. He might have given part of his prize money away."

"Who'd he give it to. You?"

"Of course not. He might have given a tiny bit of it to that insurance CEO guy."

"You mean that guy who's been following you? The one who presented the check?"

"Yeah, him."

Gertie processed that bit of information as the elevator came to a halt on the garage level. "Edna, this is dangerous territory you're entering. Stay out of it."

"I can't. Elvis Aaron looked like he was sorry he made that deal. I know he's a good boy at heart." Gertie was nearest the elevator door and turned to face her friend. "Now, Edna, you'd better listen—"

Edna shot past Gertie, searching wildly for Elvis Aaron and a bus with an older woman at the wheel. "Where are they?"

As Edna passed by, Gertie caught her friend's shoulder and clamped down hard. "Stop."

The elevator door closed, narrowly missing both of their bodies but caught the flaring cape in its jaws. Edna came up short, her neck in a stranglehold of plastic. "Ugh." Her hands flew up to her neck trying in vain to untie the cape strings.

"Here, stand still and let me help you." Gertie paused to get her reading glasses out of her purse, placed them on her nose, and moved in close to untie the knotted strings.

Edna shot daggers that missed their mark as Gertie took her sweet time to untangle the mess. The strings finally loosened, and the entire cape fell to the ground in a wrinkled heap.

An engine backfired, a cloud of noxious fumes surrounded the girls, and a refurbished bus with more rust than paint, ground into gear and rumbled past them.

Edna watched the taillights disappear as the bus rolled out of the parking garage and into the Las Vegas night toward parts unknown. She picked up the limp plastic cape, released it from the jaws of the elevator doors, wadded it into a ball, and tossed it into a nearby garbage can.

Edna leaned forward and took a sip of her pink-umbrella drink. With her elbows resting on the table for two, she cradled her chin on her folded hands. A largish hunk of frizzy, silver hair fell forward over one eyebrow.

"I'm lower than a skunk's belly," she said.

Gertie tipped her head and clucked her tongue. "Don't take it so hard. This is Las Vegas. You can't expect all these people to live squeaky clean lives."

"You can say that again." Edna pushed her hair back with two fingers so it stood straight and tall again.

"I don't think I've ever had three drinks in one day in my entire life." Gertie licked some salt off the edge of her glass. "Can you keep a secret? Promise not to tell anyone?"

Edna nodded.

"I'm sort of enjoying this trip into sin city. I feel like a kid again. I mean, all the sneaking around and getting caught by security—I certainly didn't enjoy that. And the Elvis impersonators are of questionable character. But ... well, when I'm with you, I do things I'd never get a chance to do back home. I feel spunkier—like maybe I've held back since Donald died. I'm actually having fun."

Edna relaxed and grinned. "Good for you, my friend. Hearing that lifts my spirits. But, dang, I never thought Elvis Aaron would stoop so low as to offer a bribe to the head of that lousy insurance company. He would have won without doing something underhanded like that."

"I know, people do disappoint."

"I could just cry. And to think I trusted his mama while she was part of the whole thing."

The two friends grew quiet, sipping and thinking somber thoughts together. The bar was an alcove set off to the side of one of the slot-machine lounges, and the ladies' thoughts were perforated with the incessant clangs and beeps of the machines.

Edna stood and slapped both hands on the table. "I've made up my mind." She scrabbled through her handbag.

Gertie jumped at the loud noise and clutched her drink in both hands as if to protect it. "What are you doing?"

"Desperate times call for desperate measures, Girlfriend. I already lost my money for the day, but this isn't just any day. This is the day we stand up to injustice. This is the day we rise above underhanded dealings and take control of our destinies. I'm busting into my emergency fund. Are you with me? We missed the ten o'clock shuttle anyway—can't catch the next one until midnight."

Edna reached deeply into her bag, unzipped a zipper, and took out a small, leather coin purse. She opened it and pulled out a bill folded into a square. She unfolded it. "This here is meant for times when I'm in serious trouble. I'd say Elvis Aaron's behavior sent me down into a nasty funk, and this here hundred dollar bill will raise me back up out of it. Let's go."

Edna set off at a fast clip, halted, and turned to gesture for Gertie to follow. They headed into the bowels of the slot machine beast.

CHAPTER TWELVE

Edna parked herself at a slot machine that sported cats, kittens, dishes of cat food, and bags of kibble. Every time she won a few credits, it meowed. "I'm gonna play this one for a while. Reminds me of Big Bertha. If we get separated, I'll meet you at the shuttle station at eleven forty-five. I think I have a winner here."

Gertie looked at the adjacent machines. Creepy-looking wizards on one side and lions and tigers on the other. "I'm not much for animal machines. I'm going to look for some sevens and cherries."

"Atta girl. This is the new you—full of courage and ready to take on the world." Edna refocused her attention on her game. Four cans of cat food lined up, and the machine emitted a yowl as it surrendered thirty credits.

Gertie wandered up and down the aisles. Nothing caught her eye. She watched an elderly woman play a poker machine, cigarette smoke spiraling over her head, her walker parked neatly by her side. Then she spied a bank of machines through a doorway—all sevens and cherries and pretty oval buttons with X5 and X10 on them.

She spotted an empty seat at the far end of the row and hurried to claim it. "Darn, the smallest I have is a twenty." *Oh, well, this is the new me—not so timid and shy. I can play until I run it down to ten dollars and quit anytime I want.* Gertie slid the twenty into the appropriate slot and watched as the machine ate it. It sang a little song as it rang up the credits. Make that credit. Only one credit? She pushed the play button.

All hell broke loose. The lights on the top of the machine lit up and bells clanged. A siren pierced the air. Gertie covered her ears. Every player in her row gathered around as she gaped at the screen. A flashing row of sevens sparkled and an "X10" button burned alternating purple, silver, and blue.

"What was the progressive?" a man asked.

"Huh?"

"How much did you win?" asked the woman to her right. "Looks like ten times whatever those sevens are worth. Look at the top of the machine."

Gertie peered at the rows of sevens and cherries plotted out in dizzying array above the screen. "I pushed the button once, I'm not sure what I got."

"Well, at twenty bucks a pop, you shoulda got something good," the man said.

Gertie sat amid the noise and confusion, wringing her hands. Her cheeks flushed red, and she fought a wave of dizziness. *How did this happen?*

The woman to her right patted her shoulder. "Don't worry, honey, an attendant will come any minute. They like to let the noise attract attention for a while, and then they pay out."

A stocky, uniformed woman with keys dangling from her belt approached and offered congratulations. "Looks like we have a winner!" She opened the door of the machine and turned off all the bells and whistles. "This is your lucky day, ma'am. You won a total of $1,397.52. Come with me, and we'll take care of you."

Gertie stood and meekly followed her toward the cashier's cage. Her mind raced, but no coherent thoughts emerged.

The woman opened a door and led the way to a small office. She gestured to a chair in front of her desk, and

Gertie sat. "Do you always play high stakes?" the woman asked.

"High stakes? You mean like real gamblers play—a lot?"

"Yes, ma'am. You won on a twenty-dollar machine."

"Twenty dollars? Every time?"

"Yes, ma'am. Now, would you be interested in having your photo taken with the floor manager as a souvenir of your win? And may we have your permission to use the picture in our promotional materials? Also, your winnings are subject to a thirty percent tax—anything over $1200. Sign here, please." She handed Gertie a tax form and pointed to a line at the bottom.

Gertie woodenly signed her name.

"That's fine about the taxes, but no pictures, please." *Oh, where is Edna?* "Can you page my friend for me, please? Edna Gratzer? She's outside in the next room playing on a cat machine."

"Yes, ma'am, we can page her for you. You stay here while we make up your check. Or would you prefer cash?" The woman did a quick calculation on her computer. "You'll receive $978.26."

Gertie stared at the woman for a long moment. She stood and lifted her chin. "The old me would have taken a check and put it in my savings account when I got home. But this is the new me. I'll take cash, please." Her heart did a kerthump in her chest.

"Yes, ma'am." The woman left the office and proceeded back into the casino proper. Gertie heard the sound of a microphone: "Paging Edna Gratzer, paging Edna Gratzer. Please meet your party at the High Stakes cashier's cage."

Gertie opened her handbag, drew out her wallet, and waited for her payout.

A soft rap pattered on the door of MGM suite 703. "Room service."

Edna roused off the comfy couch, pulled the sash on her robe tight, and sashayed to the door. She peered through the peephole, squinted at the young man dressed in black and white carrying a tray, and opened the door.

"Come on in."

"Your champagne and strawberries, ma'am."

Gertie appeared, peeling a fifty-dollar bill off a wad of money. "Here, keep the change."

"Thank you, ma'am." The young man set the tray on the granite counter of their kitchenette, bowed politely, backed out of the room, and closed the door discreetly behind him.

"Good thing I tended bar for my Uncle Louie's wedding, or I might not know how to open one of these." Edna grasped the bottle and popped the cork. She poured the bubbly into two tall, elegant flutes and lifted one in a toast to her newly liberated friend. "Here's to you, Gertie. This is the life. You thought of everything—toothbrushes and toothpaste, champagne, and this here tray of strawberries, and you got us a room with a Jacuzzi. Cheers." Edna drank. "Let's slip into our bathing suits and drink the champagne in the tub."

Gertie sipped her champagne. "I thought to myself, *Gertie Hansen, this might be the only chance you ever get to stay in a fancy hotel in Las Vegas. No more slinking around. It's time to go right up to the counter and pay for a nice room.* They even gave me a special deal on the champagne being I was a high roller and all." Gertie stopped to take a breath and glanced around at the spacious, well-appointed suite. "I know we don't have pajamas with us, but these robes will do, and we can always rinse out our undies and hang them to dry over the heat vent."

"Sure, why not?" Edna drained her glass and chuckled. "I didn't think you had it in you. Playing in the high stakes room, winning big, and then springing for a double queen room with the works."

"I couldn't face that awful room at the MGM Too when I had all this money in my hands. But the high-stakes part was an accident. I put in a bill and pushed once and—"

"Hey, I don't care how you did it. You won." Edna fired up the knobs on the Jacuzzi, and hot water gushed into the huge, oval tub. "Let's relax and enjoy these hot water jets on our tired muscles. Then how about we watch a movie and sleep in late tomorrow? We can have us a nice brunch right here in the room. We'll catch the shuttle back to that dive, gather up our stuff, and have plenty of time to catch our bus at four o'clock."

"Sounds good to me. I'm exhausted after all that excitement. The Jacuzzi is calling my name. Where're our suits?"

Edna grabbed her handbag, pawed through it, and pulled out a twisted plastic bag. She pulled out two soggy lumps. "They're right here—still a little damp, I'm afraid." She separated the suits and held them at arm's length. "Hell's bells, Gertie, let's jump into the tub in our birthday suits. No one's here, and you can wrap in a towel if it makes you feel better."

Gertie downed the rest of her champagne and poured a second glass. "I guess one more black mark by my name won't matter at this point." She gathered up a huge, fluffy, white towel and disappeared into the bathroom to disrobe.

Edna rested her head against the seat of the Greyhound bus and stretched her limbs. "Ah, that was quite a night. I slept like a baby."

"Me too. I never had room service before, and I never ate breakfast at noon. Those flaky croissant things were worth all the trouble we went through." Gertie stashed her handbag by her feet and looped the strap over her knee.

"I could get used to the good life, my friend. Think of the stories we have to tell back home."

"Now, Edna, we aren't going to talk about *all* those things. I can't even tell my friends at church about winning the money—they wouldn't approve of gambling like that."

"I thought you were the new and improved Gertie—you know, wild and free." Edna's mouth broke into a wicked grin.

"Maybe I got a taste of wild and free, and that was enough for me. I like my nice, quiet, *safe* life, thank you."

"I know you do, but admit it, you have more fun when you travel with me."

The girls settled back for the all-night ride. Edna had trashed the cheese puffs and chips in favor of a tidy little bundle of mini croissants and butter pats housed in an MGM ashtray and wrapped in a hand towel.

They rested quietly as the bus moved out of the MGM Too's parking lot, ground its gears onto the highway, and reached maximum speed.

Edna sighed. "I can't help thinking about Elvis Aaron and his mama. What a life they lead, traipsing all over the country in that ratty bus and trying to win contests. It's kinda sad when you think about it."

"Yeah, and what happens when he's too old to do all that gyrating and carrying on?"

Edna clucked her tongue and shook her head. "No one said the entertainment business was easy."

They rumbled on in silence until soft music crackled over the loudspeaker. "Listen to that. The driver is either psychic or he loves George Strait as much as I do."

Gertie listened. Strains of "Amarillo by Morning" filled the air. "Amarillo by morning is right. I'm looking forward to my nice, quiet apartment. I wonder how Big Bertha did at Rose's?"

"Yeah, I wonder too." Edna chuckled. "If there are expenses, I know who to ask for a loan."

"I think I'm going to donate the rest of the money to the garden club." Gertie's voice took on a thoughtful tone. "It doesn't feel right to keep it."

"The garden club? Those snooty dames have more money than they know what to do with. Give it to the Senior Center or the Elks. Maybe they'll be able to afford someone to clean the place once in a while. The last dance was disgusting. I swear the same flies stay on the windowsills from one month to the next..."

But Edna's words fell on deaf ears. Gertie had closed her eyes and was snoring softly, a tiny smile turning up the edges of her mouth.

EDNA AND GERTIE: A SINGLES CRUISE TO NOWHERE

CHAPTER ONE

Edna Gratzer clomped up the front steps of the Elks' building, shifting two loaded grocery bags to her left arm. She leaned back, hauled open the heavy oak door, and whooshed through before it could smack her in the backside.

"Rose? You here?" she shouted down the stairwell toward the combination lunchroom and bar. Balancing her bags on the handrail while she caught her breath, she focused straight ahead through another set of doors that led to the main floor. Towering over the entrance, Mr. Elk Head's glassy eyes greeted all comers. He looked a little crazed as if he couldn't figure out how he'd exited his serene meadow and landed in this dingy establishment. Edna knew this room well. She was a regular at the monthly dances held there on the old burnished-oak wood floor, the one saving grace of the dilapidated structure.

"I'm down in the kitchen." Rose's voice sounded thin and far away.

Edna hoofed it downstairs, bags up to her chin, praying she wouldn't tilt forward and roll to the bottom in a heap. She breathed a sigh of relief as she reached the last step and made her way across the ancient, concrete floor to the Formica counter that sectioned the kitchen off from the rest of the room. A plywood panel had been unhooked and raised to open the window into the kitchen. She plopped the grocery bags onto the counter.

"Whew, this stuff is heavy. Good thing we got permission to have the party here. My apartment is way too small. Thanks for coming over to help, Rosie."

Rose pushed her pink rhinestone eyeglasses back up the bridge of her nose and carefully placed stray strands of fine, brown hair back into the do that always ended with a bun on the top of her head. Today she'd accessorized with poodle-head drop earrings. She was a walking advertisement for her shop.

"That's okay. Thursdays are slow at the Pet-o-Rama anyway. It's Fridays when the mad rush arrives with weekenders wanting the kennels and Saturdays when we get lots of nail clips and shampoos. Our *Spa Day for Fluffy and Fido* is real popular. You should bring Big Bertha over for that sometime."

"I doubt it, but thanks for the offer. BB is a great cat, but I gotta watch my nickels and dimes these days. I spent a wad on this party for Gertie. Not to mention her gift. Of course, I don't mind. Gertie's my best friend, and she could use some cheering up. She goes up and down since Donald died. I'm tickled to death to throw this surprise party. I don't think she has a single clue."

"Probably not, being as she won't usually set foot in this place." Rose finished wiping down the counter and ripped open the wrappers on four, red-plastic tablecloths.

"I know our Gertrude would rather hang out with the garden-club women at the country club, but those dames make me tired with all their airs." Edna shook her head and harrumphed. "Give me a nice, comfortable Elks club any day of the week. We can breathe easy here and not worry about all their fussy rules."

Rose opened her mouth, but Edna cut her off. "And don't say we can't breathe easy because the air stinks from the smell of cigars. I know it does—that's why I bought a bunch of air fresheners to plug in around the room. I got two lavenders and two spring gardens. That should do the trick." She ripped open the packages and bustled around to every outlet, plugging in plastic aromatic cover-ups in the shapes of spring flowers.

Rose got busy spreading out the red cloths on the long, rectangular tables. "What did you decide on for the menu? I brought three cans of fruit punch and grabbed some little pizza doodads I had in the freezer. We can heat them up in the oven."

"Sounds good." Edna began unpacking the paper bags. "I got caramel corn and chips. And I sprang for a couple of fancy flavors. Let's see ..." She rummaged in the bag. "I got cheddar horseradish and barbecue pork rind. Mary Jo is bringing cocktail weenies in her crock pot, and Madge said she'd bring a six-pack or two. I don't expect more than a dozen will show up—sort of short notice. I got everything arranged the day before yesterday when Uncle Louie's money came in."

"Your Uncle Louie who got married a while back?"

"Yes, God rest his soul. He got married to that gold digger in January and died two months later. Everyone thought she'd get the whole shebang, but my Uncle Louie always had a fondness for me—his big girl, he always called me—and he left me a little bit."

Edna folded up the first paper bag and attacked the second. "This is the one that weighed a ton." She pulled out two eight-by-eight Pyrex dishes. "Red Jell-o squares in this one, and lime with pear cubes in the other. The red and green will look nice with the tablecloths. I couldn't find red plates, so I went with these cardboardy ones. But I got red napkins and cups. And ... "

She pulled out the pièce de résistance and held it high. "A bee-youtiful box of wine. It's called Summer Blush. I guess it doesn't matter that it's still springtime. Anyway, we got alcohol, and your fruit punch for the old fuddy-duddies that come."

"What about a cake? Can't have a big birthday bash without cake." Rose organized plates, cups, and napkins in neat piles along the counter.

Edna checked her Timex. "Holy cow, I gotta go pick up the cake right now. I only ordered it yesterday what with all the last-minute rush. The lady at Fiesta Foods said it would be ready by six, and it's nearly that now. Are you still gonna be able to pick Gertie up and bring her here?"

"Yes, ma'am. She's expecting me at six forty-five. I told her we were going to my book club. She won't know anything until I pull up outside, and then I'll get her in the door and down the stairs real quick so she doesn't have a chance to ask too many questions."

"Thanks, Rose. I'll get back as soon as I can." Edna clenched her fists, did a little jogging in place, and giggled like a teenager. "I can't wait to see the look on her face. Especially when I give her my gift. Leave the door unlocked if you go before I get back with the cake. It's gonna be chocolate with cherry filling and red and white icing. Tootles."

Gertie Larsen sat in Rose's passenger seat. She did enjoy a good literary discussion with well-read women. Rose signaled a left turn and drove through the bumpy, gravel parking lot to a spot right by the front door of the Elks Club.

"Rose, don't tell me your book club meets at this musty, old place. I swear, when they do their annual budget, they draw a red line through the custodian's wages." Gertie added a tiny sniff to her disapproval of the Elks Lodge building.

"Well, now that you mention it, we don't usually meet here, but Dolores's husband came down with the flu, and she didn't want to expose the club to his germs."

Rose opened her door and smiled an encouraging smile in Gertie's direction. "Come on, you'll love this group—so cultured and friendly too."

"Where's your book?

"Huh?"

"I said, where's the book we're discussing? You promised to get a copy for me too so I could at least follow along with the discussion. I hate not having read it beforehand. My book club wouldn't put up with women who don't do their homework before a meeting."

"Yeah, well, this group is a mite more relaxed. I was here earlier. The books are downstairs. And they begin right on the dot of seven, so let's get a move on." Rose's face flushed pink. She scurried out of the car and onto the gravel, crunching her way toward the front stairs.

Gertie exited the car and stood by its side a moment to gather courage. She'd had her hair done the day before and felt presentable in white slacks and a soft, lavender top that would fit in well with a new gathering of her peers. "Okay, I'm coming, but if I stay in the group, I sure hope they find other places to meet. Edna dragged me to a dance here a while back. The place smells like a pool hall."

Rose reached the top of the stairs and held the door open. She motioned Gertie to take the lead down the stairway.

Gertie whispered over her shoulder, "And here I am in white slacks. They'll probably be grey after we sit on those grimy old folding chairs."

The room at the bottom of the stairs was a dark hole. Gertie held tight to the handrail as she descended. "Are you sure there's someone down here?"

"Surprise, surprise!" The lights flashed on, exposing a cluster of partygoers wearing bright-red party hats. The group may have been small in number, but they'd made up for it with hearty shouts.

Gertie stood stock still, hands to her face and mouth wide open.

Edna shoved past the others to embrace Gertie in a big bear hug. She stood back, leaving her hands on Gertie's shoulders. "Did we surprise you? I sure hope so, 'cause you looked like we did. Man, that was fun. I wish we could send you up the stairs and do it all over again."

Gertie took a step backward. "But ... my birthday isn't until next Monday." She moved her hands from her face to her heart, where it pounded in her chest. "Rose, you misled me. My goodness, you all scared the life out of me."

"Now don't be mad at Rose—she was my decoy. I know your birthday isn't until next week, but you're gonna be busy by then. That's part of the surprise, but I can't tell you just yet." Edna placed an *over the hill* black sash over Gertie's shoulders and crushed a black paper crown on her head, and Gertie cringed. "Come on in, most of the gang is here."

Rose hurried to the kitchen where the aroma of something hot and charred emanated. She opened the oven door, and smoke billowed out in smelly clouds. She hollered through the serving door, "Edna, did you put those pizza thingies in the oven at 450? They look like lumps of coal." Smoke billowed from the kitchen into the dining area, and Rose followed, flapping it away with a kitchen towel.

Edna waved her arms to dismiss the smoke. "Don't worry—there's plenty of other stuff to eat. Good thing this joint doesn't have a working smoke alarm. Dump 'em in the garbage can, Rose, and let's get this party started. Gertie, you know Madge and Joan. And this here is Harold and June, from this very Elks club. And I met Mary Jo at the line dance classes at the Senior Center a while back. I asked a few more, but I had to put this thing together in a hurry."

"It's nice to see all of you." Gertie's voice wavered, but she forced out a tight smile.

"Here, Gertie. You come and sit down in the seat of honor at the head of this table. We got the food spread out over there, and Rose will get you a nice plate with a serving of everything. Relax while I get you some Summer Blush." She led Gertie by the elbow and deposited her into a brown, metal folding chair with three red balloons tied onto the back.

"Edna," Harold said, his deep voice booming through the hall. "Are you two dames gonna keep all this grub to yourself or can a hungry guy dig in?"

"Shh." June gave the stink-eye to her rotund husband.

"Well, if I gotta be the only guy at this party, at least I'm not gonna starve."

Edna hurried back to Gertie with two red plastic cups of wine in hand. She offered one to Gertie and held the other up high. "Here's to Gertie and her special day. Oops, guess the rest of you don't have drinks to toast with. Oh well, it's the spirit of the thing. Here's to my best friend in honor of her birthday." Edna tapped the two cups together and downed the contents of hers in one big gulp.

"Hear, hear," Harold bellowed as he filled his plate with chips, Jell-o squares, and weenies in spicy tomato sauce.

Rose arrived at Gertie's side with a heaping cardboard plate. She handed over a red plastic fork and napkin. "Sorry to tell that little white lie, Gertie. But all's fair in love, war, and surprise parties. Eat up. There's plenty of everything."

Gertie sat meekly in the rickety folding chair. The crown on her head had surely squashed her lovely hairdo. She took a sip of her wine and waved the other arm in a vain effort to fan away the smoke still spiraling from the kitchen. She opened the red napkin and spread it over her lap, then eyed the food. One of the weenies and its sauce had landed in the middle of the red Jell-o square. She shuddered. Orange-colored potato chips were tinged red where they met the Jell-o.

"I'm not very hungry right now. I'll just have a few pieces of the caramel corn."

Edna patted her friend on the shoulder. "That's all right, Gertie. You've had a big surprise, and you're overwhelmed is all. Eat what you want, and on this special occasion, you get cake even if you don't eat your dinner. Is that wine okay, or would you rather have a beer?"

"The wine is fine." Gertie glanced down at her white slacks. Somehow a big drop of the weenie sauce had missed the red napkin and landed on her thigh. She took several large sips of the Blush, closed her eyes, and tried a deep, cleansing breath to clear her mind.

"In fact," she said, holding out the red Solo cup, "I'll take a refill."

CHAPTER TWO

The dim basement room had the look of a bomb shelter, sirens blown long ago, the occupants more than ready to move toward the light of day. Drinks had been drunk, plates now were empty, and the food table looked like yesterday's dog dish. Red and green Jell-o sat half-melted, and little circles of oil lay congealed atop the unplugged crock-pot of weenies in spicy sauce.

"Happy birthday to you, Happy birthday to you, Happy birthday, dear Gertie—" Harold's deep voice out-decibeled the women as they finished, "Happy birthday to you."

"And many more, cha, cha, cha." Edna finished with a flourish, her large, square hips emphasizing each cha, back and forth. "Go ahead and blow out the candles."

Gertie sat forward on the flimsy folding chair, black crown atilt, and gave a half-hearted attempt to blow out the seven and one-third black candles.

"I didn't want to waste money on seventy-three candles, so I did the math and broke one into thirds. Had to dig some of the wax off to light it, but—"

Gertie waved her hand to stop Edna. "Am I supposed to cut it, or are you?"

Edna yanked the candles out of the red and white icing. "You, my friend, are the guest of honor. You sit there and enjoy every minute. Rose and I can serve." The two women bustled to move the sheet cake to the Formica counter where they sliced it into large slabs. She leaned over to speak to Rose. "I didn't bother with ice cream. The rest of the dinner was so rich."

"That's okay." Rose, ever the encouraging friend, said. "Everything is perfect the way it is."

Edna handed two cake-laden plates to Rose and wiped her hands on a paper towel. "Rose, you pass these out. I need to find my handbag." Edna hustled into the kitchen and delved into the bottom of her purse, coming out with a slightly bent, legal-sized envelope. She stuffed the envelope into the waistband of her slacks and used both little fingers to create an ear-splitting whistle.

"Okay, everyone, listen up. This here is the highlight of Gertie's special surprise party. We're gonna enjoy the cake now and give Gertie our presents."

Guests shuffled their feet and averted their eyes as they shoveled hunks of cake into their mouths.

"I wanted to get one of those whoopee cushions," Harold offered. "But June wouldn't let me."

Rose wiped her hands on her apron and pulled an envelope from her pocket. "Here, Gertie, I didn't have time to get a present, but I brought a gift card." She handed it to Gertie who smiled politely and opened it.

"A ten-dollar gift certificate good toward all goods and services provided by the Pet-o-Rama. How thoughtful of you, Rose. Thank you."

Rose beamed. "Well, you have that cute little Yorkie, and maybe you can use it for him sometime."

"She sure wouldn't need it for herself," Harold broke in, chuckling. "That's taking the pampering one step too far, I'd say."

June jabbed a sharp elbow into his side, and he glared at her.

Edna strode to Gertie's side and placed one hand on her shoulder. She took in a deep breath. "Gertie, it isn't every day that a gal turns seventy-three. It's one of those landmarks we all hope to hit one day and look as good as you do. And being as I'm your best friend and came into a little money unexpected like, I thought it fitting that I sprung for something special this year. So, I wrote you a poem. See if you can guess what I got you. Well ... got us."

Edna pulled the envelope from her waistband, opened it ceremoniously, and unfolded a type-written page. She cleared her throat.

> On my friend Gertie's special day,
> A birthday past her sixties,
> I didn't give her Cadillacs,
> Or vodka, schnapps, or whiskeys.

Edna looked out over the group to gauge their responses thus far. Blank faces, dull as sheep stared back at her. She refocused, took a deep breath, and continued.

> Instead, I signed us both up for
> Four days of thrills galore.
> From Galveston, we'll soon embark
> On a cruise that goes off-shore.

More blank stares.

Edna handed the opened envelope to Gertie and clasped her hands together in front of her heart. "I'm so excited about this I could hardly sleep last night. I wanted to find something to rhyme with cruise, but I couldn't think of anything but *bruise*, and that didn't seem right."

"You sprang for a four-day cruise for Gertie's birthday?" Harold broke in. "Man, I got a birthday next August. Where'd you get bucks like that?"

Gertie slid the remaining paper out of the envelope and opened it. She raised an eyebrow, "It's a receipt."

Edna clapped like a seal. "I know. Read it out loud."

"It says, 'Paid in full. Two fares on the *Bountiful Lady's* Senior Singles Cruise to Nowhere.'" Gertie squinted as she reread the words. "What does that even mean?"

"It means you and me on a four-day cruise in the glorious Gulf of Mexico. And instead of wasting time and money on excursions, the cruise ship tools around in figure eights for four days and gives us lots of time on the ship to get to know everyone. I've heard the fishing is good." Edna waggled her eyebrows meaningfully.

"Fishing?"

"Yeah, you know. Four days at sea with a whole boatload of eligible bachelors."

"Bachelors?" Gertie's crown slipped over one eye.

"Oh, Gertie." Edna crowed, "We're going to have the time of our lives. Now, let's all get busy and clean this joint up. We have to be out by nine. Plus, you need to get home and get to bed at a decent hour because our meet and greet is tomorrow afternoon at three, and then we leave."

Edna hustled around to every electrical outlet and unplugged the plastic flower air fresheners. "No need to be wasteful," she muttered.

CHAPTER THREE

Edna pulled up in front of Gertie's condo. Gertie sat beside her, hands folded in her lap. "You haven't said one word all the way home. I guess the party surprised you, all right."

"Thank you, Edna," Gertie said. "I know you went to a lot of trouble to plan the party, and everything was ... unique."

Edna shook her head modestly. "I couldn't have pulled it off without Rose. She knew I was short on time, and she pitched in and did anything I needed."

"Yes, Rose is very thoughtful."

"So, as I said, tomorrow afternoon is the meet and greet, and then, we hop on a short flight to Houston at six. I got us a room there for tomorrow night, and then, we catch the shuttle to Galveston and board the *Bountiful Lady* nice and early on Saturday. You got all tomorrow morning to pack. Be sure to bring a nice variety of outfits—you'll need something a little sexy for the date nights.

Gertie didn't respond.

"Gertie, did you hear me? You look kind of funny."

"I heard you. But nothing is computing."

"Okay, here. Let me try again. Tomorrow morning you pack a nice suitcase for our cruise. Bring a couple of fancy tops or something. Then at three, we have a meet and greet downtown at the Quality Sleep Inn. That's sort of like a cocktail hour where we visit with some of the other passengers and play a few games and things. This is only for the local single folks who signed up. Sort of a head start on the whole cruise. Don't worry, I already filled out your interview questions for you."

"Interview questions?"

"Yeah, they want us to get a chance to match up with some of the other guests in the most appropriate ways—you know, find guys we have things in common with."

"Edna, I don't want to sound ungrateful, but this is—"

"I know. No need to thank me. When Uncle Louie died, and I found out he left me a little stash, I wanted to do something extra-special for once. And it gives me pleasure to see you happy. We always have fun when we travel together, don't we? You had a great time in Vegas. But it's time for another pick-me-up. You've been sort of down since Donald died, and this here is your chance to shine again."

"I don't think I'm up to shining, Edna."

"Now you hush. Seventy-three years old is just a spring chicken. And you're the pretty one of the two of us. All I have going for me is my charm and wit." Edna chuckled at her joke. "And my hair, of course." Edna patted her silvery, spiky hair and then Gertie's shoulder.

"You better get a move on. I want you to get a good night's sleep, and then, you'll have time to pack your suitcase and take care of little what's his name."

"Oh, my! Chester. I'd forgotten about him. Maybe I won't be able to go, Edna. I can't go off and leave Chester alone for four days."

"Of course not. You can leave him with Rose. And you have that coupon for ten dollars off at the Pet-o-rama. Perfect. I'll pick you and Chester up at two-thirty tomorrow and away we go. I'm leaving Big Bertha there too. And don't worry about a thing—I've got you covered."

Gertie got out of the car, steadied herself, and walked to her front door in a robot-like daze. She turned once as if to make her way back to Edna, but instead feebly waved to her, unlocked her door, and disappeared.

Edna revved up her engine and tore off down the road. "Hoo boy. That couldn't have gone better if I'd had a month to plan it." *Edna, old girl, you've still got it going on.*

Edna pulled into Gertie's driveway, hopped out of her old beater, and opened the passenger-side back door. Big Bertha let out a distinctly unhappy yowl. "I know, BB, you hate being cooped up in that crate. Let's hope Rose sees fit to give you a bit of freedom to roam around this time." She hustled to the back of the car and opened the trunk, then hurried to Gertie's front door, pushed on the doorbell, and added a few taps with the door knocker for good measure.

Gertie opened the door.

"You ready? Wow, you look great. Is that a new outfit?"

Gertie stood decked out in classic navy dress slacks with a cream-colored, long-sleeved blouse. "I bought it for the Garden Club's fundraising dinner. This is only the second time I've worn it." Gertie's words were soft and distant.

"You okay, Gertie? You look a little tired."

"I am tired. I didn't sleep much last night with all the fuss over my birthday and this sudden trip to get ready for."

"Yeah, that was a wing-ding of a party. Where's Chester?"

"He's already in his carrier. And he's not a bit happy about it either."

"I know. Big Bertha's a bit miffed too. Let's get going. The sooner we deposit them at the Pet-o-rama, the sooner they'll get some freedom to move around. Hey, are you as excited as I am? This is gonna be a real adventure."

Gertie glanced around her tiny, perfectly appointed living room. "I'm too exhausted to be excited right now. Let's see, the heat is down, the alarm is on, and all the windows are locked. Help me with my bags while I carry Chester to the car."

Edna grabbed Gertie's suitcase and handbag, pulled the door closed behind them, and followed her to the car. Gertie placed Chester's carrier on the backseat alongside Big Bertha, who flattened her ears and hissed. Chester, unconcerned about the gigantic feline a mere eight inches away, circled his crate twice and lay down for a snooze.

Edna stowed the suitcase in the trunk beside hers.

Gertie settled in the passenger seat with her handbag at her feet. "Edna, tell me again about this meeting at the Quality Sleep Inn. I think that's what kept me awake half the night. You know I don't enjoy chitchatting with people I don't know."

Edna started the engine. "That's the whole point, Gertie. This here entire trip is designed to get us back in the game. We'll meet all kinds of new people, have a lot of laughs, and, if we're lucky, we might meet someone special." Edna held up her hand to forestall Gertie's disparaging words. "And don't you pooh-pooh that idea. It would be nice to have some gentlemanly company once in a while, and you know it."

The furrows in Gertie's brow deepened. "My idea of a gentleman and yours don't exactly match. Case in point— Ramon." Gertie tipped her nose upward and sniffed.

"Are you gonna bring that up again? I've apologized a million times for dumping you during my one romantic moment in Tuscany."

"A moment! You deserted me the whole evening." Her voice lowered. "And besides, he was creepy."

"That's water over the dam and under the bridge, my friend. But if it makes you feel better, I promise not to ditch you on this singles cruise. I'll stick to you like glue." Edna stopped at a red light, looked over at her timid friend, and spoke from her heart. "Come on, Gertie, let's think positive. This is a whole new experience, and I have a good feeling in my bones. Just think, four luxurious days and nights on *The Bountiful Lady* with a whole slew of eligible men and all the great food we can pack away. What's not to like?"

Gertie remained silent.

Edna gunned the engine and headed for the Pet-o-rama.

"Ooh, look at that flower arrangement. It's ginormous! Glads have always been my favorite." Edna led the way into the Quality Sleep Inn's lobby. She marched up to the check-in desk. "We're here for the *Bountiful Lady's* meet and greet."

"Shh," Gertie stood behind Edna, her head turning in all directions to see who might have heard. "You don't have to tell the whole world what we're doing."

"That would be in the Desert Sands room, ladies, down this hall." The young clerk in a crisp, white blouse and black pencil skirt gestured to her left.

"Thanks." Edna directed Gertie away from the desk and toward a potted plant in the corner. "Now, Gertie, I know this is out of your comfort zone. But here's the thing. This here is just a practice round, and by the time we get on board the *Bountiful Lady* and get all settled in for the cruise, we'll be old pros. So, relax and try to enjoy yourself."

"Practice round of what?" Gertie's voice squeaked.

"You know, as I said, it's a meet and greet. We're gonna meet some guys and talk with them for a little bit. Let's find the room and see if there's anything to drink."

Edna forged ahead down the hallway, stopping at each double doorway to read the name. "Let's see, this one here says Sierra—that one on the other side says Oasis." She kept moving. "There, this is it. Desert Sands. You ready, Gertie?"

Edna disappeared through the double doors leaving Gertie no choice but to follow. "Yippee, there's a bar. Oh shoot, it looks like it's mineral water. Oh well, let's grab some before the round begins."

"What round?" Gertie's words floated away in the general hubbub of voices coming from several clusters of folks milling around the room.

113

Edna hiked over to the drinks table, took a healthy scoop of ice cubes, and clunked them into a tall-stemmed glass. Gertie arrived at her side. "This here's gonna be a first-class trip all the way. Look at these fancy glasses." Edna opened her mineral water and dumped the contents into the glass, splashing large drops onto the white linen tablecloth.

Gertie followed Edna's lead, delicately added ice to the glass, and then carefully poured the water. She turned to scan the rest of the room. "Goodness, there's quite a large bunch here. What are all those little tables and stools for?"

A portly gentleman in a gray suit with a too-short red tie flopping on his belly approached. "You ladies here for the meet and greet? I see you found the drinks. Welcome. Your bios and score sheets are already on the tables. Find a spot. We'll start in about five minutes."

Gertie's eyes grew to the size of the cake plates from the night before. "I thought we were just going to talk with people."

Edna took stock of the situation and morphed into motherly mode. She placed a steadying hand on Gertie's shoulder. "We *are* just talking, but the whole idea is to spend some time with everyone. That way they can match up the information from our applications with our gorgeous faces." Edna turned her head as she spoke, taking in the other meet and greeters. "Look, for once there's as many guys as gals. Guess it has to come out even for this thing to work."

"Edna, you're scaring me. What in the world are we doing?" Gertie's big eyes were now snapping with what came as close to spunk as she ever got.

"Calm down, Gertie. It's called speed dating, but it's not that big a deal. It's only a three-minute chat with a guy, and then we move on to the next one. Well, in this case, I think the guys will move, and we'll sit politely and wait for the next handsome face."

"Ladies and gentlemen, may I have your attention?" Mr. Gray Suit stood at the center of the circle of tiny tables with two stools on either side. Edna counted fifteen tables. "Please find a spot. I'll give you a minute or two to glance over your bio sheets, and then we'll begin. For first-timers, you'll want to think of ranking your interviews as you go. Once aboard the *Bountiful Lady*, you'll have the opportunity to spend some quality time with any lucky matches made today. So, relax, have some fun, and let's meet and greet!"

Edna pulled Gertie along by the elbow, placed her water glass on the table, and hiked herself onto one of the stools. "Go ahead, Gertie, get on up there and read up on each guy. There's your bio sheet. After you read through that, you'll be able to take notes on your score sheet after each little meeting."

"Mercy! How did they get this information about me? My word, Edna, this sounds like I'm a streetwalker." Gertie's voice had started high and ended in a growl. "Edna, did you tell them I'm a wealthy widow who loves a good time?"

"I didn't put it quite like that. I said something like 'Lovely well-to-do widow enjoys long walks on moonlit nights.' Don't get your knickers in a twist. I had to fill out the application and questionnaire before the surprise party—I couldn't ruin your special night. And I had to say nice things about you. It's important to think about the image you want to present on these here mini-dates. You don't want to attract the wrong kind of guys. So being you *are* a real lady, I put down things that would—"

Mr. Gray Suit tweeted one short blast on a whistle. "One minute until round one."

Edna gave a last encouraging word to her friend. "Now don't worry about a thing. If you don't care for someone, you can smile and nod and wait for the next guy. We won't be doing any real dating until we're onboard, so you don't have to say anything ugly to anyone, even if he's a real loser."

Gertie glared at her, sighed, and picked up her pencil. She ran her eyes down the bio sheet for the men.

The whistle blew, and the men trotted into the circle of tables like steers at an auction house. They perched themselves on random stools.

Edna sat face-to-face with a chubby fellow in a wool plaid jacket. His hair lay parted neatly and slicked down over his mostly-bald head, and he had a circular, dented-in line around his head, loudly proclaiming a cowboy hat. His forehead beaded with sweat. He shifted on the tiny stool in an effort to balance his hefty hindquarters. "Howdy, ma'am. My name is Boyd Osterman. How you doin'?"

Edna glanced over at Gertie and did a double-take. The spitting image of Boyd sat across from Gertie. Same plaid jacket, same dented-in balding pate with a few strands of hair pasted down. She eavesdropped enough to hear him begin, "Howdy, ma'am. My name is Floyd Osterman. How you doin'?

Edna hauled her attention back to the twin in front of her. "I'm fine, Boyd. Nice to meet you." She discreetly picked up her pencil, scanned down her score sheet, and marked a two for appearance.

CHAPTER FOUR

Edna mopped her brow with a napkin from the drinks table. "Woo-Eee, that was hard work. My bottom feels like there's a permanent round indentation from that stool. I sure hope they have better accommodations on the *Bountiful Lady*. Did you circle your top three guys?"

Gertie's forehead was creased, and her mouth had a pinched look about it. "No, I didn't circle anyone. I don't like the idea of meeting men that way. It's degrading. Made me feel like I was being inspected. Besides, I was embarrassed about those things you said about me. I felt ridiculous trying to explain that I'm not wealthy. Or a party girl."

"Oh, phooey. You don't have to say anything about that. Those bios are just a way to start the conversation. Every man here could see you're a classy lady. And how about those Osterman twins. Aren't they a hoot? They must have practiced their lines. They both said the same things. 'Howdy, ma'am. What's your favorite ice cream?'" Edna mimicked the twins' low-pitched southern drawl. "I wonder how old those two are? They seem a mite younger than us. Everyone on this here tour is supposed to be past retirement age."

Gertie folded her scoresheet in half and tossed it into a nearby trash can. "I thought they were sort of cute. Of course, I wouldn't want to date them." Gertie glanced around the room at the few remaining speed daters. "What do we do now?"

"That's the beauty of this whole trip. We sit back and relax. They have everything planned for us. I can leave the car here. We'll take a nice shuttle to the airport, and away we go to Houston. They got us booked at another Quality Sleep Inn there. Meanwhile, we have a light supper in the Oasis room until it's time for the trip to the airport. It's all here in our itinerary." Edna handed several stapled pages to Gertie. "Here's your copy. Don't you love living in the lap of luxury? When Uncle Louie's money came in, I didn't have much time to make all the arrangements, so thank heaven I found this package deal."

"Your last package deal ended us up in Las Vegas at the MGM Too. Have you forgotten that little disaster?" Gertie hoisted her handbag onto her shoulder and started toward the door.

Edna followed. "Does this look like the MGM Too? This here is a high-toned place. Look at the draperies and the carpets. They're plush. Thanks to Uncle Louie, you and me are going to live large for four full days. Our light supper is at five. We have a little time to kill." She stopped at the doorway, stretched, and bent to do some toe touches. "Let's find somewhere to sit. My heinie needs to rest on something soft for a bit."

Edna lounged on a plush couch in the Quality Sleep Inn ladies' room. She held her score sheet in hand. "Hey, Gertie, what did you think of number nine? Bert Harris, the former construction worker. He had a big belly, but I liked his eyes. Crystal blue like Old Blue Eyes."

Gertie wiped her hands on a paper towel, peered into the mirror, and patted several curls back into place. "Honestly, they all run together in my mind. Well, except for the twins. I was so overwhelmed by the entire event, I don't remember much."

"See? That's the reason we needed to do this little practice session. When we're on board, we'll do it up right, and then we'll have a real-life date right there on the ship. I can just see the romantic décor in a fancy ballroom full of hunky guys all dressed up, looking handsome and ... eligible."

"Good grief, Edna. Did you see anybody hunky or gorgeous in this last lot? We'd be smarter to talk Boyd and Floyd into being our dates for the whole cruise, and then we could relax and enjoy ourselves. Anyway, I'm not in the market for a man like you are."

"I wouldn't say I'm in the market, but if a Mr. Right came along ..." Edna shoved her score sheet into her handbag. "I guess I marked the best three of this lot. We'll see if any of them chose me. That's how it works. That way we can let the men down easily. We don't have to reject them to their face. One guy was downright rude. Said he wondered how I slept at night with my hair spikes poking into the pillow."

Gertie surveyed Edna's stiff, porcupine-like head. "They do look a little ... crunchy."

Edna fingered the spikes. "I see my updated hairdo as one of my best features. It doesn't pay to be behind the times. I say, 'full steam ahead'."

"Well, Madam Full Steam Ahead, let's chug on toward our light supper. I was too nervous to eat much earlier, and now I'm starved."

"Good for you, Gertie. That's the first spark of life I've seen since we surprised you at the Elks Club. Let's get this party started."

The girls returned to the door marked *Oasis* and peeked inside. White linen-covered tables lined the wall and red-aproned servers stood behind them. Large, steaming, stainless metal trays and huge platters of fresh fruits and vegetables sat in neat rows on the buffet. A yeasty aroma from baskets of rolls wafted their way. Someone had artfully arranged and filled three-tiered dessert stands with a variety of delectable-looking sweets that awaited diners at the end of the tables. Completing the meal were carafes of coffee and hot water for tea. Tall pitchers of ice water had been placed at each table.

"Hot doggies. Something sure smells good. Looks like we're the first ones here. It's almost five o'clock. Let's see if they'll let us start." Edna approached the first server and flashed her most appealing smile. "Okay if we begin? We're with the *Bountiful Lady* tour, and that meet and greet must have boosted our appetites. We could both eat a horse."

The young man doffed his chef's hat and gave a slight bow. "You ladies go right ahead—the trays are piping hot—you'll get the first pick of everything. Sad to say, horse is not on the menu, but I trust you'll find other dishes to suit your taste."

Edna played along. "I like a man with a sense of humor. You aren't a senior citizen in disguise, are you?" Edna batted her eyelashes at the young man who grinned back at her.

Gertie elbowed Edna and whispered into her ear, "For goodness' sake. Mind your manners."

"I am minding my manners. I'm being congenial to the help. That's what we're supposed to do on this here whole trip. The tips and such were already included in the package deal. So, we can be as friendly as we want and not feel obligated to dole out big gratuities at the end of the cruise. That was a big relief to me because I want to use Uncle Louie's money in the most sensible way."

"Yes, that's what folks say about you. You're the epitome of sensible." Gertie's words held an atypical edge.

"No need for sarcasm, Gertie Larsen, it doesn't become you. Let's load up." Edna pulled a warmed plate from the stack, grabbed a wrapped utensil package, and made her way down the length of the tables, sampling everything.

"Mm, chicken *and* roast beef. What did I tell you? This is a light supper—nothing compared to the spreads they'll serve on board. I may gain a few pounds in the next four days, but it'll be worth it."

Gertie forked up a perfectly browned chicken breast. "It does look good. Lots of healthy choices." Her voice softened. "Thank you for planning this trip and including me. It took me a while to get used to the idea, but now I'm going to try to relax and enjoy myself."

"Atta girl. Uh-oh." Edna lit out for a table in the furthest corner of the room.

Gertie finished filling her plate and hurried to join her.

"What's the matter with you? You acted like your pants were on fire." Gertie placed her plate on the table and hung her handbag over the back of the chair.

Edna kept her voice low. "It's that guy, Marvin something or other. He's the one who made fun of my hair. I don't choose to spend my light suppertime being insulted by him. Where is he? I'm going to sit with my back to the rest of the room."

Gertie took her seat and unwrapped her silverware. "My word, I thought you were sick or something. You scared the daylights out of me. Again."

"Sorry. Let's eat the warm stuff, and then, I'll sneak back to get my dessert." Edna buried her head in her dinner plate.

Two chubby shapes approached the corner table. The first one spoke. "Howdy, ladies. How you doin'?"

Edna looked up from her plate. "Are you Boyd or Floyd?"

"Thanks for asking, ma'am. I'm Floyd. Boyd is right here behind me. We tend to stick together. You all mind if we join you two lovely ladies? This is a Texas-sized spread. Reminds me of the way Mama used to cook for us back at the ranch, don't it, Boyd?"

Boyd placed a large Stetson hat at the far end of the table, away from the women, and Floyd laid his alongside it.

121

Gertie swallowed her bite and smiled politely at the two men. "Why, of course, have a seat. We were so hungry we headed straight here from the ... event. You gentlemen must be genuine cowboys if you grew up on a ranch."

"Yes, ma'am. Practically lived in the saddle growing up. Right, Floyd?"

"That's right. We're cattle ranchers through and through. When Mama passed, we had to step up and take over all the chores. Papa died when we were little."

"Now that's right sad," Edna said. "My ma passed some time ago too. We didn't exactly get along, but a gal always remembers her mother. Do you boys cook for yourselves then?"

The brothers shared a meaningful look. "Floyd here just finished a special class in French Cuisine. The community college offered it, and he stepped right up and took it."

Floyd's face lit up in childlike glee. "And brother Boyd took the Italian Cuisine class. We thought we should branch out and not do everything together. The classes were right across the hall from each other."

Gertie's gaze ricocheted back and forth between the two identical faces, and she shook her head. "I'm sorry, gentlemen, but I can't tell you two apart."

The twins sat across from the ladies. One began to tuck his napkin into his shirt collar but seemed to take a cue from Gertie who smoothed hers out on her lap. Both men followed suit.

"That's all right," one said.

"Yes, ma'am, we're used to it," the other said.

Edna led the way from the Oasis Room to the hotel parking lot. She unlocked the trunk of her car. "Let's grab our bags and wait for the shuttle in that nice, little, outdoorsy area by the entrance. We sure don't want to miss our flight. It's three hours to Houston and then there's the shuttle ride to our next home away from home. That's why we had our light supper so early—they don't want us senior citizens to get pooped out before the trip even begins. I got us a second-floor room so's we're safe from burglars and ax murderers." Edna guffawed.

"My heavens, Edna, your sense of humor sinks a bit lower every day." She lifted her suitcase, set it on the pavement, and rolled it toward a patio space with river-rock pathways winding amongst cedar Adirondack chairs.

The patio area included small cocktail tables, and clusters of hotel guests enjoyed the cool of the evening and a gentle breeze as they nursed their before-dinner drinks.

Several *Bountiful Lady* guests lounged in the patio area as well, waiting for the shuttle. Edna barged up in front of one of the sturdy cedar chairs, leaned her suitcase against its side, and plopped down. "I've always wanted one of these here Adirondacks. They remind me of rich folks from the Northeast. I could pretend I'm sitting on a beach in Martha's Vineyard or maybe on one of them big estates in Kennebunkport."

A shadow towered over Edna. "I'll bet you've never even been to the Northeastern states." Marvin's voice held a challenge. "I don't remember Martha Stewart cutting her hair to an inch long and gluing it up in points."

Edna's face flushed as she hoisted herself up from the chair. "Okay, Mister. Let's get one thing straight right from the start or this is going to be a lousy four days ..."

Gertie was startled and turned toward Marvin. She took in a deep breath and said, "My friend is right. There's no need to be rude."

In a flurry of boots, plaid, and cowboy hats, the Ostermans appeared on either side of Marvin. They locked arms with him. "Looks like the ladies aren't interested in hearing your opinions, Mr." The words were spoken softly but did the trick.

123

Marvin froze.

"Yes, sir. You heard brother Floyd. Move along if you can't be respectful to the ladies."

Marvin threw a disgusted look in both directions, yanked his arms free of the twins, and stomped off to wait for the shuttle at a distance.

Edna slapped the boys on their shoulders and chuckled. "Thanks, fellas. You should have seen the look on his face. That was more fun than a barrel of monkeys. I think you two scared that creep away for good."

"Thank you, gentlemen," Gertie chimed in. "You were wonderful. I appreciate men with a sense of honor."

"Shucks, ladies. Mama always taught us to respect our elders."

Boyd's eyebrows shot up to his hairline. "What Floyd means is Mama always taught us to stand up against big-mouth bullies. That Marvin was plain rude, and we see red when ladies are mistreated. I hope you didn't listen to the things he said, ma'am." The boys put their hats back on their heads.

Edna patted Boyd on his plaid shoulder. "Of course, I didn't listen to him. He's just a loud-mouthed loser."

She looked at Floyd, who had suddenly become tongue-tied. "Thanks, Floyd—at least I hope it's Floyd."

Floyd lifted his head and touched his hand to the brim of his hat. "Yes, ma'am. You're welcome."

Gertie continued to search Floyd's flustered face.

Edna scanned the horizon. "Hey, everyone. Grab your stuff. Here comes the shuttle."

Boyd and Floyd stepped back to allow the ladies to move to the head of the line.

"Oh boy, Gertie, this is it. Houston, here we come."

CHAPTER FIVE

Edna led the way as she and Gertie snaked through the airport security line. When they reached the conveyor belt, Edna burst into action. She flung her suitcase onto the belt, removed her jacket and shoes, and tossed them into a bin along with her handbag. She clutched her paper boarding pass in her hand.

Gertie followed, managing the tasks with less mayhem.

"I'll be glad to get on board the plane," Edna said. "We'll be one step closer to the *Bountiful Lady.* Such a highfalutin' sounding name, isn't it?"

"I'll admit I'm eager to see the ocean and get aboard," Gertie said. "I do love the water."

Edna stood next in line for the x-ray machine. When the TSA agent beckoned, she got into the position, feet apart and hands in the air.

Red lights suddenly flashed, and more agents approached. They escorted her to an area off to the side and surrounded her, their backs to the rest of the line.

"What's going on?" Edna sputtered.

The agents didn't speak, but one of them wanded Edna's body from top to bottom while a female agent proceeded to poke and prod her upper torso. The woman leaned in and spoke into Edna's ear. "Are you wearing an underwire foundation garment, ma'am?"

"You mean my Wonderbra caused all this kerfuffle?" Edna said. "For goodness' sake, don't you people have better things to do than harass a senior citizen?"

The agents stepped back and allowed Edna to rejoin Gertie who had managed the entire process without a hair out of place.

Edna glared at her. "Not a word. Let's get down to our gate. I want to grab a snack before we board."

Thirty minutes later, Edna greeted the young steward in his crisp, white uniform who led the way down the narrow aisle of the plane, wobbling her carry-on behind her. "Let's see, we're twenty-six C and D. I hope one of those is a window seat. I love looking out at all the clouds and the shapes they make. Sometimes it looks like you could step out and walk on them."

Gertie followed close behind. "I don't mind sitting in the middle. I always had to when Donald and I flew. I'm used to it."

"Thanks, Gertie. A big girl like me has a hard time in those tiny middle seats. I feel like a sardine by the time we get anywhere.

Edna eyed the number twenty-six above a row of seats and grunted as she hoisted her suitcase up into the storage bin. "Want some help with your bag?" she asked Gertie.

"Yes, please." Gertie paused in the aisle as Edna flung the bag up above and then ducked and rolled her way into the window seat. Gertie sat first in the aisle seat and slid over to the middle. She stowed her handbag on the floor in front of her feet and fastened her seatbelt.

Edna slid open the window shade and peered out. "I guess all airports look the same on the tarmac. Nothing but concrete. It sure feels good to sit down. That security line keeps getting crazier and crazier. Imagine setting off an alarm with one piece of underwear. They practically make you undress these days and then stand there with your arms in the air like you're being robbed ... and on top of that, to be wanded in front of everyone ..." Edna tossed her head in disgust at the memory.

"Well, Marvin seemed to enjoy the spectacle." Gertie cinched her belt tight and folded her hands in her lap.

"Marvin is going to get a fat lip if he even so much as mentions my Wonderbra. Besides, a girl needs a little help to stay perky at our age."

"Must be the giant, economy-sized underwire if it set off the alarm." Gertie lowered her voice. "And I wouldn't say Wonderbra too loudly if I were you. No telling who's within earshot, and every last one of these people are heading for the cruise ship. We might have to ..." Gertie shuddered as she spoke, "meet and greet them later on."

"I'm looking forward to the speed dating on board. There's bound to be better pickings there—more *fish* to cast our lines toward." Edna dug her elbow into Gertie's side and cackled.

Gertie turned her head toward the aisle. "I don't want to think about that right now, Edna. I'm going to take a nap. That big meal and then the shuttle ride made me sleepy." She closed her eyes as the plane took off.

Edna grasped the armrests with both hands and waited until the ground receded. "Okay. But one of these days you and me are gonna travel first class. Don't you wonder what those folks up there are doing right now? Did you ever notice how smug they look when us peons come down the aisle, and they're already in their big, oversized seats with drinks in their hands? We're gonna get exactly one bag of pretzels and about three ounces of Coke while they guzzle gin and tonics and put their feet up on little footrests."

"They pay rather dearly for the privilege, my friend, so don't complain. I *would* enjoy one of those little, hot towels though. They're so comforting." Gertie sighed. "The flight is only three hours. I don't think you're going to see many clouds out the window now that it's nearly dark but relax and let me take a little snooze." Gertie closed her eyes.

A bulky form collapsed into the aisle seat, jiggling the entire row. Gertie's eyes flew open, and Edna turned from the window, her mouth agape.

127

"Well, hello there, Wonder Woman. And I guess this is your little sidekick. I was in twenty-four E and saw you two ladies were starved for companionship." Marvin guffawed at his joke as he buckled his seatbelt. He ogled the two women.

Edna threw a scowl in Marvin's direction and leaned on the button to recline her chair. "I'm taking a nap too. See you in Houston, Gertie."

Edna punched the too-soft Quality Sleep Inn pillow and doubled it to get her neck high enough for comfort. "I'm still fuming. I paid good money to buy us this relaxing four-day cruise, and that Marvin is hell-bent on ruining it for me. That man never stopped bad-mouthing me the whole flight. I have a mind to make a formal complaint to whoever is in charge of stuff like this."

Gertie reached to turn off the table lamp on her nightstand, then settled back down in her bed. "You know, I've been thinking about him." She raised her arms and clasped her hands behind her head. "He reminds me of those little boys who used to tease the girls in third or fourth grade. They pulled hair and burped, made armpit noises, and went out of their way to get our attention. And they did it all because they liked one or the other of us. Boys only tease the girls they like."

"Aw, geez, Gertie. Don't tell me you think Mad Marvin has the hots for me. He hasn't said one nice thing since I first laid eyes on him." Edna snapped a hairnet over her spikes.

"My point, exactly. Maybe he's one of those grown men who are still about nine years old emotionally, and he just doesn't know any other way to get your attention." Gertie rolled over on her side, facing Edna. "What if you called his bluff and killed him with kindness? You might find there's a nice guy underneath all that bluster."

"Well, if there's a nice guy hiding inside that blowhard, I'm happy to leave him there." Edna gave her pillow one last whack and closed her eyes. "Besides, if he's gonna spill the beans about my Wonderbra, that could jeopardize my chances for finding my Mr. Right. Yup, I'm gonna lodge a formal complaint and warn that louse he'd better leave me alone. G'night, Gertie. Tomorrow is boarding day. Can't wait." Edna stopped talking.

"I still say you should try to make peace with Marvin. I don't look forward to three more days of verbal skirmishes between the two of you." But Edna was already snoring. Gertie sighed and pulled the covers up to her chin. Nothing was ever simple with her friend Edna.

Edna puffed with the effort of hauling her carry-on up the endless ramp. "My goodness, look at the size of this ship. And the *Bountiful Lady* is one of the smaller ones." She wiped the sweat from her forehead with her sleeve.

"Donald and I only cruised once—a trip up and down the Baja Peninsula. Rather disappointing, I must say. The weather was cloudy, and Donald didn't want to do much. He said every time he turned around someone tried to sell him something."

The line of guests checking their luggage came to a halt, and Edna parked her suitcase on its wheels and breathed a sigh of relief. "Yeah, Donald wasn't exactly a barrel of laughs."

"No, Donald was a serious man. Sensible and quiet most of the time. Sometimes I would have enjoyed a bit more ... enthusiasm, I suppose." Gertie's voice had taken on a wistful quality.

"Boy, howdy. I know what you mean. Fred was my man until his health took a nosedive, and Sam was a ton of fun until he hightailed it off with that blonde floozy. That's why we need to set our caps for a Mr. Right, Gertie. There are great guys out there—we just have to 'use the right bait' as they say."

"Who says that?" Gertie's strict sensibilities were back in place. "I say we live a nice, clean life, and if a romance is meant to be, it will happen naturally, not by 'meeting and greeting.'"

"That's a nice sentiment, my friend, but the fact is fate needs a kick in the pants now and then." Edna pulled at the sides of her Wonderbra and wiggled a bit to get things back into place.

The line began to move again, and they scooted steadily ahead. The sound of luggage wheels bouncing up the gangway turned both the girls' heads.

"Thanks for saving my place, ladies. I overslept and missed the shuttle." Marvin's nasty smile pulled his lip up into a sneer.

"Get lost, Buster," Edna growled.

"Now, Edna, remember what we talked about?"

"Er, yeah." She turned to Marvin with a sweet smile and motioned for him to take his place with them. Edna took a deep breath and scrunched up her face in an effort to make nice. "Okay, Marvin, you step right in here with us, and we'll get this luggage stowed away in no time. That's too bad that you missed the shuttle—must have been scared you'd miss the whole trip."

Marvin's eyes bulged and his mouth fell open. "Thanks. And, yeah, I saw my cruise dollars going down the drain. I saved a whole year to scrape the money together for this trip."

Gertie nudged Edna's arm with her elbow and raised her eyebrows as if to say, *See*?

Marvin shuffled his feet and spoke in a softer voice. "After Anna died, I sort of lost my zest for life. I thought

130

maybe this singles cruise would help me start over, but I always seem to put my foot in it. Anna used to say my sense of humor left something to be desired."

Gertie patted Marvin's shoulder. "Losing a life partner is about the worst thing we can experience. I lost my Donald too. I'm sure this cruise will be ..." Gertie faltered for a moment, remembering the speed dates ahead. "Well, it will be fun if we keep our wits about us."

Edna chimed in. "You betcha, Marvin. Good for you. There's lots of fish in the sea, and I intend to fish to my heart's content."

Marvin opened his mouth to speak, but the three had arrived at the check-in counter. A flurry of questions and paperwork ensued, then the girls handed their bags to the porters. With a lull in the action, Edna looked up and saw Marvin off in the distance. "Look, old Marvin got ahead of us." As she spoke, he turned back toward them and gave a tiny wave of his hand before he scurried up a ramp and onto the ship.

"Hm, maybe you were right," Edna said to Gertie. "Maybe there's a decent human being in there somewhere after all."

CHAPTER SIX

Edna retrieved her key from the slot in the cabin door and stepped inside. "I didn't expect the Ritz, but this is the tiniest room I've ever seen. It looks like it's built for midgets." She took three giant steps and reached out to touch the back wall.

Gertie followed. "Cruise ships are known for their compact living quarters. We'll be fine here although a view of the ocean would have been nice." She moved further into the cabin and sat on her narrow bed. "And aren't these towel animals cute? I wonder if this is meant to be a dog or a fox or—"

"Look, we got our bags already, and hot dog! Here's a tray full of bathroom stuff—lotions and shampoo and hairnets. That's good because I lost my other net at the Quality Sleep Inn last night. Must have dropped down behind the bed." Edna opened the hairnet package and placed one on her nightstand.

Gertie stared at her best friend's stiff-as-a-board silver spikes. "Why would you need a hairnet for that hairstyle?"

Edna raised her chin, ready for any insults to her spiky do. "I find the spikes stay in place better when I protect them a bit. Any other questions?" She glared in Gertie's direction.

Gertie busied herself unpacking. She opened her suitcases and removed neatly-folded stacks of clothing.

"I think I'd like to hang up my clothes and get organized before we do anything else. What time is lunch?"

Edna dug through her handbag and pulled out her itinerary. "Let's see ... lunch at twelve-thirty, and we get our meet and greet results then too. I don't have my heart set on any of those guys, but number nine wasn't too bad. We get the "one-ways" too—the guys who chose us even if we didn't choose them. Can't hurt the old ego, right? And then maybe we'll have an opportunity to give them a second chance at a later date."

"Whatever you say. I don't remember marking any favorites. I just wanted it to be finished." Gertie opened a tiny cupboard closet built-in above her bed and hung her outfits.

"Guess you'll get some surprising results then." Edna saw the panic growing on Gertie's face. "Come on, Gertie. Remember, we're here to have a good time. Relax. If all else fails, I'll loan you Marvin now that he's tamed." Edna chuckled at her own joke.

"I don't think Marvin would be such a bad escort. I may borrow him if all these results get too overwhelming. Or one of the twins. They seem safe."

"I can't argue with that. They are about the safest two men I've ever met. Kinda endearing though—the way they stepped up to save me from Marvin."

Gertie placed her last hanger inside the tiny closet and closed the door. "Chivalry is not yet dead. We need to remember not to judge books by their covers, Edna. Those twins may be short and a bit overweight, but they seem to have hearts of gold. That can be another lesson to us."

"I don't know about you, girlfriend, but I've graduated school, and I'm done with lessons. I'm ready for a little walk on the wild side. Let's go get some lunch and see our meet and greet results. I hope we can fit all the guys into our time slots. Cocktail hour is at five o'clock, and they only gave us three mini-dates before dinner. Then after dinner, we get to the real deal—three half-hour meet and greets to 'optimize our connections' the brochure says here."

Gertie stood, her eyebrows shooting sky-high. "Hand me that thing. You mean we spend the rest of this day carousing around from one guy to another?" Gertie browsed through the schedule and sat down on her bed. "Edna, every time you get me into one of these terrible situations, I swear I'll never let it happen again. And then, bingo, before I know what hit me—"

"Now, calm down," Edna said as she reached out and placed a steadying hand on Gertie's shoulder. "You're getting all riled up over nothing. After tonight's meet and greets, there's a lovely promenade on the upper deck and a couple of movies we can choose from, and then, tomorrow there's all kinds of activities. It's gonna be a blast, you'll see."

Gertie mopped her brow with tissue from the bathroom tray. "Mercy. Donald, forgive me. I suppose I'm stuck with all of this."

"I hate to say this, Gertie, but you need to stop talking to Donald like he's looking over your shoulder. He's gone to the great by and by, and you're free to live your life here on good old terra firma. Or floating on the ocean as the case may be. He'd want you to enjoy your life—get back in the game again."

Gertie took in a deep breath and let it out. "I agree Donald would want me to be happy. He always said the decisions he made were for my well-being, but I don't think you and I see eye to eye on the way to do that. Give me a nice, quiet garden party or a lecture at the University or—"

"Holy cow, Gertie. We gotta go. It's nearly twelve-thirty, and we don't know our way around this barge yet. Follow me." She lit out the door, her friend straining to keep up with her long-legged steps.

"This is about the fanciest salad bar I've ever laid eyes on." Edna piled miniature corn cobs atop her mountain of a salad and struggled to keep her water glass, coffee cup, and assorted bread rolls and desserts from tumbling to the ground. "Whoops! Guess I took a bit more than I should have. It all looks so tempting."

"Can we sit anywhere we want?" Gertie flanked Edna, her more modest lunch tray balanced on the drinks counter.

"Yup, the brochure says we're free to roam for breakfast and lunch. We only have assigned tables for dinner tonight. That's okay by me because we might get stuck with duds at dinner, and this way we can *troll* if you know what I mean." Edna squinted with the effort of perusing the vast array of dining tables.

Gertie let out a huff. "Quit *trolling* for Mr. Right and get us settled somewhere. I'm hungry, and this tray is getting heavy."

"Okay, don't get your knickers in a twist. How about that table over there by the portholes? We can look out at the water while we eat."

Gertie nodded and hoisted her tray. "That's fine. I do hope the formal dining room is a bit cozier. This feels like we're eating in a gymnasium."

"Well, Miss Garden Party, I'm sorry if the accommodations don't suit your taste. It looks fancy to me. They had three different kinds of salad greens and at least nine dressings to choose from. Back at the Elks, we're lucky if the lettuce is green instead of brown."

Gertie visibly recoiled. "Yes, well, this is decidedly better than the Elks. And thank you again for giving me such a thoughtful birthday gift. I don't mean to be ungrateful."

Edna set down her tray on a nearby table and gestured for her friend to sit. "I know, Gertie. You're used to a dull, routine life. And here I come along and give you excitement and adventure, and sometimes, it's all a little more than you can handle. Trust me. This cruise is going to be something we'll never forget. When we're little old ladies sitting in our rockers, we'll be talking about it."

"Some might say we're little old ladies already."

"Never." Edna unloaded her tray onto the table and handed it with a flourish to a nearby waiter. "We're in our prime, Mrs. Larsen. And don't you forget it."

Gertie chose to let that comment hang in the air while she organized her plates, cups, and glasses.

"Howdy, ladies. Can we join y'all?"

Edna and Gertie looked up into the sincere, chubby faces of Boyd and Floyd Osterman.

"Don't see why not," Edna responded.

"How is your suite, gentlemen?" Gertie pulled back the chair beside her and offered the space to whichever twin was nearest her.

"It's a mite on the small side, but we have a nice little deck overlooking the water and a great big sliding door so we can look out there whenever we want, even when we're in our beds."

"Oh, how nice. I do love a view of the ocean. But, of course, it probably cost a lot more." Gertie rushed the last words, her face flushing, and turned her attention to her salad.

Edna took a large bite. "Aw, who cares about a view? We're gonna be out and about most of the time anyway. We only sleep in that little sardine tin of a room, right boys?"

One of the twins sat down by Gertie, and the other found his place beside Edna. "Floyd here can't wait to get his results from last night. They have a table set up, and as soon as we're done eating, we'll go in alphabetical order to find out who picked us. We walked right by it on our way to the salad bar. They posted a sign saying to enjoy our lunch and come back around one o'clock."

Floyd chimed in. "'Course we need to be ready to hear that none of them ladies wanted to spend time with us. No sense in getting our hopes up and then be cast into despair."

Edna spoke right up. "Well, boys, if you ask me, those ladies would be crazy to let two fine, handsome fellas like yourselves get away without a date."

"That's right," Gertie hurried to add. "You boys make a favorable impression with your hats and all. Lots of women are interested in cowboys."

A shrill squeal from a microphone broke into the conversation. "Sorry, folks, just a few announcements." Mr. Gray Suit stood before them, coat unbuttoned and wiping a sheen of sweat from his forehead. "Soon as you folks finish your lunch, you can make your way over to the table by the east doors. Look for the signs with the first initial of your last name, and line up for your results from last night's meet and greet. There will be three, twenty-minute time slots available for your mini-dates during the five o'clock cocktail hour. Dinner is at six and then the on-board meet and greet begins at seven. The evening events begin promptly at eight-thirty. And you'll get your results from tonight after breakfast tomorrow morning. That's about all the help we can give you. After that, you are on your own." He guffawed once, blaring the sound into the microphone, and hurried off toward the alphabetical tables.

"Mercy, it sounds like we're all being herded around like cattle. No disrespect, gentlemen." Gertie took a few more bites of her lunch and then blotted her mouth with her napkin.

Edna shoved her salad plate back and wielded a toothpick to pull any lettuce bits from between her teeth. "Can't afford to scare Mr. Right off with a hunk of green between my choppers."

"My word, Edna," Gertie began. But Boyd—or Floyd— hopped up from the table and gathered all the plates and napkins in a neat pile. "Allow me to bus our table, ladies."

"Why, thank you, Mr. Osterman," Gertie took the easy way out, smiling at the gallant but stubby cowboy who scuttled to a nearby cart, deposited their dishes, and hurried back.

Edna scooted her chair back, stood tall, and cracked her knuckles forward and back. "I say we all hotfoot it over to the tables and get our results and then come back here to compare notes."

The twins glanced at one another, sharing quick smiles and tiny nods. "Sounds like a right fine idea, Miss Edna." And one twin offered his left elbow to Edna, while the other sidled up to Gertie and did the same.

"A girl could get used to this kind of highfalootin' behavior." Edna beamed down at Floyd. "Uh-oh, I gotta get in the GHI line. Gertie, you're with the boys in the LMNO line. See you all back at the ranch." Edna allowed herself a snorty chuckle at her little joke and lit out for the GHI table.

CHAPTER SEVEN

Twenty minutes later, Edna plopped herself back down at the table, her dog-eared results form in hand. "Looks like you all beat me. How'd ya do?"

"Well now," one twin said, "we pretty much prepared ourselves for any disappointing turn of events. After all, long as Mama was alive, we focused on family, and we didn't, neither of us, run around town much ..." His voice trailed off, and both boys looked off into space.

"Came up empty, huh? Don't feel bad cause I did too. Or as good as. The three guys I chose didn't respond, and the only one-way I got was from Mad Marvin. It would be a cold day in you-know-where before I'd have a mini-date with him."

"Now, Edna. That's not very charitable of you. You saw how sweet and sad he was at the check-in tables." Gertie reached out and patted a twin's hand. "You boys do me a favor and add some little thing to give us a hint about who you are. Maybe a certain color hanky or tie?"

"Now that's a right fine idea, Miss Gertie. We'll work on that when we get back to the room. Guess we have some time to kill until that cocktail hour. Suppose we'll be drinking alone."

Edna crumpled up her results form and tossed it on the table. "Well, Gertie, you're a country not heard from. What were your results?"

Gertie stood from the table, smoothed her slacks, and picked an imaginary bit of lint from her top. "Since I didn't choose any of the gentlemen back in Amarillo, I only got some one-ways. I'm happy to report that two of them are sitting right here!" She shone a benevolent smile on both of the boys.

"Who was the third?"

"Well, that Bert Harris—the one with the blue eyes you liked so much."

"I never said I liked him. I said he wasn't as bad as some." Edna glanced at Boyd and Floyd. "Not that you two aren't real special. In fact, I have an idea. Why don't the four of us meet up for cocktails at five? The only one of us with a mini date is Miss Congeniality here, and that's only for twenty minutes. We can get the lay of the land and see what the next meet and greet has to offer."

With a screech of chairs, Edna and the twins arose, and the four headed off, two by two to their respective suites.

Gertie lay on her bunk, eyes closed, one hand behind her head. "Cruises are supposed to be relaxing. We've only had one meal on board, and I'm feeling weary. I think I'll rest for a bit."

With tweezers in hand, Edna looked at her reflection in the tiny bathroom mirror two steps from Gertie's side. "I'm feeling pretty knackered myself. And I don't want any bags under my eyes for tonight's meet and greets. This here is the big one—our best chance to latch on to someone." She spied a black hair under her nose and gave it a yank. "The group that runs this whole cruise is very professional. All our paperwork was sent on ahead so tonight the guys will have seen our questionnaires. And, of course, we'll get good dope on all of them too. The itinerary says our packets will be delivered to our door an hour before cocktail hour. I'm gonna take a quick nap too and then I'll have time to pay attention to my 'toilette' before we go."

"Toilette?"

"Yes, madame." Edna stretched out the *am*. "I read about that in one of those high fashion magazines Rose keeps at the Pet-o-Rama. All the European ladies take lots of time to make sure their make-up is right, and they even have these fancy bathrooms with little—"

"Shh. Let's take a rest." Gertie waved her hand to indicate she'd heard enough.

The girls awakened to two, sharp raps on their door and a cheery call of "Here are your packets." Two fat files swooshed under the door, one after the other.

Edna stretched and yawned. "Gertie, wake up. We only got an hour to study these here packets and get dressed before the cocktail hour." She leaned over, picked up the nearest file folder, and riffled through it. "Holy guacamole, this is impressive. There must be two hundred guys here. I can tell a lot just from looking at these pictures. I can spot a dud a mile away when I get a gander at his mug."

Gertie roused. "Pictures? We have pictures?"

"Yeah, I found one of me when I sang karaoke at the Elks—pretty good if I do say so, and yours was in an old garden club brochure. I think you look very dramatic in that hat."

"That brochure is old as the hills. Isn't that false advertising or something?"

"As I said, I didn't have much time to pull all the details together. Anyhow, I'm gonna hop in the shower and get ready. You can study while I'm in the loo."

"Okay." Gertie swung her legs out of bed, grabbed her packet, and leafed through it. An involuntary chill shot through her body. There she was, big as life in her sunhat. The familiar words popped out at her with the same misleading message—wealthy, loves a good time. "Oh, mercy." She flopped back down on the bed, one arm covering her eyes, and stayed there.

Edna bolted from the bathroom. "Girlfriend, what are you doing? Get up. We got exactly forty-three minutes to look fantastic and hot to trot. Did you target three guys for the meet and greets? We gotta finalize our three, thirty-minute dates when we cruise through the happy hour."

Gertie groaned. "I haven't even looked through the photos. This is all moving so fast. I thought we were joining the twins for cocktails."

"Sure. We are. We'll have a quick drink and then go on the hunt. Dinner is at six. That's not much time to get our hit lists together before seven. If we play our cards right, we can find the guys who look the most promising and fill in our slots."

Gertie thumbed through a few pages. "Most of these pictures look ancient too. There's Boyd and Floyd. My word, these must have been their high school graduation pictures. Weren't they cute?"

"Don't waste time on them. Find yourself someone hunky. I'm gonna get dressed and then circle my top ten. Can't risk wasting those three valuable time slots with random losers."

"How you talk, Edna. You know all those men have feelings too. They wouldn't be doing this speed dating thing if they weren't lonely. And think what they might be saying about us."

Edna cackled. "Fabulous ... alluring ..."

"I was thinking more along the lines of rich and wanton."

"Are you still worried about that bio? There's nothing wrong with enjoying a good time. And Donald left you with enough to be comfortable. It's mostly true."

Gertie sighed. "I'm going to wash up and change."

"You do that. I'll be working on *Edna's Top Ten*."

Gertie pressed the elevator button and waited for the ding and an open door. "I still think you should go back and change. You don't look ... respectable."

Edna glared at her proper friend, who did, indeed, look respectable and lovely in her pale pink blouse and tailored black slacks. "I told you I didn't have a chance to try this top on with my new Wonderbra. Sure, it's a bit low, but I think the purple looks good with my hair."

"I don't think the gentlemen will be looking at your hair." The elevator opened, and the girls got on.

"Let's think positive, Gertie. We'll have a nice cocktail hour and get a little tipsy. We'll find three guys to spend time with after dinner. And dinner! Our first big meal of the cruise. I can't wait. Remember, scan the crowd, and look for the guys you like best. Who's on your list?"

Gertie stalled. "Well, I didn't make a list. I think I'd rather just see what happens naturally. You know, maybe when we do the three rounds, I'll meet someone nice. And if not, I'm happy to enjoy the meals and the change of scenery."

Edna eyed her sedate friend. She stood up tall, chest out. "Well, to each her own. I'm putting my best foot forward." She winked at Gertie as they exited the elevator.

They followed signs to a large ballroom on the second deck. "Not bad." Edna elbowed her way through the crowd.

A three-piece band played soft renditions of oldies, and tuxedo-clad waiters carrying huge, round trays offered drinks to everyone.

"Hey, Boyd and Floyd, over here," Edna called out.

The twins, resplendent in matching brown-corduroy jackets and bolo ties approached. "Howdy, Miss Edna, Miss Gertie." They both tipped their hats.

Tiny tables for two were scattered by the dozens throughout the room, and Edna hauled two of them

145

together. "Looks like you boys took our request to heart." She nodded toward the hats in their hands, now sporting a B and an F above the brims.

"Yes, Ma'am. We found this tape in a first aid kit in our room and thought it would work fine. Boyd's was a little harder to do than mine."

Gertie chimed in. "Thank you. That was very enterprising of you, and it's a great help to know which of you is which."

Edna beckoned a waiter by giving a short but ear-piercing whistle, and soon, the four had drinks in hand.

The twins had chosen champagne flutes. They seemed distinctly uncomfortable twirling the delicate glasses by the stem and didn't taste the bubbly.

Gertie selected a white wine and took a tiny sip.

Edna grabbed champagne flutes in both hands and drained one in a single gulp. She set the empty glass on the table and scanned the crowd.

"Floyd and I don't drink much. Gotta be careful not to overdo."

Floyd added, "Yeah, just a beer now and then after all our ranch chores are done. Branding and roping and … stuff."

"You boys keep Gertie company, will you? I'm gonna take a stroll."

"Oh, my. Edna's out looking for Mr. Right. I appreciate you boys staying here with me."

"Our pleasure, ma'am." Boyd and Floyd spoke in unison.

"Ooh, isn't this beautiful?" Gertie surveyed the dining room decorated with crystal chandeliers and sparkling white linens at each table for eight. "Look, flowers and candles on every table and those pretty, folded napkins. This is fancier than I imagined, I feel a bit underdressed."

Edna commandeered them through the crowd. "You're fine. Look around—some of these dames are in tank tops. Let's find our places."

They cruised the tables in search of their names set into individual silver place cardholders.

"Here we are. Good, they kept us at the same table. I was afraid they might mess that up." Edna pulled out her chair and plopped down. "Whoa, I guess those drinks went to my head. I need to get some food in me.

Gertie moved to her spot and placed her hands on the chair.

"Allow me, my dear." A tall, well-dressed gentleman in a white jacket appeared at Gertie's side. He pushed the chair back, gently took an elbow, and guided her into her seat.

"Oh, thank you."

He bowed at the waist, smiled into Gertie's eyes, and then seated himself at her right.

"Grayson Winters," he intoned, his voice soft, cultured.

"Gertie Larsen." She put out her hand.

"So very nice to meet you." Grayson brought Gertie's hand to his lips and grazed her fingers with a kiss.

Edna cleared her throat.

"Oh," Gertie startled at the sound. "This is my friend, Edna Gratzer. We're taking this cruise together."

"How nice to meet you, Ms. Gratzer," he answered, but his gaze remained focused on Gertie.

Edna studied the man. He was a looker, no doubt, with wavy, silvery hair, a gorgeous smile, and eyes that crinkled nicely at the corners. His white dinner jacket and black bow tie set him apart from the rest of the men who were mostly in casual attire. This one was a bit too high-toned for Edna, maybe, but ...

"Mr. Winters," Edna crooned, "how are you liking the cruise so far? Plenty of good eats, huh? Are you a Texas guy?"

He pulled his gaze away from Gertie to respond. "Actually, Ms. Gratzer, I've been afraid I'd made a terrible mistake coming on the cruise. He paused, sighed, and smiled slightly. "You see, I lost my dear wife six months ago, and well, it hasn't been easy. And no, I'm not a Texan. I split my time between London and Los Angeles." He turned back to Gertie and lit up with pleasure. "But now it seems the fates have led me here after all." He beamed, eyes riveted on Gertie's face. "This lovely creature has appeared to rescue me."

Gertie seemed mesmerized, eyes wide and a dreamy sort of smile at her lips. "Mr. Winters, I'm so sorry for your loss. I know how you feel. My Donald passed recently too."

"It's Grayson. May I call you Gertie?"

"Of course."

Edna tried again. "I guess lots of folks came on this here cruise to meet up with someone new. I know I did."

But Grayson and Gertie were perusing the menu, heads together, and Bill, the retired car salesman from Pittsburgh to Edna's left, vied for her attention, his gaze landing somewhere south of her chin. "Gotta love the new four-wheel-drive SUV's. They can outmaneuver those pickups ..."

A lovely meal ensued. Grayson and Gertie chose marinated vegetables and a fruit soup as starters. Then a beautifully-appointed Caesar salad with croissant followed by beef filets and roasted potatoes.

Edna followed suit. "All this fancy French is getting in the way. I wish they'd just say steak." She finished her meal with chocolate lava cake and coffee.

Bill nattered on about the car dealership he'd sold to his son-in-law, and Edna tried but failed to pull Grayson's attention away from her best friend.

"Anybody up for the movies later on? There's a couple of rom-coms playing after the promenade."

But Bill had turned to the retired librarian from Minnesota to recite his salesman of the year story, and Ted from Georgia interrupted with a discussion on conspiracies to keep the public in the dark about alien sightings in Area 51.

Edna tuned them all out and discreetly read through her hit list again. She'd run into number six during the cocktail hour and had booked him for the seven o'clock slot, but she still had two empties. Bill wasn't on her list.

She ate the last bite of cake and washed it down with coffee. "Hey, Gertie, we better get a move on. First round of meet and greets starts in five minutes."

But Gertie was gone. She caught a glimpse of her pink blouse and a white jacket exiting the door of the dining room, the man's arm at the woman's waist.

"Well, if that don't beat all." Edna slapped her linen napkin on the table and took her leave.

Edna paced back and forth from the door of their little cubicle stateroom to the back wall. She muttered to herself, giving Gertie a piece of her mind and rehearsing what she'd say when she saw her. *Can't believe you'd do such a thing.* Other words peppered her speech as she wore a path in the cheap carpet, *ungrateful,* and *just plain rude* amongst some saltier ones. She'd only been angry at first, seeing Gertie waltzing out of the dining hall without a decent goodbye, but now she began to worry.

She stopped pacing, collapsed onto her bed, and glanced at her watch. Ten-thirty. Gertie had been with that silver-haired devil for nearly four hours. She and Mr. Wonderful could've trotted around the promenade a hundred times by now. A tingle of worry shot down Edna's backbone. She'd strangle him if he hurt her best friend.

Muffled conversation penetrated the door along with the sound of the key sliding into the lock. *Finally.* The door opened slowly. Edna tensed as Gertie paused, back turned to her for several long moments before she closed the door and turned, breathing out a small, satisfied sigh.

Edna exploded. "Gertie Hansen, where in the world have you been? I've been worried sick about you. And what did you think you were doing traipsing off from the dining room without even a 'fare thee well?'" She stopped to catch her breath.

Gertie's eyes widened and one hand flew to her chest. "Edna, I'm surprised at you. I was so excited to share my evening with you and tell you every little thing. My goodness, you were the one who brought me on this cruise to meet someone special. Well, I'll thank you to know that is exactly what's happened." She pulled out the tiny desk chair and sat, resting her handbag on the desk. "Mercy. You've upset me. I expected you to be happy for me." She reached for a tissue and dabbed at the corners of her eyes.

"Well, now that I know you're safe and sound and not thrown overboard or something, I feel some better. But honestly, you could've said goodbye and let me know where you were going."

"You're right. That wasn't very thoughtful of me, but oh, Edna. Grayson is the most wonderful man I've ever met. We clicked the moment he sat at our table and … well, he's not just handsome, he's genteel and kind and such a gentleman. We walked around the promenade under the stars and slipped into a tiny, little bar for a glass of champagne and—"

"I don't care about all of that right now. It's happened too fast. Why is he so keen on you when you just met? Sounds fishy to me."

"Fishy? How can you call Grayson fishy? You heard what he said. He's lost his wife and he's lonely. He nearly canceled his ticket, but as the fates would have it, he came. And we met and, oh my, he's everything I've ever dreamed of." Gertie closed her eyes, and the corners of her mouth turned up in a beatific smile.

Edna softened her voice. "I gotta admit he's good-looking. And smooth—maybe a little too smooth." She sat down on the edge of her bed.

"As opposed to the twins or that sleazy Ramon guy of yours? You wouldn't know smooth if it slapped you in the face." Gertie reached down and removed her shoes.

"No need to get nasty." Edna struggled to gain some composure. "Why don't you come over here and sit down and think about this whole thing."

"There's nothing to think about. Grayson is a wonderful man who happens to have taken a fancy to me. He said some of the loveliest things—I'm beautiful and intelligent. It's been a long time since anyone spoke sweet nothings in my ear. And if the truth be told, Donald never was very good at expressing his feelings. I enjoyed it, Edna. You're just jealous."

Gertie stood and removed her necklace and earrings. "And I want to get right to bed because Grayson is picking me up in the morning. We're going to have brunch together."

"Now, wait a minute, Gertie. Let's take some time to process all of this."

"Nothing to process. I like him. How was your evening? Did you find any suitable men at the meet and greets?"

"Naw, more of the same. By the way, Bert was looking for you. You had that one-way from him."

"Bert? Oh, yes. Well, there's no obligation to meet with one-ways, since I didn't choose him. Anyway, I've found the only meet and greet I care for. Thank you so much, Edna, for giving me this birthday trip and a chance to fall in love again."

"Love? You're already talking about love? Gertie, you've known this guy for exactly five hours. You need to slow down a little and ..." But Gertie had gone into the tiny bathroom and turned on the shower.

"Holy smokes, she's got it bad." Edna wriggled out of her tight purple top and slacks and into her pj's. "Well,

Edna, old girl, you'll have to keep an eye on her and keep her out of trouble. Dang, I'd give my eye teeth to have a guy like him chasing after me."

CHAPTER EIGHT

Edna awoke to a pungent aroma and wrinkled her nose and sneezed. She reached for a tissue and blew her nose. "Holy cow, Gertie. No one wears perfume anymore. Everyone's allergic these days."

Gertie fluffed the sides of her hair and checked her teeth for lipstick smudges. "Grayson happens to be partial to it. It's French—Guerlain ... something, I forget. He bought it for me last evening."

"Hmph. He must have bucks then."

"Yes. He comes from a very well-appointed European family. However, the wealthy don't advertise their incomes, so don't ask." Gertie smoothed down her soft, heather-green, hip-length knit top.

Edna scrambled out of bed. "Yikes, it's later than I thought. What time is your brunch?"

"Grayson reserved a table in the Bliss Lounge for eleven. He said the food is 'ever so much better' than the open buffet."

Edna began her morning exercise routine. "Us peons will have to settle for the bargain-barrel brunch, I guess."

Gertie turned to face Edna. "No need to get nasty. I'm looking forward to a mimosa in the quiet ambiance of the Bliss. *And* with the handsome man of my dreams by my side. I would think you'd be happy for me. You know how hard it's been for me to be alone."

Edna finished her toe touches. "I know, Gertie, but I hope your dreams don't turn into nightmares. All I ask is that you slow down a bit." Edna wrangled on her slacks and her top, then adjusted her cleavage.

Gertie's eyebrows arched. "My word, Edna, this blouse looks as bad as yesterday's. Maybe worse."

"Well, as I told you, I didn't have time to try these tops on with my new Wonderbra, and now I've got no choice. It's either this or ..." She grinned wickedly at Gertie. "Nothin.'"

Gertie shuddered. "I'm going now. I'd like a quick stroll on the above deck before I meet Grayson. All this rich food can add pounds to a girl's figure."

While Edna tried to think of a witty comeback, Gertie opened the cabin door and exited, trailing an invisible veil of fancy French perfume behind her.

"Oh, man. Gertie, what are you thinking?" *I better watch her like a hawk.*

"Hey, you two! Over here," Edna hollered over the chatter of the crowd loading up on Sunday brunch items. Four long lines moved down the sides of two endless tables heaped with tempting arrays of everything from fresh fruit to cheese platters, and from mini quiches to serving pans piled high with aromatic slices of ham and crunchy, thick-cut bacon. Everything looked and smelled delicious.

Boyd and Floyd, breathless, joined Edna and tipped their hats politely to the people next in line. "Where've you boys been? Good to see you. Gertie's run off with that Grayson guy, and it's no fun to eat alone."

Boyd with a B spoke up. "Me and Floyd thought since it's the Sabbath and all we'd pop into the little chapel for 'a song and a prayer' as the brochure said. Weren't but seven of us, but the service was right nice, wasn't it, Floyd?"

"Yup, a sort of peaceful way to begin the day," his brother agreed.

"Well, that's nice, boys. Can't remember the last time I darkened the door of a church. Probably when I married Fred at eighteen. Me and Sam got hitched at the court house." Edna grabbed a plate from the stack, then selected her utensils and a white linen napkin. She craned her neck to see what kept the line from moving. "Looks like the make-on-demand omelet bar is holding up the show. I think I'll make an end-run around that and see what's further down. I'll grab a table for the three of us."

They settled themselves at a table near a wall with a padded bench on one side and chairs on the other. They unloaded their trays and handed them to a passing waiter.

"Man, it's hard to choose from all that bee-yootiful food. Look at these pastries and all the breakfast meats a person can hold." Edna held up her champagne flute and made a toast. "Here's to us, boys. May we all find what we're looking for." Boyd and Floyd held up their orange juice glasses and clinked them together. Everyone enjoyed their meal.

An announcement rang out from somewhere near the entrance to the dining area. "Ladies and gentlemen, we hope you're enjoying your senior cruise and are having the time of your lives. Don't forget to sign up for the afternoon's events before you leave. There's something for everyone. But be sure to save plenty of time to gussy up for tonight's dinner which begins promptly at seven. And if you haven't found that *someone special* yet, maybe you'll bump into him or her in the conga line." The announcer hit the mic on something as he set it down. It made a loud thunk, and he uttered a muffled curse.

Boyd whipped out a cruise program and turned to page six. "Here's our choices for this afternoon. By golly, you couldn't do all this stuff if you tried. Me and Floyd want to give shuffleboard a try and maybe a hand or two of pinochle. We used to play cards when Mama had our Aunt Cora over some evenings."

Edna twisted her head to read the choices. "I'm more of an action-oriented gal. I might go for the zip line and a belly dancing lesson. Always did wonder how those women got their tummies to go in and out like that. But then I gotta remember it would be good to find a date for tonight's dinner. Probably won't be many guys in the belly dancing class."

Boyd and Floyd both sported Cheshire-cat grins and stared at her.

"What?" Edna searched their pudgy faces.

"Well, me and Floyd sort of hit the jackpot this morning at the little Sunday service," Boyd said. "We saw a couple of nice, quiet, young ladies sitting in the front pew, and we got to talking after service. They spoke right up and asked us to the dinner tonight. They're cousins from North Dakota, Eunice and Norma, and they took a shine to our cowboy hats. Said it reminded them of home." Boyd sat back in his chair and wiped his brow after his long speech.

"Well, I never," Edna said. "You boys surprise me. Those gals stepped right up and invited you to dinner, did they? And right after church too." Edna shook her head and tsked a few times. "They sound like little hussies to me."

Boyd and Floyd's eyes had grown wider and wider until Edna let out a guffaw to let them know she was giving them 'the business.' "Naw, I'm happy for you, boys. That's what this here cruise is all about. But it puts me in a pinch, doesn't it? I better figure out some activities where the men will flock to. What do you think of salsa lessons?

Edna wiped the sweat from her brow and pulled at her neckline to make sure everything was in place. She'd waited forever for her turn at the zip-line. The ship had rigged the line to run from the sporting deck over the pool and onto a platform on the other side.

Marvin sidled up to her. "Mind if I cut in line? I want to witness you riding that thing. You sure you want to try it?"

"Why wouldn't I? You tryin' to tell me what I can and can't do?"

"Whoa, there, little lady. Don't get all exercised. Fact is, I kind of admire your spunk. Have you looked down? I'd probably lose my brunch if I tried that thing. No offense intended."

Edna backed down. "Well, okay, I guess. No one ever calls me 'little.' What other activities have you tried? I checked out the salsa dance class, but there were only about five people there, and the instructor was a skinny little guy with sideburns and a mustache who sort of gave me the creeps."

"Oh, I've been wandering around. I'm not used to *activities*. I'm used to a normal life where you get up, get dressed, eat, do your chores for the day, and maybe watch a little television. I'm not interested in lessons on this and that. Probably shouldn't have come on this cruise." He looked down at his feet and shuffled them back and forth. "Don't fit in with the rest."

"You surprise me, Marvin. One minute you're mouthing off like a big bully and the next you're beat as a whipped puppy." She paused. "Hey, I'm tired of waiting in this line. Why don't you and me go get a drink somewhere? What do you say?"

Marvin perked up, a wide smile stretching out his mouth. "Sounds good. There's a mini-bar down by the pool. We can watch these bozos zip overhead while we relax."

Two mojitos later, Edna leaned her chin in her hand and sighed. She'd made the mistake of asking Marvin about his late wife and had been treated to a very long and detailed tour through his long years of marriage to the perfect woman. Marvin had loved his wife and was now one of the loneliest people she'd ever met.

He paused for breath, and Edna took the opportunity to jump into the conversation. "It sounds like Anna was a great woman, and I'm glad for the time you had together. My first marriage was a good, long one too. But he died, and I was in the same boat as you. I hated living alone. But I'll tell ya, Marvin, there's only one thing worse than living alone, and that's living with a lying, cheating bum. I did that too. Sam stuck around for four years, and we had some good times, until one day he took off and never looked back. Left me for a woman young enough to be his daughter. I learned my lesson. Don't be in too big a hurry to find another Mrs. Right. There are a lot of mistakes lurking out there."

"Yeah, suppose you're right." Marvin doodled around with his glass. "I'm gonna ask you something, but you can say no if you want."

Edna felt a tiny niggle of dread run down her spine. "What's that?

"I wondered if you'd have dinner with me tonight. Not a date, really. Just friends. I'm tired of running around this boat all by myself. Feel like a darn fool." He turned his gaze on Edna and his eyes reflected both hurt and a hint of hope.

"Why, sure I'll eat dinner with you. I feel kinda out of the loop too. Thought it would be a hoot to do the speed dates and all, but really, it's sort of ... well, different than I thought. I'll meet you in the dining room right before seven. Thanks for the drinks." And Edna took her leave with a bit of an ache in her heart at the memories Marvin's wistful stories had unearthed inside her.

Edna fussed with her spiky hair do, trying to get all the points in exactly the right spots so she didn't look like a hedgehog on top. She'd changed into black pants and a sequined top in purples and pinks. She planned to hold back her snazziest top for the moonlight ball on the last night. "Shoulda brought at least one dress," she grumped. "If I had one."

She finished with her hair and stepped back to thoughtfully look in the full-length mirror squashed between the beds and the dressing table. "Not bad. You still got it going on, old girl." But her shoulders slumped as she tried and failed to pull in her tummy. "Dang, no one to please but Marvin. Not to worry. Now, where is Gertie? She should've been here hours ago to get ready for tonight."

Edna paced and fumed for the next hour, checking her watch every five minutes. But Gertie failed to make an appearance. Six forty-five, six fifty-five. She leafed through the cruise brochure. Page seven was glittery with ads for jewelry and hair and nail appointments as enticements to spend money getting "princess-perfect" for the moonlight ball on Monday night. The big finale. "Phooey." Edna tossed the brochure clear across the little room where it landed on the floor beneath a pint-sized television.

She left the brochure where it landed and headed out the door to find Marvin.

CHAPTER NINE

Marvin and Edna arrived at a table for eight just as Boyd and Floyd showed up with their women in tow. Boyd, always the first to speak, introduced the girls. Eunice was on Boyd's arm and Norma on Floyd's. Both women were on the chubby side and dressed in drab, polyester dresses cut from the same pattern—high neckline with no adornment on the bodice and a simple A-line skirt with a two-inch sash tied in the back. The dresses looked like someone's home economics project. Eunice was in gray and Norma in brown—two little sparrows lost at sea.

But Boyd and Floyd walked with shoulders back and heads held high as they set about seating the ladies with a flourish. They opted to wear their hats as the table left no room for such large accessories.

"Marvin," Edna said, "you remember Boyd and Floyd from earlier, don't you?" Marvin mumbled something that sounded like "How could I forget," but he kept the words close to his chin.

"Well, everyone, it's prime rib night—can't beat that with a stick." Edna wanted to put the girls at ease with some light repartee.

"Eunice, here, is a vegetarian," Boyd said the word as if it were naughty. "Not sure what you're gonna do to fill yourself up."

"I've made arrangements with the staff for the entire cruise," Eunice spoke slowly and evenly in a nasal voice.

"They bring me salads and vegetables, and I do fine, thank you very much." Her tone made it clear the topic was not to be addressed again.

Boyd cleared his throat and asked Norma if she was 'one of those' too.

"Not on your life," she answered, "I like my beef so rare it could jump right off the plate. Just because we're cousins doesn't mean we do everything alike. Although Eunice is a whiz at the sewing machine and whipped up our entire cruise wardrobe in under seven days. I count it a miracle." Norma beamed at each face around the table.

Floyd struggled to enter the conversation. "Well, you girls look real nice. Boyd said at the service this morning you both looked like 'right nice girls.'" That's all he had.

Edna and Marvin took their seats. There were two conspicuously empty spots at the table. "I suppose we should hold these spots for Gertie and what's his name," Edna said. "Hey, Boyd would you tip the chairs up against the table, so nobody comes and takes them?"

Eunice chimed in, "That's a bit tacky, don't you think? Let's just tell people they're reserved."

Norma nodded her head in agreement. "Sure, we can tell them."

"Whatever." Edna had her nose out of joint. "What do you think, Marvin?"

"I think we should let Gertie do what she wants," Marvin answered. "If she shows, she shows. I, for one, am going to order a drink and dig into a nice, juicy prime-rib dinner. I think there's chocolate mousse on the dessert list too. The food is about the only thing that makes this cruise worth all the dough I laid out."

Edna huffed. "Thanks a lot. Guess my good company is just chopped liver, huh?"

Marvin opened his mouth to either upgrade the argument or make peace, but he had time for neither because Gertie and Grayson flew into the dining hall and up to their table on wings of joy.

Grayson had Gertie's hand and delicately seated her, then bowed to the rest of the table guests.

Gertie's face shone with happiness. "Hello, everyone. And my goodness, Boyd and Floyd, please introduce me to your lovely ladies. I'm sorry we're late, but we had so much to do before tomorrow. I just now carried my dress to our cabin, and then, we had to make sure the captain had the schedule and ..."

Everyone froze. Edna's mouth hung open, and she was half-standing at the table.

Marvin's face registered surprise with a touch of 'are you kidding' and the twins looked flummoxed.

Eunice and Norma waited to be introduced.

"What the heck are you talking about, Gertie?" Edna sputtered. "What dress? What schedule?"

Gertie looked at Grayson, and they shared a secret, ecstatic smile. "Well, we were going to wait to share the news until dessert time, but we're both so excited we can't help ourselves." She beamed at Grayson again. "You tell them, darling."

"Darling!" Edna was up now. "Did you call him *darling*?"

Grayson had remained standing and now addressed the table as if he were a professor in front of a classroom. "You all know we experienced love at first sight when I met Gertie at our first dinner together. We've both felt it—fate pulling us together." He sent a dazzling smile in Gertie's direction. "We've both been lonely. Now that we've found one another we don't want to waste a minute. We want to spend the rest of our lives together. And what could be more romantic than a wedding on the high seas? We already got permission from the captain, and he had the licenses necessary, so we're getting married tomorrow night before the Moonlight Ball. We're hoping you'll be matron of honor, Edna, and the first mate will be my best man."

Edna clenched both fists. "Now wait a darn minute, Gertie, you must have more sense than this. What are you thinking? You just met this guy. You can't get married tomorrow night. It's your birthday, you—"

"Edna, calm down." Marvin placed a restraining hand on Edna's forearm. "Let's all sit down and not cause a scene."

Boyd and Floyd dutifully nodded. Eunice and Norma sat there with their mouths open and their eyes agog. They'd followed the conversation, heads turning back and forth as if watching a tennis match.

Boyd put his oar in the water. "Gertie, are you sure about this? Mama always said it's not a good idea to rush in where angels fear to tread."

Gertie folded her hands. "Thank you all for your care and concern." Her voice was soft but determined, and she sounded as if she'd prepared her speech in advance. "Goodness, I'd almost forgotten about my birthday. If I were in your shoes, I'd probably be thinking the same thing as you, but …" She turned to Grayson, her eyes mushy with love. "Grayson is absolutely everything I've ever wanted in a man. We found each other here on this cruise ship, and we count it the Lord's blessing on two lonely people. Both of us lost our spouses and have been in darkness and despair for some time, but now we've found a new chance at happiness. We only ask that you support us and share our joy."

Grayson kept his hand on Gertie's shoulder during her speech and then shifted to catch her hand and hold on tightly. He appeared totally at ease, the perfect gentleman.

Marvin opened his mouth to speak, but Edna elbowed him in the side. "Gertie, do you know anything about this man? Where does he live? Are you going to move from Amarillo to God knows where and go gallivanting all over the world? What about your nice, quiet life? What about your kids? Have you told them about this crazy scheme?"

"My family will know in time. It's been such a whirlwind. I admit it's sudden and rather impulsive for someone like me, but I know this is right, and it's what I want. I'm a grown woman. I know my own mind. Please respect that, Edna."

Edna slowly lowered herself into her chair. For once she was out of words.

"Grayson and Gertie," Boyd said, "I want you to meet Eunice and Norma. They're our dates for tonight's dinner. Eunice is a vegetarian," he added helpfully.

The servers brought in dinner rolls and salads with a special tray of greens and roughage for Eunice, and everyone focused their meals. Edna shot meaningful looks at Gertie whenever she got the chance, but Gertie was blissfully engaged in quiet, intimate conversation with Grayson. He remained a charming, attentive, betrothed gentleman.

Boyd and Floyd carried on a farm-and-ranch kind of conversation with the girls with a heavy emphasis on their cattle and how they tended them each quarter of the year. The girls nodded and smiled politely but had little to add about their own farm lives.

When the last bits of chocolate mousse had been scraped from their dessert bowls, Gertie and Grayson were first to offer words of departure. "We still have some planning to do, and we both want to get a good night's sleep."

Edna scowled in their direction and refrained from making any snide comments.

Boyd and Floyd rose and escorted their women a few feet toward the exit sign.

"Hey," Edna hissed in their direction. "You boys meet me back here. We need to talk. How about nine o'clock? Does that give you enough time for ... whatever?"

"Norma and I will take our leave right now," Eunice said. "We've both had headaches coming on all afternoon, haven't we, Norma? I think maybe mine has turned into a migraine. Thank you, Boyd and Floyd, for a lovely dinner. Good night, everyone." Norma allowed Eunice to lead the way, following closely behind, making good on their escape.

"Humph," Boyd said, "Guess we didn't make much of an impression on the girls. Not sure I want to truck with one of them vegetarians anyway."

"Yeah," Floyd agreed. "Norma's probably not my type either. But I kinda enjoyed sitting with someone and not being left to eat all alone. I expect they're not really ranch gals but more like small-town girls who yearn for the ranching life."

Busboys swarmed all over the dining hall, so Edna, Marvin, and the boys stood to get out of their way. "Let's take a bathroom break and meet up at the little coffee shop down the way. Marvin, are you in on this? We need a plan to rescue Gertie from making a tragic mistake."

"Sure, I'll go along for the ride. Seems like a darn fool thing for her to do. Don't know as we can change her mind, but I'm in."

Edna checked her watch. "It's eight-fifteen. Let's meet up at eight-thirty. Everybody, think hard between now and then."

Lattes in hand, the four friends put their heads together over the back table of The Big Grind.

"Okay, Edna said, "Let's approach this here problem like we're detectives. What do we know? I'll start. Fact number one—I sort of started this whole thing with the bio I wrote for Gertie. It said she was a wealthy widow who liked to have a good time."

Marvin stared. "You did?"

"Yeah, I did, and now I regret it. I think probably that rat Grayson read the bio and decided to go after a rich widow. Probably wants to get her to sign over her property and bank accounts and then plans on dumping her later."

Boyd and Floyd looked at one another, their plump faces red and sweaty. Boyd spoke up. "I know this might not be the time to say this, but me and Floyd need to get something off our chests. We've been feeling more and more guilty. Y'all have been so nice to us, and now we feel terrible. This whole cruise has been a mistake, and we want to make it right, don't we, Floyd?"

Floyd nodded.

"Right," Boyd went on. "Here's the thing. Me and Floyd saw the brochure for this trip when we went through some of Mama's papers and stuff. The brochure was an old one, but we looked up the new one on her computer, and we made a plan. We've been mighty miserable since Mama's passing, and we thought we might be able to find a willing woman to sort of live in with us. No hanky panky, you understand, just live with us as a housekeeper in exchange for room and board, and we wouldn't have to eat our own cooking. Truth is, we're not really cattle ranchers at all. We run a turkey farm and send the toms and hens up to the butchers at the right time each year."

Edna scrunched her face into a question.

Marvin began to laugh. "You mean you two are turkey farmers, and you wanted to go on a senior's cruise to snag a housekeeper? That's the funniest thing I've heard in years."

Boyd nodded. "Yeah, that's about the size of it. We aren't proud of it." He looked at his brother, and they both hung their heads. "We thought cattle ranchers would sound better than turkey farmers, and we got these hats to make us look more like cowboys. We aren't the dating type, but we thought there would be a lot of nice, eligible ladies on the cruise. We're not even old enough to be here. Had to fudge the numbers on the applications. Right, Floyd?"

"Yup. Feel downright sorry about it all now." Floyd picked up a stray napkin and wiped his brow.

Edna took a long pull on her latte and plunked it down hard enough to splash coffee out the vent hole. "What in the world does any of that have to do with Gertie getting married to a guy she barely knows?"

Boyd shook his head and muttered. "Well, we kind of took a shine to Gertie. Thought she might be the one for us. But now, we see she's a real lady, and we're ashamed we tried to trick her like we did. We want to help if we can."

Edna stared the boys down for a good, long while. "You are a couple of dumb bunnies if I ever saw them. But we have bigger fish to fry and true confessions time is over, boys. I don't give a hoot why you came. But if you thought me or Gertie was gonna give up our nice, free retirement years to wait on you two hand and foot, you got another think coming. Now let's get back to business. We got fact one, anyone got number two?"

"This Grayson seems too good to be true," Marvin said, "and you know what they say. All that bowing and talking like a movie star."

"Exactly." Edna went with it. "He seems like he's acting because he's a great big fraud. Now, what are we gonna do about it before my Gertie gets her heart broke?"

"I think it's too late to fix that," Boyd said and Floyd agreed.

"Maybe so, but listen, I have an idea." And Edna laid out her plan.

CHAPTER TEN

Edna paced back and forth in the little room and thought about the way her birthday gift to Gertie had gone belly up. *How in the world did this happen?* She owned her part in the fiasco, having written a bio that made Gertie a prime target for a con man. But how had her intelligent, well-bred friend stepped into the trap without a thought for her safety and well-being? *Maybe she's been as lonely as I am sometimes.*

She glanced at the nightstand where her pretty little package tied up with a pink bow sat waiting for Gertie's birthday. A special gift for her best friend—a heartfelt gift for both of them. Now Grayson overshadowed all of it, and Edna's stomach clenched with the thought of the pain to come. Gertie's would-be wedding dress, a gorgeous lace and chiffon affair in powder blue hung from a hook on the closet door. A Moonlight Ball special she'd purchased at the Bountiful Boutique. The gown was so lovely it brought tears to Edna's eyes. What a disaster.

But she and the boys had done what they could, and now the chips had to fall where they might. Edna was prepared for Gertie to make a late night of it. She'd want to spend as much time as possible with old lover boy. But when the ax fell, and it surely would, she'd be devastated. She'd avoid facing her friends as long as possible.

No way would Edna get to sleep, so she closed her eyes and determined she'd lay there until Gertie got back to the cabin safely.

Gertie rattled the pass key in the door and fell into the room. Once inside, she turned and leaned against the door, head back as tears streamed down her face, her eyes puffy with pain. She stood there crying for a bit and then tossed off her clothing in an effort to get herself into bed where she might stay for a week or two. But no, she'd have to deal with the consequences of her folly sooner than that. Just not now. She stumbled a bit in search of her pajamas, then collapsed on the edge of her bunk.

Edna roused from a deep sleep. "Gertie, is that you? What time is it?"

"It's me, and it's about three in the morning." Gertie's voice was flat, lifeless, even to her own ears. She pulled on her pajamas over her bra and undies and sat there, head down.

Edna bolted upright in the bed and turned on the lamp. "Oh, no, look at you. I'd like to smack that Grayson right in the middle of his perfect face."

Gertie looked up at Edna and sighed.

"Are you okay? Where have you been all this time?" Edna pivoted so her feet were on the floor, her knees mere inches from Gertie's. "Wait a minute. What happened to your arm? It's bleeding."

"Oh, it's just a scratch. I guess I hit it on the edge of the Captain's desk when I fainted."

"Fainted?" Edna's voice screeched.

"Well, maybe not fainted all the way. I sort of had a lights-out moment. It didn't last long."

"Holy cow, Gertie—"

"It's all gone up in smoke. Everything. Grayson, the wedding, everything." She turned her swollen eyes on Edna and made a heroic effort at a wry smile. "You were right, of course."

Edna grabbed a box of tissues and handed it to her and Gertie dabbed at the scrape on her arm. "Well, that doesn't matter now. You go on and tell me all about it and get it all out. I can see your heart is broken all to bits." Edna leaned forward and patted Gertie's shoulder then waited.

Gertie spoke as if in a trance. "Well, after we left the dinner table, we took a walk and enjoyed the night air, and then, we had an appointment to go over the wedding details one last time, assuring the captain we had people to stand up with us and all." She stopped and gave Edna another mournful look. "So, we went into his office and sat down, and before I knew what was happening two men in uniform came and 'detained' Grayson ... or whatever his real name is.

"One man said they were with Cruise Security, and they had a warrant. They handcuffed him and escorted him back to his room. The captain says he'll be under guard there until we dock Tuesday morning. Then I don't know what happens. The captain was so kind, and I could tell he felt sorry about the entire mess. He had me sit with him for a bit and gave me a cup of tea. He asked if I wanted to press charges when we dock."

She took a fresh tissue and dabbed at her eyes. "But ... Oh, Edna, he's a flim-flam artist. He cons silly old women into trusting him and then makes off with their jewelry or gets them to add him to their bank accounts and all kinds of sordid, illegal things. I was such a fool." She shook her head and blew her nose.

"I can't say I'm surprised," Edna said, "but I'm so sorry this happened to you and on your birthday cruise too."

Gertie let out a little yelp meant to be a laugh. "Yes, happy birthday to me, the biggest fool on the entire cruise ship."

"Aww, don't say that. We women long for someone to romance us, and I guess old Grayson was pretty good at it. How did they catch him?" Edna leaned forward, homing in on the details.

171

"The captain said someone came to him and suspected Grayson was up to no good. So, they ran a computer check on him, did some research, and there he was in mug shots from several states. He's had a whole string of names. After the captain told me the story, I wandered around the ship—around and around the decks—anything to keep my dream alive a bit longer. But it all evaporated into thin air, didn't it?"

Gertie turned her gaze to her closet where the soft blue gown hung. "Oh, my dress." And she broke down again. She cried for a bit then sniffled. "I guess I'll return it. It's too fancy for anything at home."

"*Can* you return it? Didn't Grayson buy it?"

A sad little smile curved Gertie's mouth. "No, something was wrong with his credit card, and it wasn't accepted, so I paid for it. I bought the Gherlain perfume too. I should have sensed something was wrong right then. But, oh Edna, even though I'm embarrassed and angry and sad, I have to tell you these last two days *have* been a dream. I so wanted to believe it. I felt like I was standing outside my body, watching as I acted out a wonderful fairy tale.

"He really *was* everything I've always wanted—gentle, attentive, full of lovely words and compliments." Her voice dropped to a whisper. "And kisses." She shook her head as she remembered. "I don't suppose it was worth getting my heart broken and my reputation besmirched, but I *will* remember how it felt to be cherished." She let out a long, ragged sigh.

The two friends sat there for a bit, both quiet, letting the information and the events of the night sink in. "Seems a shame for that rat to get away without doing some jail time. If they have a warrant, he's wanted by someone somewhere, and they'll transport him once we dock."

Gertie blew her nose again. "I don't know. Even now I don't wish him any harm. I suppose they need to stop him from hurting other women though. But how in the world am I going to face everyone after this?"

"Well, there aren't too many *everyones* to worry about," Edna kept her tone soft and kind. "Marvin feels sorry about the whole thing, and the twins have confessions to make to you, so you'll sort of come out even with them. Don't worry about any of that tonight. Let's get some sleep. Here, let's clean off this scrape and put a Band-Aid on it."

Edna puttered around and found the first aid kit, swabbed the area with a cleansing wipe, and carefully dabbed on antibiotic ointment before covering the scrape with a bandage.

"You stay in bed as long as you want in the morning, and I'll wait to have a late breakfast with you. Then we'll relax for the rest of the day. I don't think any of us want to attend the Moonlight Ball anyway. We'll think of something else to do. Okay?"

Gertie nodded. "Thank you. I feel all used up. But in a way, I feel kind of relieved too. Everything was happening so fast, and I felt like I was spinning out of control. And now I'm ... tired."

"Sure, you are. You lie down and go to sleep. I'll see you in the morning." And the two friends settled into their skinny beds.

Gertie quieted immediately. She sank into the mattress and allowed the exhaustion to take her.

The main dining hall was relatively empty from a lull between the breakfast eaters and the brunchers. Gertie selected an array of fresh fruit and one bran muffin. The coffee sat at the end of the buffet line, and she poured herself a cup. Her eyes felt as swollen as they'd looked in the mirror, and lines of grief ran across her forehead, but mostly she appeared pale and was bone tired.

"I suppose the boys all ate earlier," she said to Edna.

"Probably, but we'll find them and make some plans for the rest of the day. I think all of us have pretty much given up on the dating part of this thing." Edna piled scrambled eggs on her plate and squished them over to make room for little pig sausages and rashers of bacon. "Let's sit over here."

She'd chosen a table off to the side and near the back exit. A quiet oasis. "How are you doing? Feeling better?" Edna took a large forkful of eggs.

Gertie tipped her head as she examined her feelings. "I feel ... quiet inside. Like I've been ill and am starting to recoup. It's like I don't have to be part of things quite yet." She gave a Mona Lisa smile.

"That's okay. You take all the time you need to get yourself back together. This here day is all about you and honoring your birthday and forgetting about the past. Oh, here's the boys now."

Gertie turned and sure enough, the twins and Marvin— the three musketeers—all stood in a line and looked like they weren't sure if they were welcome or not. "Hi guys, come on over and join us. Did you all eat already? Or are you back for seconds?" Edna guffawed.

Boyd spoke up. "Yes, ma'am, we did eat breakfast earlier, but we wanted to find you two and sort of pay our respects. Miss Gertie, we're awful sorry about what's happened." The twins had taken off their hats for their speech.

Gertie squinted her eyes and asked, "How do you know what's happened? Who told you?"

The only response from the three was a general looking off into the distance and then down again at the tops of their shoes and boots.

"Were you boys the ones who spoke with the captain? Did you poke your noses in where they didn't belong?" Gertie's voice had a hint of hysteria in it. But then she stopped and gazed at each one of the three in turn. "Well, you ruined my wedding, but you probably saved me a world of sorrow in the long run." She looked at them with another serene smile. "Thank you."

Edna came to the rescue. "Sit down, boys. Get yourself some coffee or something, and let's make plans for the rest of Gertie's birthday. This young lady is seventy-three years young today, and it's gonna be a happy day if it kills all of us."

CHAPTER ELEVEN

Gertie and Edna stood outside the Bountiful Boutique where Gertie had returned her dress. Gertie had her handbag open, and she placed three, one hundred dollar bills into her wallet. "I'm glad to get this back. It's a lot of money to lose on my income. I'll keep the Gherlain. They say aromas are a trigger for memories, and I guess I'll remember this little venture for a good many years."

Edna sighed. "We all will. And just to set the record straight, I went along with the boys to do that little intervention with the captain. You can be mad if you want, but I'd do it again in a minute to save you from disaster."

Gertie studied Edna for a moment. "I've had some time to think about the whole fiasco, and I believe I've come to the realization I've been more unhappy living alone than I understood. I do keep busy with my church and garden club activities, and I see people. But the evenings and the long nights alone—that's when it hurts most, doesn't it? Sleeping all alone is so ... cold and sad." Gertie's face was a mask of pain, and Edna reached out to pat her hand.

"You're right. I hate it too, but like I told Marvin, there are a lot of bums out there, and it's better to be alone than to be bamboozled."

"It's funny when you think about how all five of us—you and me and Marvin and the boys—were all looking for something on this cruise, but none of us found it." Gertie gave a wistful, little smile. "I guess that should be a lesson to us to let life happen and not try so hard. Both you and I have happy marriages to remember, and that's more than some women have. We need to be thankful."

Edna nodded. "Yeah, I'm thankful for Fred and all those good years, but I still could run a stake right through Sam's heart. Much as I'd like another chance at being blissfully wed, I'm still gun-shy. Don't know if I could ever trust a guy again. I'm surprised you don't feel more bitterness toward old Grayson."

"Imagine him sitting there all alone in his cabin, knowing he's going to be arrested for bilking women out of their worldly goods and be taken away by police officers." Gertie pursed her lips and shook her head. "I still can't believe it."

She hung her handbag strap over her shoulder and continued, "Well, just between you and me, I *have* fantasized about wrapping this handbag strap around his neck and pulling ... hard." She gave one of her sweet, innocent smiles as she said it.

Edna's eyes widened, but she pasted a big smile on her face. "Okay, now it's your special day, and we have a little surprise for you, but you have to stay in the cabin until I come and get you. Okay?" She escorted Gertie back to the cabin and deposited her there. "Be glad you're not married to that crumb, and he won't have the opportunity to drain all your bank accounts. Now I'll be back in a jiffy. Sit tight." And she was off.

"We'll have two large pizzas—one pepperoni and olive and one Bountiful Supreme." Edna rummaged in her purse for some cash. "And five beers."

Marvin sprang into action. "I'll cover the beers while you go grab us a table. Pretty empty in here. I suppose most everyone is at the Ball."

"Well, we'll have our own celebration right here." Edna looked down on her snazziest top—a silver and gold number with shiny beads everywhere. She'd insisted the boys wear whatever they'd brought for the Ball. No one was going to spoil Gertie's birthday celebration.

Marvin looked respectable in a navy suit.

Boyd and Floyd showed up with a pink bakery box tied up in twine. They wore their brown corduroy suits again, but this time they'd accessorized with polka-dotted bow ties. Boyd's dots were dark green, and Floyd's were midnight blue. They'd left their hats in their cabin. "We couldn't find a nice cake, but we got chocolate éclairs. They had candles too, so we got some pink ones."

"Good work, fellas. Now, the pizzas will be done in about twenty minutes. You guys sit down over there and set the table real nice with the éclairs in the middle. We won't do the candles until after we eat the pizza. I'm gonna go and get Gertie from the cabin now. And you all remember to keep the conversation light and cheerful. No mention of you know who."

"Got it," the twins said in unison. Marvin nodded. They set about their tasks.

Edna hurried down staircases and through hallways to their cabin. She unlocked the door and put on her happiest, most carefree face. "Hi there, birthday girl. It's time for your second surprise party. Don't know very many ladies who get two birthday parties."

Gertie stood tall with her shoulders back and her chin out. She wore pale-green slacks with a shell top and an ecru linen jacket. She looked fragile but lovely.

"Wow, Gertie, you look great. You wear clothes so well. It always made me jealous back when we were in high school. You could pick up any old rag right off the rack, and it looked terrific on you."

"Thank you. I don't know if I'm ready yet to enjoy a party, but I'll do my best. Thank you for going to all this trouble for me." Gertie gathered her things.

179

"No trouble for my best friend. Now, we better hurry because the main course is about ready." They hurried out the door, Edna in the lead and Gertie struggling to keep up with her.

Gertie didn't seem fazed to find her birthday party was happening in an onboard pizza parlor.

"Sit down here at the head of the table, and we'll all fill in the spots. Hope beer is okay—we could get you a glass of wine if you want."

"No, the beer is fine. I enjoy a glass of beer now and then." Gertie smiled at each of the guys in turn.

"Now, before we go any farther, the boys here, Boyd and Floyd, have something they want to say. Oh, dear, where's your hats, I can't tell you apart."

Boyd grinned. "Take a good look at our bow ties," he said. And sure enough, when Edna looked closely, she could see the tiny B and F in the middle of each tie. "We stitched them. Mama always said her boys needed to know how to fix their own clothes, so she got each of us an emergency sewing kit. Wasn't too hard, just fussy work."

Gertie looked expectantly at the twins. "You have something to tell me?" She sipped her beer.

"Yes, ma'am, and we are thoroughly ashamed of ourselves about the whole thing." They proceeded to relate their sad tale of losing their mama and practically starving to death on their cooking. Their adventure into the culinary arts at the cooking classes held at their community college had done little to solve their problems. Plus, they hated doing housework on top of feeding the turkeys and taking care of their pens.

"Our work is never done," Floyd complained.

Gertie squinted her eyes and focused on the chubby cowboys. "And you pretended to be cattle ranchers while you were actually in the market for a housekeeper? Why didn't you post an ad on your community bulletin boards? And what does all of this have to do with me?" Gertie seemed more perplexed the longer they talked.

Boyd dropped the final shoe. "Well, you see, ma'am, we took a liking to you right away. You're pretty and kind, and we thought maybe we could convince you to share your life with us, so to speak. We would have offered a stipend along with the room and board."

Gertie's mouth dropped open. Then her eyes teared up, and Edna wasn't sure if she was going to cry again or scream. Instead, she began to laugh, first in her throat and then way down to her belly. She grabbed the edge of the table and laughed long and hard until the tears streamed down her face.

The rest of the gang stared and then joined in the laughter. Tentatively at first, then all five of them held their sides and let loose. The young men firing the pizza ovens for the night looked a bit alarmed.

Edna was still hooting. "Picture this. Gertie all dolled up in a ruffly apron, serving the boys their dinner every evening promptly at six. And with a stipend." She mopped her eyes with a napkin.

Everyone finally settled down. "Ooh, boy, it felt good to laugh hard like that." Edna was the first to have enough breath to speak. "You know, everyone, we paid good money to come on this cruise, and it's been disappointing in nearly every way except for pretty good eats. We just have tonight to make some memories we'll want to pull up in the future. Let's dig into the pizza and have our dessert and then go out and have us a shuffleboard tournament. Winner gets bragging rights and maybe the extra éclair."

The mood of the group hit an all-time high. Even Gertie seemed invested in making it a night to remember. They devoured the pizza, sloshed down more beer, and laughed and joked all through the meal. Gertie finished two beers and ended up with a smudge of tomato sauce on her cheek.

"Okay, now, boys and Gertie, I have one more little surprise for our birthday girl, and here it is." She produced the small gift box from her handbag and offered it with a shy smile to her best friend. "Here."

Gertie reached out to cradle the box in both hands. "You shouldn't have bought me anything after all you spent on this trip. I won't ever be able to repay you. We'll both be broke if we try to one-up each other every birthday."

"We can make a pact to just exchange cards from now on if that makes you happy." Edna grinned. "Open it."

Gertie unwrapped the box carefully, trying not to see the sale sticker on the bottom reading $11.99. "Well, they say good things come in small packages," she said. She pulled off the lid and a soft piece of cotton batting covering the surface. She lifted out a silver necklace with interlocking hearts on a long chain. "Why, Edna, this is beautiful."

"I got one for me too. Thought since we're best friends we can wear the same thing close to our real hearts." Edna pulled out the matching necklace from under her snazzy top.

"What a beautiful sentiment. I love it."

"Well, I'm glad. I tried to order some jewelry through the Elks. They got some real pretty bracelets and necklaces with bona fide elk teeth in them, but I couldn't get them here in time for your birthday. Had to settle for something more conventional, but I'm glad you like it anyway."

"Elk's teeth? How ... unique." A shadow of dread passed over Gertie's pretty features, but she settled her face into a sincere smile. "Thank you, Edna. Thanks for being a true best friend."

"You're welcome. Let's pack up the rest of this pizza, and I'll stash it in my purse. I've been known to eat cold pizza for breakfast. Now, let's get this shuffleboard party started."

CHAPTER TWELVE

Everyone packed and left their bags standing neatly by their beds. Stewards would take them to the dockside where they'd retrieve them and head for the shuttle to the airport later in the morning. After the previous evening's shuffleboard tournament, which, to his surprise Floyd had won, they all agreed to meet for breakfast—one last meal together before parting ways.

"Morning boys," Edna greeted Boyd, Floyd, and Marvin. "Wowee, did we have fun last night or what? I think we made Gertie's birthday special and helped her forget all her troubles, didn't we?" She clapped Gertie on the shoulder, and Gertie nodded her agreement.

"We did have a good time. Thank you, everyone. And I even slept well, which I didn't expect."

Marvin spoke up. "Let's get in line, I'm starving."

Edna couldn't resist. "Holy cow, Marvin, what are you gonna do when you get home and don't have all these tables full of food waiting for you every mealtime?"

A wistful look passed over Marvin's face as he scanned the breakfast feast awaiting them. "Yeah, what I'll do is I'll go back to canned soup and frozen dinners. Maybe throw in a peanut butter and jelly once in a while. Not looking forward to it."

Edna recanted. "Well, don't get all down in the dumps. Let's enjoy the grub while we have it." She herded the group toward the beginning of the line, and they all loaded up their plates. "Do you think I can get away with stuffing some of these muffins in my purse for later? I'm not sure if we'll have time to eat before the flight home."

Gertie tsked and shook her head. "Who would want to eat muffins that have been rolling around in the bottom of your purse for hours? I'm sure we'll have time to get something along the way. The people who plan these affairs think of all the details."

"Guess you're right. Saving last night's pizza was a mistake. My bag still smells like pepperoni."

Marvin led the way to a nearby table, his two plates overflowing with breakfast bounty. "Might as well get my money's worth," he grumped.

Boyd plunked his cowboy hat down on the floor under his chair. "Me and Floyd thought maybe we shouldn't wear these hats anymore now that our cover is blown, but we've sort of got used to them. Makes us a little taller I guess."

"And there's the added benefit of us knowing which one of you is which," Gertie added.

The twins nodded.

Marvin ate a sausage whole. He chewed. When he'd swallowed, he put his fork down and leaned in toward the others. "Hey everyone, I got something I want to run by all of you. The twins and I got to talking last night on our way to our cabins, and we said how we're gonna miss being together. I don't know when I've had as much fun as we all did last night."

Boyd chimed in, "Me and Floyd agree, and after we got back to the ranch—our little cabin that is—we remembered something. When Mama was alive, she and her sisters used to do this round-robin letter thing. They weren't the friendliest family in the world, and sometimes the letters were full of gossip and downright meanness which came back around and fired the burners for the next round, but of course, if *we* all did it, we'd tell what we're doing and maybe figure out some times to get together and all. We're all Texas folks, so it's not like we'd have to travel for days to see each other. Meanwhile, the letters would give us something to look forward to. What do y'all think?"

Edna slurped her coffee and rummaged in her purse. "That's a real friendly idea, boys. I got a pen in here somewhere and a hunk of paper. Why don't you guys write your names and addresses on it, and Gertie and I can start the first round. I'll write something and send it on to Gertie and then she can get the ball rolling. What do you think, Gertie?"

Gertie took her time before answering. "I told Edna last night that every one of us came on this cruise hoping to satisfy a need. Seems like we're all lonely and in need of support of one kind or another. Look what that got us. This cruise appeals to folks who are a little desperate, doesn't it? But kindness won over desperation. I won't forget how all of you rescued me from a truly dangerous situation. And how wonderful it will be to go home with new friends— people we trust because we've been through some difficult experiences together."

"Must be like soldiers who come home and never forget their buddies," Edna added. "Or maybe like the guys on those survival shows who live on bugs and dirty water."

Gertie's serene face clouded over for a moment. "Well, something like that, I guess."

"Not sure I'll be able to think of much to write about, but I can't remember the last time I got a real letter in the mail," Marvin said. "It'll be kinda like going back to the good old days when people took time to write down their thoughts. Feels good to me."

Edna beamed. "Okay, it's settled then. Here's the pen and paper. Once you get the first letter you can keep our addresses and then we'll go round and round." She stopped talking, and her face went from happy to near ecstatic. "Man, I got a great idea. We need a name. You know, like a team name. We're brave and true. We're together through thick and thin. What's our name?" She looked expectantly at each one in turn.

"Comrades in Arms?" Marvin offered.

"The Five Musketeers?" Gertie asked.

Boyd shrugged and said, "The Friends in Need?"

Still enjoying the high from his shuffleboard tournament win, Floyd took a long time thinking, his face all scrunched up. "The Posse," he said. "We went on a mission, and we got our man."

The other four turned stunned faces toward Floyd, which one by one morphed into sheer joy.

Edna clapped her hands. "The Posse, I love it. What do you all think? Doesn't that capture us? Daring, sort of independent and feisty?"

Gertie's approval sealed the deal. "The Posse it is."

The Posse sat in all their glory at a table in the main dining hall. They had only minutes left to spare before departure. The only barrier to leaving lay in the survey papers and blue ballpoint pens sitting before them. No survey, no departing.

"I hate surveys," Marvin said.

Gertie read through the page. "Am I extremely satisfied, satisfied, neutral, less than satisfied, or extremely dissatisfied that I have to do this?"

Boyd chimed in. "There's some simple yes or no questions too. Will you sign up for another Senior Singles Cruise?"

Edna's eyes got dreamy. "Reminds me of one of George Strait's best songs: 'Check Yes or No'." She began to hum the song as she circled answers and tossed down her paper. "There, good enough. One of the things I missed on this trip was my playlist. I have George singing to me all day long when I'm at home. I miss him."

Gertie gasped, her hands flew to her mouth, and she stood all in one motion. "Look," was all she got out.

All eyes turned. There, heading toward the exit gangplank, was a contingency herding Grayson through the dining hall and off the ship. He was flanked by two security guards, and several uniformed officers stood ready to receive him at the doorway. His hands were cuffed behind his back.

At Gertie's exclamation, Grayson slowed his pace, turned in her direction, and scanned the area. Their eyes locked. Gertie tipped her head and frowned a wistful little frown. She gave a slight shake of her head.

Grayson mouthed something back. Then he turned and disappeared into the jaws of the law.

"I think he said, 'I'm sorry,'" Gertie said. "Anyway, that's what I'm going to believe."

Edna bit back seven or eight comebacks before she settled on, "He oughta be sorry, and he'll be sorrier when they lock him in the slammer."

"Such a handsome man. What a shame he's allowed himself to sink to such depths. I want to believe he still has some remnants of goodness inside." Gertie wiped a tear from her eye.

The Posse made their way off the ship, found their respective luggage, and managed to stay together as they boarded one of the waiting shuttles. Marvin and the twins helped Edna and Gertie hoist their bags while the girls found five seats.

"Houston to Amarillo," Edna said. "Sure glad we only got a three-hour hop to get home. Seems like we've been gone forever."

Marvin chuckled and said, "Edna, you better make some arrangements for getting through security this time if you don't want another exciting foundational experience."

"I'm gonna forget you said that now that we're all part of The Posse. We got each other's backs, right? Besides, I got a plan. I'll have a little chit-chat with one of those TSA folks before I go through the machine. Kinda like the folks with bionic knees. No problem."

"Yeah, right. Sorry." Marvin hung his head like a schoolboy caught pulling a pigtail.

Gertie scanned the twins' cowboy hats for her clue, "Boyd, what are you two going to do about finding a housekeeper?"

Boyd nodded. "Yes, ma'am, Miss Gertie, we'll probably take your advice and go on down to the library and the community center and so on and put out advertising cards. We'll tell the truth and ask for the help we need. We'll see what happens. Just might work."

"Good for you," Gertie gave them both a smile. "Honesty is the best policy." She sat back for a bit, bumping along with the shuttle's ups and downs. "And I want to thank everyone again for rescuing me and making my birthday one I'll never forget. There will always be a bit of sadness when I remember this trip, but you all are the silver in the silver lining."

"That there, was a nice speech, my friend." Edna put her hand out like she was playing one potato, two potato. "Here everyone, let's do a group handshake. On the count of three let's say, 'To the Posse'."

And they did.

Edna and Gertie Ride the Range

CHAPTER ONE

Edna Gratzer slammed her car door and tromped up Gertie's primrose-lined sidewalk. She leaned into the buzzer beside the front door and added a quick rap for good measure. "Open up, Gertie!" she hollered. A glimpse in the window beside the door reflected one or two wayward tufts of hair. She leaned toward her image and straightened the silvery spikes in her short, sassy hairdo.

A momentary pause, and Gertie Larsen, hairbrush in hand, opened the door. "My goodness, you startled me. I've barely had time to get dressed." She stood back to let her best friend enter.

"Sorry, once I heard the round-robin had arrived, I hightailed it over. I can't wait to hear what the boys are up to. I was afraid they'd poop out and not answer us. You know how most men hate to write." Edna tossed her coat on the back of a stately, floral-upholstered armchair and plopped herself down. "Where's the envelope?"

Gertie took her time, first returning her hairbrush to its rightful spot in her bathroom and then returning to open her secretary desk. She retrieved the large manila envelope. "Here it is. It came in yesterday's mail, but I waited to open it until we could read it together."

Edna nodded her appreciation. "That was nice of you. I wonder if the twins found a new housekeeper?"

Gertie grasped the letter opener and neatly slit the top of the envelope. "I guess we'll soon find out. Those two. Imagine pretending to be cattle ranchers and going on a singles cruise to find someone to cook them three meals a day."

Edna chuckled. "Boyd and Floyd, what a pair. And Marvin—well, he turned out to be a pretty good guy after I stopped wanting to throttle him."

Gertie let out a long sigh. "Talking about the cruise still reminds me of Grayson and how foolish I was." She shook her head and studied her feet. "I wonder where he is now?"

Edna shifted in the armchair. "Now, Gertie, don't get all melancholy on us. That cruise is ancient history. Besides, we met the boys there and formed the Posse. That was the good that came out of the bad, as they say."

Gertie blew into the envelope and pulled out a sheaf of papers. "You're right—the silver lining and all, but if I'm honest, it still hurts when I think of him."

"I know. He was a handsome devil for sure, but what a rat. Maybe he's finally behind bars where he belongs, but I wouldn't be surprised if he charmed his way out of trouble again."

Gertie closed her eyes for a moment. *You look so lovely tonight, my dear. How wonderful the fates that threw us together.* "Mm—well, let's see what the boys have to say. I sent our letters about a month ago, and they went to the twins first. The return address is Marvin's, so I guess they've all had a chance to give us their two cents. Should I read aloud?"

"Sure."

"This top one is from Marvin. I think I'll start with Boyd and Floyd so we can keep the letters in order. Here we go."

Dear Edna, Gertie, and Marvin,

This is Boyd writing for both of us. We haven't written a letter since we were Boy Scouts writing to Mama from summer camp. But we'll do our best. It was good to hear you girls got home safely and that you're keeping busy. We were just talking the other day about our pizza party for Gertie's birthday and the shuffleboard tournament. Floyd won, but I bet I'd make a comeback and win if we had another go at it. Hah, hah.

The turkeys have had an off-year, sad to say. We got a bout of fowl cholera and lost most of our chicks. But we have a new batch coming next week. That's the ups and downs of turkey ranching.

Edna cackled. "Fowl cholera. Never heard of it."

Gertie glared at Edna. "The poor little things died, Edna. It's nothing to laugh at."

"Yeah, yeah, keep reading." Edna fanned away the criticism with one hand.

We still miss Mama. We hired one lady after we got home from the cruise, but she only lasted a few weeks. Said we were too fussy about the food. Mama was a good cook. It'll be near impossible to replace her. A new lady is starting next week. She sounds pretty good although a mite old. Well, she sounds old on the phone. It's not polite to ask a lady her age, so we'll wait to see her in person.

Edna started to make another comment, but Gertie's stern look changed her mind.

We've been talking to Marvin once in a while, and he's been trying to get us to take a little vacation at some dude ranch his cousin runs. Little place in Colorado. It sounds good, but it's hard for us to get away with the feedings and watering and all. But both Floyd and me are pretty interested in western things since we kind of role-played being cattle ranchers. You know, cowboys. Every kid wants to be a cowboy. Hah, hah.

Gertie laid the papers on her lap. "I do miss those two. You couldn't imagine two peas in a pod like them if you tried."

"That's a fact. Is that all?"

"Pretty much, just a 'Hope to hear from you soon' and their signatures, Boyd Osterman and Floyd Osterman."

193

Edna nodded her head. "Let's hear from Mad Marvin then. Boy, he sure got my hackles up when we first met him."

Gertie shuffled the letters, placing Marvin's on top. "I remember. He *can* be a bit abrasive."

"Are you kidding? He's more than a *bit* abrasive—I came close to knocking his block off more than once."

"Yes, that's when Boyd and Floyd came to your rescue. Bless their little hearts. Thinking of their gentlemanly spirit always makes me smile." Gertie took a moment to enjoy the memory.

"So, what does Marvin have to say?"

Gertie read:

Dear Posse,

This will be short. I hope you're all doing good. I talk with the twins pretty often, and we've been hatching a plan. Seems my cousin, Bert, is running a dude ranch up in Colorado, and he says they'll give me a discount if I bring a group in for a long weekend. Their numbers need a boost, and they want to get some photos for a new ad campaign.

Anyhow, I thought of our little posse. It would be fun to get together again and reminisce about the cruise and how we helped Gertie out of a tight spot. And it would be something new. Life gets kinda boring here. There's lots of activities besides horseback riding at the dude ranch, but you can do that too if you want. The twins seem interested. How about you ladies?"

Let me know,
Marvin

Gertie squared up the letters and carefully slid them back into the envelope. "What do we do with the letters we sent—leave them in or toss them?"

"Who cares? What do you think?" Edna leaned forward in the armchair.

"About what?"

"About the vacation, what else? The boys are all set to visit a dude ranch in Colorado. I've always wanted to go there. All those mountains and rugged cowboy types. Robert Redford lives there, I think. Oh, and Kevin Costner." Edna was on a roll. "And Duane 'Dog the Bounty Hunter' Chapman, that great big blonde guy ..."

"Mercy." Gertie moved her hands to her throat.

Edna closed her eyes in thought. "And John Denver, of course"

Gertie's hands dropped to her lap. "He's dead."

"Gertie, don't be such a party pooper. It's about time we get out of our rut and have some fun. Let's check it out at least. Do we have Marvin's phone number?"

"Yes, I added the boys to my Rolodex when I got home from the cruise. And it isn't that long since we got home. I'm enjoying getting back into my schedule again." Gertie returned to her secretary's desk and opened a drawer. "Here it is."

"Schedule, schmedule. It's been over four months. Let's call and see what he has to say. It'll be nice to hear his voice."

"I guess Colorado *is* beautiful. I used to see pictures in magazines about romantic ski vacations in the mountains. But then Donald never was one to splurge on family vacations."

"Splurge?" Edna said. "That man pinched every penny till it squeaked."

"He did tend to be overly careful with our funds." Gertie scrolled through her Rolodex cards and pulled one out.

"Here, hand me that." Edna squinted to see the numbers on the card and began punching them on her cell phone. "Rats, it's going to voice mail. Hey, Marvin, it's Edna. Me and Gertie are itching to get the Posse together again. And Colorado sounds like just the ticket. Give us a holler when you hear this, and keep your phone with you so we can reach you." Edna returned her cell phone to her back pocket.

"My, that wasn't very friendly." Gertie held her hand out for the Rolodex card and filed it back into its slot.

"Marvin isn't fragile. He's just a bit thick between the ears. I bet he calls back as soon as he gets the message. Now, let's get going on planning our cowgirl stuff."

"What stuff?" Gertie clasped her hands together and pinched hard.

"You know, boots and those shirts with pearl-button snaps, and leather with fringe—things like that." Edna's eyes took on a faraway look. "I see a big adventure ahead, Gertie."

Gertie's hands had flown back up to her neck. "Oh, mercy," she said.

Edna moved down another aisle of the discount clothing store. "For Pete's sake, this is Texas—you'd think there'd be racks full of western wear." She shoved a bunch of hangers to the left and heaved a sigh of disgust.

"Maybe we need to shop at a bit nicer store." Gertie pulled her hand away from an orange blouse with a long, pointy collar. "I hate to even touch these garments. They seem … well, rather old and used."

"Of course, they're old and used. This is Thrift City—everything here is old and used, including you and me." Edna laughed at her own joke and came to a halt. "Whoa! I think I hit the jackpot. Look at this." She held up a dark-brown suede jacket with long fringe hanging from the sleeves. "Hmm, size XXL. Well, I'll cut out the tag. No need to advertise." She flipped the jacket over her shoulders and worked her arms into the sleeves. "How's it look?" she asked Gertie.

She marched down the aisle in search of a mirror and found an old, silvery, cracked one by a costume jewelry counter, and standing tall, she admired the view. Gertie caught up with her. "A mite large, but I'd say it fits the bill. Wearing it makes me feel like a real-life cowgirl. I wonder if I could ride fast enough to feel the wind in my hair."

Gertie remained silent while several different looks of horror washed across her pretty face. Her nose wrinkled. "That thing is hideous. It's old as the hills, and besides, you can't wash leather. Who knows where it's been?" She paused and took a breath. "And second, your hair wouldn't move if a tornado went past it. When's the last time you rode a horse?"

Edna pulled her hands together and mimicked a jockey bouncing along and whipping the horse's flank. "I rode my Uncle Louie's old nag a few times—maybe my senior year of high school. But he said I was a natural. His big girl, that's what he always called me. And quit going on about my hair." Edna placed her hand behind her head. "It is a conscious choice. It empowers me. I like my spikes."

Gertie moved back from the racks of dowdy clothing. "You're right. The way you wear your hair is your choice. But *I'm* right about the jacket. It looks ridiculous on you."

"Apology accepted. Let's go ring it up."

CHAPTER TWO

Edna had pulled into the Pet-o-Rama parking lot when her cell phone cranked out its new "Back in the Saddle Again" ringtone. "Hey, Marvin. Good to hear from you. Can I call you back in about half an hour? I'm at the Pet-o-Rama picking up Big Bertha from her kitty flea dip and nail clip. She hates it like anything, but Rose always does a good job, and I don't have fleas hopping all over my apartment. Oh, and I'm working on Gertie. She's always shy when it comes to new things. Thanks, Marvin, I'll call you as soon as I get home. Toodles."

She hurried up to the front door and swooshed through it amidst the cheerful tinkle of the entry bell. Rose bustled through an inner door and up to the counter, her black-and-white, Dalmatian drop earrings swinging as she came to a halt.

"Hi, Edna," Rose greeted her. "Boy, Big Bertha was in rare form today. Good thing I was wearing my protective gloves, the ones that go all the way to the elbow. Otherwise, I think I'd have to charge you for damages." She wore her usual, friendly smile to soften her words and pushed her pointy, rhinestone glasses back up her nose as she took Edna's credit card and rang up the bill. Yips and yaps of pets waiting to be sprung from their cages filled the air. "Whew, we're sure busy today. I'll bring her out. I didn't want to let her out of the cage until she sees you. She isn't getting any tamer in her old age."

Edna bellied up to the counter and leaned in. "Hey, Rose, before you get BB, I want to ask a favor. I'm trying to convince Gertie to go with me on a long weekend trip to Colorado. Some of the guys we met on the singles cruise have invited us for three days at a dude ranch up there. I'm dying to go, but Gertie's dragging her feet."

"What do you want me to say? I don't know a thing about dude ranches."

"Maybe tell her she needs to get out more, something like that."

"I suppose I could do that. But I know Gertie has her book club and her garden club and lots of church activities. I don't think she's bored."

"Yeah, well, there's *activities* and then there's fun. I'm ready to have some fun. I want to ride horses and go on hayrides under the moonlight and maybe find a nice, rugged cowboy to cozy up to."

"Good luck with that." Rose, armed with her elbow-high gloves, disappeared into the back of the store, and returned carrying a huge, orange, hissing Big Bertha. She placed her in the loving arms of her owner. "There, and I still have most of my blood inside my body."

"Thanks. Big Bertha was a gift from Sam, that rat of a second husband of mine. Maybe some ugly rubbed off on her. But she's my baby now." Edna ran her hand down Big Bertha's back and grinned as a loud purr began to rumble. "See? She just needs her mama. See you, Rose."

"Edna?" Marvin's voice boomed into her ear.

"Hey, hi, Marvin. Thanks for letting me call back. I got BB all settled at home now. Anyway, we got your letter, and now I'm jazzed about the trip. When are you and the twins going?"

"I was hoping you'd want to go. Is Gertie on board?"

"Sort of. You know Gertie. She usually needs a little kick in the behind to try anything new. Luckily, I'm available to give it to her."

Marvin laughed and paused. "I'm still working on the twins. Those two need encouragement too. I keep pushing the Texas cowboy agenda. They're suckers for that."

"Got any dates in mind? I hear the weather in Colorado can be tricky."

"Bert says their numbers slump in May, when the winter sports are done, and it's not as warm and sunny as the summer. So, he wants me to rustle up some tenderfoots and do a photoshoot of turning them into full-fledged, satisfied ranch folk."

"May sounds good. I don't have anything planned. Well—there's the Elks spring dance, but I'm tired of hauling myself there solo, so ..."

"How about the second weekend? Bert wants us to show up on a Friday and hang around until Monday noon. He has a whole raft of activities to feature in a new brochure he's doing. He's not the owner—that's some rich guy from New York City. He's the manager, and it sounds like he's nervous about the place going under."

"Okay, that would be May twelfth through the fifteenth. I'll take care of Gertie. You get the twins in line. You got a car that could fit five? Probably best if we travel together to save gas money. And how much is this discounted weekend gonna cost us? Better be cheap if they're using us as guinea pigs for their advertising."

"How does *free* sound? I did a few rounds with Bert, and he agreed. There'll be other folks there, so we have to keep our freebie to ourselves, but it's all on the house. And, yeah, I have a big Econoline. We'll leave your car and the twins' pickup at my place and go from there."

"Okay, sounds good. I can't wait to get the Posse together again. Good memories. Tell Bert it's a go."

Edna clicked off her phone and grinned. *Gertie, old girl, you're gonna have the time of your life.*

Gertie squinted, trying to get her bearings. "Why in the world did you choose this musty old place for lunch? It's so dark I can barely see."

The Big Boy BBQ sat short and squatty on the tail end of Main Street. The dark-brown paneling and Naugahyde booths screamed 1960s.

Edna led the way. She pushed through the saloon-style, swinging doors, and slid into one side of the nearest booth until she hit a pothole in the seat. "Ouch! Holy cow, they must not have updated this place in decades. And to answer your question, I thought a nice barbecue lunch might get us in the dude ranch mood. I don't know why you're fighting this trip. I can hardly wait to see the boys and have a little fun down on the ranch."

Edna wrestled her way to a smoother part of her seat. "Plus, it's all free. Marvin's cousin, Bert, is gonna host us for a nice, long weekend in cowboy land."

Gertie sat quietly for a bit, scanning the cowboy motif. "This place rivals the Elks Club for grit and grime. I'm not sure I want to eat here."

"Aw, it'll be fine. You can't hurt barbecue—everything is cooked for hours. Kills all the germs."

"Very reassuring."

A waiter brought two glasses of water with no ice. "What'll you have?" he said.

Gertie reached for a menu propped between the salt and pepper shakers.

Edna spoke up. "What's your most western lunch? You know, what's most authentic?"

"That'd be our Cowpoke Special—pulled pork, coleslaw, and beans, $8.95. The Buckaroo runs a close second—ribs, beans, and cornbread."

"What do you think, Gertie? I'll take the Cowpoke and a Coke."

Gertie squirmed and dipped her napkin in her water. She wiped the sticky spots from her side of the table. "I'll have the same, I guess, and some iced tea."

The waiter disappeared into the recesses of the dark kitchen.

"Marvin has a big Econoline, so we can park our rigs at his place and all go together. Second weekend in May. That gives us a few weeks to work on our wardrobes. I got my jacket and jeans, of course. Now I gotta find some boots and a few western-style shirts. You got anything western yet, Gertie?"

"It does sound like fun to see the boys again, and Rose thinks it's a good idea for me to get out more. I think I have some gabardine slacks that look a bit like denim. My boots aren't western, but I guess I don't mind if they get mud on them or ... other things."

"That's the spirit. Let's do our best to be *ranch-ready*. I checked online for The Colorado Pines, and it looks like they don't have a website yet. Guess that's why they want us to be part of a photoshoot—we could end up famous— smack-dab in the middle of their home page."

Gertie sat quietly, observing Edna in her excitement. "You know, Edna, that's what I admired about you back in high school. You always found a way to make even the most mediocre situation seem like an adventure. I was so timid in those days, and you helped me to get up a little gumption and try things. Sometimes I forget. Thank you."

Edna took the compliment in stride. "Sure, no problem. Life is short and then you die, huh?" She laughed. "Remember

Scotty Ripkin? The scrawny, pimply kid who had a crush on me. I was twice his size but talk about a mediocre situation. I finally agreed to go to the fair with him. He ate three corn dogs and an elephant ear and then threw up."

Gertie looked at Edna for a good, long time, then shook her head. "That's not exactly what I meant, but yes, we did have some wonderful times back then. And I felt sorry for Scotty. He tried so hard to make kids like him. I heard he did fairly well for himself—has a nice car dealership somewhere in East Texas."

The two meals arrived, pulled pork piled on oval platters with sticky baked beans oozing into mounds of coleslaw. Edna doused her pork in barbecue sauce from a nearby bottle and dug in.

Gertie made a futile attempt to separate her food into three distinct piles.

Marvin stood on the tiny deck of his neat and tidy-looking modular home, ready to greet the travelers. He waved a big welcome to the girls as they pulled up and parked in a gravel area off to the side of his driveway. His home sat on the edge of Meredith Lake, a fishing hot spot for the retired, and fit in nicely with the woodsy locale with its forest-green trim.

"Hey, Marvin. Great to see you. Could we pop into your place and use the facilities? Don't want to begin a long trip with a full bladder." Edna hopped out of her car and headed toward him.

"Sure. Good to see you two too. Go on in, Edna, it's the first door on your right down the hall."

Gertie moved at a slower pace toward Marvin's little abode. "Hello, Marvin, what a wonderful day we have for our little adventure." She climbed the stairs, and Marvin offered his one-and-only deck chair to her.

"I'll stand, thank you," she said. "I know we'll be sitting for a few hours, and it's good to stretch my legs."

The twins arrived in a swirl of dust and gravel and parked beside Edna's old heap. They bounded out of both sides of the battered pickup and hauled their bags out of the bed of the truck.

"Hey, Marvin, Gertie. Did you leave old Edna back home in Amarillo? We cruised through there and shouted out a howdy to y'all as we went. But since you're already here, maybe you didn't hear us." Boyd chuckled at his little joke.

Gertie fanned away the cloud of dust that had enveloped them. "No, Edna's inside for a minute."

Marvin stepped off the deck to shake the boys' hands. "You boys seem mighty eager for this trip. It's sure gonna be fun having the Posse together again."

Floyd pumped Marvin's hand, and said, "Yes, sir. We're about as excited as little kids on Christmas morning. We can't wait to rope and ride and such."

Edna emerged through Marvin's front door. "Hey, boys, good to see you. Anyone else need the facilities?" She looked from one face to another. No one responded. "If not, let's get this show on the road."

All five of them clambered into the large, white panel truck. "Wow, Marvin, this here van is perfect. Five people plus all our junk and still plenty of wiggle room." Edna wiggled her shoulders to prove her point.

Marvin pulled away from the curb. "Glad you like it. I bought it for a song from a guy going out of the plumbing business. That's why it's grimy around the edges ... Well, the truth is he had a Clean-as-a-Whistle Sewer Service franchise. I scrubbed it up pretty good."

Gertie remained silent, but a shudder ran down both shoulders. She and Edna sat in the middle row, and the twins had been relegated to the back of the van. Gertie tightened her seatbelt and frowned at the frayed edges.

"How was your ride from Lubbock, boys?" Marvin bellowed over his shoulder. "Hit much traffic?"

Boyd hollered back they'd done fine after getting out of town.

Edna elbowed her friend. "Are you as excited as I am?" The fringe from her leather jacket sleeve trailed over Gertie's arm. Gertie shuddered again and crossed her arms.

"I *am* looking forward to some beautiful Colorado scenery. I'm not sure about the rest. I've never ridden a horse. They're so big and unpredictable. I may skip some of the activities. I've brought along some reading materials—a nice memoir and a poetry anthology."

Edna huffed. "I, myself, prefer to live large in my own life. Who needs to get bored to death reading about someone else's ups and downs? On the other hand, poetry can be a hoot. I love those limericks."

"You gals like poetry?" Marvin chimed in, "Bert says they like to cook up a little cowboy poetry around the campfires at the ranch. You know, a nice fire, a can of beans, and some witty words. Hah!"

Gertie sat back in her seat and closed her eyes. "I was thinking more about Wordsworth and Blake," she said softly.

"Me and brother just love Blake," one of the twins added from the back seat. "In fact, we love all country music. Boy, oh boy, this dude ranch is gonna be a barrel of fun."

Marvin maneuvered the van onto the highway and fiddled with his GPS. "Glad you all agreed to cut this trip in half. It'll be about six hours of driving total. I booked us into the Bide a Wee Motel for tonight—right at the Colorado border. Me and Anna stayed there once before she passed, and it wasn't too bad. Cheap.

"Then we'll get to Colorado Pines sometime after lunch tomorrow. It's off Highway 297 between Pueblo and Colorado Springs. Bert has a schedule set up for us with some professional photographers ready to go.

"They're aiming for the senior angle, you know, us old folks living it up in our active golden years. Being as all this is free, I told Bert we'd cooperate with whatever they ask us to do. 'Course it'll all be fun stuff anyway."

"I hope they give us time to relax and enjoy the natural environment," Gertie said. "I'm not one to push my limits or do anything dangerous. My bucket list is rather short. I want to read and enjoy nice meals and take in the scenery."

Edna sat up straighter and slapped her hand on her knee. "Not me. I plan to make this here trip an adventure. I want to try everything they got to offer. I can't wait to ride the range and maybe ride around those barrels like they show on television rodeos. Man, those girls look great turning those tight corners, holdin' onto their hats, and then galloping like crazy to the fence."

"We're with you, Edna," a twin said from the back of the van. "We want to ride and rope and sit tall in the saddle. Me and Floyd are tired of being pretty near to city slickers even though we turkey ranch. We want to be authentic cowboys."

"We brought our hats along, and we both got new belts with big, silver buckles. We wondered if there might be a square dance or some such thing where we can socialize in the evenings. What do you think, Marvin?"

"Don't know, boys. We'll get the schedule when we arrive. Bert's been awful busy setting up our weekend, and he said to 'hold our horses and be ready to have some dude-ranch fun.'"

"Horses." Edna breathed out the word in a voice soft as a prayer, "Horses and trail rides, campfires under the stars, and big, Marlboro-handsome cowboys waiting to fulfill our every wish. Oh boy, Gertie, Colorado Pines, here we come."

CHAPTER THREE

Edna leaned forward and poked Marvin on the shoulder. "Hey, Marvin, I could use a bite to eat whenever you find something. It's been a long time since breakfast."

A chorus of "Yes" and "Me too" sealed the deal.

"Okay, I need to gas up anyway. Let's keep our eyes open for a gas station."

The Posse scanned the highway, and in a minute or two, a gas station with a convenience store right out of 1950 appeared to the left of the highway. The two gas pumps were rusty, and a garbage can overflowed between them.

A rickety-looking, red-barn-wood building set back off the road sported an Orange Crush sign in the window next to a handwritten *Cold Beer Inside* sign. A wood-framed screen door hung crooked at the entrance.

"What do you think? This okay?" Marvin hopped out of the driver's seat before he finished the question. "I'll gas up, and you all go on inside to find some grub. Looks like they saw us coming and set out a nice little picnic table over there by the johns."

Edna stepped out of the sliding door and stretched.

Gertie slid out and did the same.

The twins hunched over to clear the ceiling of the van and exited next.

"Sure feels good to stretch my legs," Edna said. "Think I'll see what they got for lunch. My stomach's growling."

"Me and Floyd will catch up with you. Gotta visit the john first."

As Edna pulled open the screen door, it let out a mighty squeak. "Wow, it's dark in here, I can't see where I'm going." She stopped still in the entry to let her eyes adjust, and Gertie came close to bumping into her backside.

Within a moment, her eyes adjusted to the dim light. "There, that's better." She moved a few steps further into the stuffy little convenience store. To their right was a counter with a soda dispenser and a roller-grill twirling greasy hot dogs around in circles. To the left were several aisles of various kinds of junk food. The closest rack contained cupcakes and cookies, much of the packaging gray from a layer of dust on top.

"What can I do for you gals?" A skinny, forty-something woman stood behind a cash register, coffee mug in hand. "We got tuna and egg salad sandwiches made fresh this morning."

Gertie scooted past Edna and browsed the aisles. The refrigerated foods ran along the back wall. "I think I'll get some cheese and crackers. I don't like to eat things made with mayonnaise unless I know they've been properly handled."

Edna eyed the hot dogs. "Give me two of those dogs on buns and a package of corn chips." She tilted her head back toward the front window. "And I'll have one of those cold beers you advertised."

Gertie added a bottled iced tea to her cheese and cracker combo, and then the girls headed toward the picnic table.

Boyd stood outside the men's bathroom, waiting his turn. He'd donned his big Stetson with the B on the front and nodded politely to the girls.

Edna plopped down on one side of the table, bouncing the legs off the ground on the other side. She opened tiny packages of mustard for her hot dogs.

Gertie sat opposite Edna to balance things out a bit.

Floyd exited the bathroom, and the twins disappeared into the convenience store. Marvin, having filled the gas tank, approached, wiping his hands on his jeans. "These old roadside places are kind of fun, aren't they?" He boomed out the words.

Edna made a note to ask Marvin if he was getting hard of hearing.

Gertie nibbled on her cheese-topped cracker. "They do have a nostalgic quality to them," she said, "if you can avoid ptomaine poisoning."

Marvin laughed loudly. "Think I'll go grab something to eat. Those hot dogs smell good." He headed back to the store.

Edna took a huge bite of her first hot dog. "This is nothing compared to what the ranch will be like. Colorado Pines. I picture it on a scenic river hopping with trout, and I bet the horses run wild and free all day in meadows of grass three-feet high."

Gertie sipped her bottle of iced tea. "Don't get your hopes up so high—we haven't even seen a picture of this ranch yet. You might be setting yourself up for disappointment."

Edna chewed and swallowed. "And it might be even better than I'm imagining. It's all in how a person thinks. I choose to think positive."

The twins joined them at the table. "Floyd asked if these were turkey dogs, but the skinny lady looked like we were nuts. Can't beat a good turkey dog." Boyd slathered his hot dog with ketchup and mustard while he talked. "But I'm hungry, so I guess a mystery dog will have to do."

"They aren't bad if you wash 'em down with beer," Edna said as she started in on her second dog.

Marvin returned with a beer and two tuna sandwiches. "Anna used to make the best tuna sandwich in the world. She always added pickle relish and slices of tomato and onion. I don't suppose these will even come close, but—"

"Now, Marvin, me and Gertie have a deal to not talk about past relationships, don't we, Gertie?" Edna had taken on the voice of a schoolmarm. "I think this here trip is a chance for every one of us Posse members to be forward-looking. Time to live in the moment as they say. Me? I'm in the market for a nice, tall cowboy. No sense living in the past, I say."

Edna's speech seemed to startle all four of the other Posse members into a long silence.

"Those were words of wisdom, Edna," Boyd finally said. "Me and Floyd have been living in the past for too long, trying to replace Mama, you know. We thought we were on to something on the cruise with the cousins from North Dakota. But Eunice was a vegetarian and all. Didn't work out. But that's not to say we can't keep our eyes peeled for some nice little cowgirls at the ranch."

Gertie remained quiet, and Marvin got serious about eating his sandwiches. The Posse finished their lunch about the time a whirlwind of dust blew over the table.

"Excuse me, everyone. I'll use the restroom before we go." Gertie carefully gathered up the remains of her lunch and deposited it in the trash barrel at the end of the table.

"Hey, Marvin," Edna said. "I been meaning to ask, are you wearing one of those invisible hearing aids? You practically holler when you talk." She wiped her mouth, and the napkin came away all yellow with mustard.

Marvin raised his head and looked across the table to Edna. "Sorry, I'll try to tone it down a little. Anna always … well, I'll try to tone it down."

Edna reached out and patted Marvin's hand. "Hey, that's okay, Marvin, I just wondered."

Gertie returned and sat on the bench with her back to the others. She tipped her head up to the sun. "Mm, the warmth of the sun on one's face is one of the real joys of life."

Edna stood and hauled herself away from the table. "Yup, give me a minute to tinkle, and I'll be ready to hit the road again."

Everyone stood and wandered around the area to let their lunch settle and to move their bodies before confining themselves to the seatbelts in the van.

Gertie stopped beside Marvin. "Thanks for doing all the driving, Marvin. And don't take Edna's rudeness too seriously. You know she's all bluster and wouldn't hurt anyone's feelings for the world."

Marvin shuffled his feet in the gravel. "Yeah, I know. It's kinda gotten to be a habit with me, talking about the past. Don't have much goin' on in the present. Gets lonely living by myself. But, in a way, Edna's right. When I first laid eyes on her, I felt a kinship there. You know, iron sharpening iron, that kind of thing. Guess I do need to live more in the moment, as they say."

Edna suddenly came flying out of the women's bathroom, eyes the size of saucers and suede fringe flapping. "Ride!" she said. "I mean it, everyone, get your fannies in the van, and let's head out of here."

A general flurry of bodies crawling into their respective spots ensued as Marvin fired up the engine. "What in the world got into you, Edna?"

"Darn toilet is clogged up, and it's overflowing all over the floor. I didn't think that skinny woman with the pointy nose was gonna take kindly to me flooding their stinky bathroom. Whew, sure hope the accommodations at the Bide a Wee are better than that."

The van roared away, leaving a scattering of gravel in its wake. "Now, if the previous owner of this van had left his toolbox inside," Marvin said, "I probably could've fixed the problem in the john. But, oh well, guess that's why they invented plungers." He settled in to focus on the road.

"What a sudden end to our lunch break," Gertie said. "I wonder if there might have been another way to solve the problem, but what's done is done."

"Don't judge, Gertie, I barely got out of there without needing hip waders."

Everyone sat in silence for a few moments.

"Hey, everyone, let's play the alphabet game," Gertie suggested. "Donald and I always played that on long road trips. I think I had the advantage because he did all the driving, but then I was better at word things. He was more of a mathematics person."

"I thought we weren't gonna talk about old relationships," Marvin's voice had a glum sound to it.

"Right," Edna said. "Let's play. Can you boys see okay back there?"

"Yes, ma'am, we can see fine out these side windows. Don't have eyes in the back of our heads, do we, brother?" Both twins laughed.

"On your mark, get set, go!" Edna immediately looked for a sign that started with an "a."

CHAPTER FOUR

The Bide a Wee Motel was a pleasant surprise to Edna who'd been expecting a flea-bitten row of rooms with saggy rooflines and even saggier mattresses. Instead, ten neat, white cabins sat in a sort of circle with a grassy central gathering area and a fire pit in the middle. A scattering of chairs and benches surrounded the pit.

They drove into the covered office area, parked, and Marvin headed for the door.

"Why, how lovely," Gertie said. "Those little cabins look like Goldilocks and the Three Bears could step out at any minute."

Edna opened the side door of the Econovan and stepped out. "Yeah, this is terrific. I better go make sure Marvin gets the rooms right. You and I can share, and the boys can figure out if they want one cabin or two."

She hustled off toward the office as Marvin came back out. "It's all settled up," he said. Us boys will share cabin three. They'll roll in a hide-a-bed for me. And you gals have cabin four."

"Did you pay for both rooms?" Gertie asked.

"Yeah, I did. I appreciate you all joining in on this little venture, and it's my way of saying I'm glad to have the Posse together again."

"Well, that's right nice of you," Boyd and Floyd chimed in one voice.

"Yes, it surely is," Gertie added.

Edna gave a big, toothy smile in Marvin's direction and said, "You're a regular gentleman these days. Must have reformed after the cruise." She softened the blow by adding, "Just kidding, Marvin. Thanks."

Marvin gave an "aw shucks" kick of his boot in the gravel and grinned at her.

Everyone busied themselves with hauling out suitcases and jackets as Marvin handed out keys to the cabins, one for the girls and one for the twins.

"I don't know about you guys, but driving makes me sleepy. I'm gonna see about my hide-a-bed and take a nap. I seem to remember a family restaurant up the road a mile or two. We can probably get our dinner there later—I'll ask the manager."

Edna rolled her purple-flowered suitcase toward cabin four with Gertie right behind her.

"I think I might take Marvin's advice and have a little nap too," Gertie said.

Edna inserted the old-fashioned skeleton key into the lock under the brass, curlicued number four, and turned it clockwise. She grabbed the door handle, twisted, and pushed. "You were right, Gertie, this is the cutest little room I've ever seen."

Red-checkered curtains framing the windows, braided rugs on the floor, and cedar-paneled walls made the room feel cozy. Both beds were covered with bright-white chenille spreads.

"Man, that bed looks just right," Edna said as she rolled her suitcase under the closest bed and plopped down. "Whew, those hot dogs are trying to bite me back. Guess I'll rest for a bit too. Dang, these boots are a lot of work. It's one of the challenges of being a real cowgirl, I guess." She hauled the boots off one at a time, lay back on the bedspread, and sighed.

Gertie carefully rolled her bag around the first bed and shoved it under the second. She sat down and brushed her hand back and forth over the raised chenille patterns. "Look, Edna, my spread has a design on it. I think it might be roses, or maybe lilies. I must say, this place is such fun. I love it. And how wonderful to have the Posse back together again." She lay back and relaxed.

"Wonderful," Edna mumbled as her eyes closed.

"Well, for an older diner stuck out in the middle of nowhere, I must say the food is delicious," Gertie said.

The Posse had bellied up to a large, round dining table in Ma's Golden Spoon Diner. Everyone had ordered the Mile-high Mushroom Burger with fries and were plowing their way through their meals.

"Man, I wanted to order some of their homemade pie, but I'm not sure I'm gonna be able to eat all this," Edna said through a mouthful of fries.

"Yeah, I forgot this place is all about big portions." Marvin wiped his mouth with a paper napkin. "Sure tastes good though. Maybe we can order pie and eat it later back at the Bide a Wee. We gotta get goin' anyway if we're gonna make it back in time for the campfire sing-along at eight."

Boyd and Floyd had shared a root beer float and finished with several slurps through their straws. Floyd grinned and smacked his lips. "Mm, mm. Now that was nigh unto as tasty as the floats Mama used to make for us when we did all our chores real good."

"Hey, guys." Marvin stood and scooted back his chair. "My phone is vibrating all over the place. I'm gonna go outside and take the call."

"And since you paid for the rooms, me and Floyd are gonna pay for this dinner. Right, Floyd?"

"You betcha," Floyd answered.

Edna and Gertie stacked their plates and silverware while the twins went off to pay the bill.

Gertie eyed her half-full plate. "I'm afraid I can't eat any more. I'm disappointed because that apple pie with the glaze on top made my mouth water." She added her plate to the top of the stack.

"How about if I buy the whole pie to take back with us?" Edna took her wallet out and headed to the counter.

"Why, how thoughtful of you." Gertie gathered her purse and sweater and followed. "You know, I was a bit worried about this trip, but it's turning out to be quite wonderful."

The Posse scrambled into the van, and Edna placed the pie carefully at her feet. "Too bad we won't have any ice cream to put on top."

Marvin put the rig in gear, and they headed back toward the Bide a Wee. "Hey, everybody, I got a call from Bert. He's all fired up about our weekend. Said he can't wait until we get there, and he has our costumes ready."

"Costumes? Why would we need costumes?" Gertie's voice had gone from blissful to tinged with worry.

"I asked, but he sort of dodged the question. Guess we'll have to wait until we get there tomorrow to see what he's got up his sleeve."

Edna put her feet on either side of the pie to steady it. "It had better be just his arm. I don't want my perfect weekend on the ranch messed up. I got my mind fixed on lots of time with a nice, tall cowboy."

Marvin huffed. "I wish you'd give that tall, handsome cowboy thing a rest, Edna. How about we go enjoy ourselves and maybe ride a horse or two?"

"Well, excuse me for living, Marvin." Edna tipped her head from side to side as she spoke. Her spikes didn't move.

"Now, everyone," Gertie spoke quickly to smooth feathers, "let's go back to our little home away from home and enjoy some songs around a campfire. We can have our dessert and get to bed. We've all had a long day."

"Yeah, okay," Marvin muttered.

"Right," Edna said. But her lips were set in a grim line as she said it.

"Home, home on the range," everyone sang. "Where the deer and the antelope play ..."

The Posse sat around the fire pit, lounged in camp chairs or perched on wooden benches. A few other lodgers sat sprinkled here and there. A dad and his son headed out on a fishing trip, evidenced by the massive gear they'd hauled into their cabin, and a salesman-type who was still in his suit and tie joined the Posse.

Heat radiated from the fire and allowed the Posse to sit with jackets open. Sparks crackled up into the air periodically, and the rangy motel manager had morphed nicely into a singing cowboy as he strummed along on his trusty guitar.

Boyd and Floyd turned out to have passable tenor voices, and they hit the chorus of "Home on the Range" with gusto.

"You boys surprise me," Gertie said. "Did you take vocal lessons growing up?"

"No, Ma'am, we sang in church on Sundays, and Mama encouraged us to do our best for the Lord, didn't she, Floyd?"

"Do you know 'You Are My Sunshine'?" Floyd asked the manager. "We know some harmony on that one. Let's do it, okay?"

Edna sat in a camp chair, her backside barely clearing the grass.

Marvin had come alongside and sat a bit higher on a stackable plastic model. He leaned back and turned his head up to the night sky. "Ah, this is the life, huh, Edna? Look at those stars. Don't see that in the cities, do we? Sure glad I moved out by the lake."

"Nope, that's a fact. Makes a person want to go back about two hundred years and live a slower, simpler life, doesn't it?" She tilted her head back and took in the twinkly array. "Hey, I'm gonna go into the office and grab us some plastic forks and napkins. We can polish off the pie while we sing a few more songs." She hauled herself up and headed for the office.

Marvin hopped up quick as a bunny and followed after her. "I'll help," he said.

As Edna came back with the pie in one hand and a wad of napkins in the other, the twins were sweetly harmonizing on "please don't take my sunshine away." Marvin held a bouquet of white plastic forks and began to hand them out to all, including the non-Posse folks. "We can cut the pie to feed everyone a nice little slice," he said.

"Kind of like feeding the five thousand," Gertie threw in.

"Mama sure would've enjoyed this evening," Boyd said.

"Yes, sir, she would've," Floyd added.

The van sped down the highway. "What a wonderful idea to get a nice, simple breakfast to go, Marvin." Gertie held her to-go coffee in one hand and a bran muffin in the other.

"Yeah, I ate too much yesterday," Edna spoke around a bite of chocolate chip muffin. "That apple pie is still fighting with the hot dogs from yesterday's lunch. Got any antacid pills, Marvin?"

Marvin rummaged around in the cupholder between the seats and came back with a none-too-clean roll of tablets.

"Here, it's a mite old, but I don't think those things expire."

The twins were in the back seat humming last night's songs in harmonizing parts.

"What time will we get there?" Edna had leaned forward and spoke into Marvin's ear over the twins' serenade.

"Should be about noon. I expect Bert will have lunch for us, but if not, we'll figure something out. Haven't seen Cousin Bert since we were both kids."

Gertie leaned forward too. "I've been thinking about the weekend on the ranch. You know, Bert said something about a photoshoot for the Colorado Pines advertising. I'll bet you they've gone and fitted us all out with old-fashioned cowboy outfits. Like the movies. You know, like the Old West with the women in long skirts and bonnets and the men in dungarees and vests and all. It sounds rather romantic when I think of it."

Edna thought for a moment. "Hm, you might be on to something. I, myself, have already done pretty good in the cowgirl clothes department, but you could use a boost, Gertie. The twins have their hats and belts. How about you, Marvin? Sounds like Bert thought ahead and will have all of us looking like real, bona fide cowpokes. Right, partners?"

Edna clapped Marvin on the shoulder and sat back. "Colorado Pines. Tall trees and tall cowboys. I can't wait."

CHAPTER FIVE

At the gateway to the dude ranch stood a roughly-carved cedar sign that read *Colorado Pines*. Decorated with three pine trees, it sat atop two, seven-foot-tall vertical logs. Marvin drove the van between them and onto a narrow, dirt road.

"I knew it," Edna crowed. "Look at those huge meadows and all the cows any cowgirl could imagine. And on this side, there's horses ... oh wait, those are llamas. Aren't they pretty?"

"We're not quite there yet," Marvin said as he checked his GPS. "Bert said they're a couple of miles off the highway. It'll be great to get away from the traffic so everything is nice and quiet."

Everyone sat at the alert, searching out the beginnings of dude-ranch paradise.

Edna, ever the optimist, luxuriated in the beauty. "Oh, my heart is thumping. Everywhere I look, it's cowboy heaven." The fields lay green and lush, and a string of horses and a herd of cows grazed in the midday sunshine. On the right side of the road, a river rushed over layers of rock, rounded, and smoothed by the currents. Eventually, Marvin cranked the steering wheel right and then left again, and there, stretched out before them, lay Colorado Pines.

"Oh, my goodness," Gertie said. "It's like a little western town from the old movies. Look, there's a saloon and a general store, and the bank. And I guess The Chuck Wagon must be where we eat. Oh, it's so cute."

Edna craned her neck as they drove through the main drag of the western town. "Look, there's signs to the stables. Must be where they keep our horses." She glanced off to the right. "And what are those white things?"

The road angled off to the right and into a loop that meandered through tall pine trees. Every twenty or thirty feet sat a wooden platform, and atop of each, a large, pure-white tent with the flaps tied back to show rustic furniture, beautifully made beds, and potted plants in the interior. Deck chairs adorned the tiny porches, and wooden pathways led from the road to the steps.

"Holy cow!" Edna exclaimed. "This here is camping in style. Look at those cute tents. And they're big too. Looks like we struck it rich, boys."

Boyd and Floyd remained quiet for a moment. "Don't look like a cowboy bunkhouse to me," Boyd said.

"Looks more like camping for city slickers," Floyd added.

Marvin drove on around the loop and back to the main road. "We need to find Bert and see what's what. I know there's a lodge here somewhere when the weather's too cold for these tent thingies. You know a dude ranch caters to people with bucks, and some of them don't want to rough it too much."

They drove a bit further, then came to a sign with the word *hotel* and an arrow directing them up a wider dirt road. They followed it to the top of a hill and arrived at a stately, two-story, pine-log building with huge upright poles sectioning off the wide veranda. Gables jutted out from the top floor and a red-tiled roof set off the whole structure like a picture in a travel magazine.

Marvin opened his door and stood. "Looks like we're here. I'll go ask around where to find Bert. Maybe he has an office inside here or something. Looks like a nice place, doesn't it?"

Edna hurried to undo her seatbelt and hauled herself out of the van. "Hey, Marvin, wait for me." He turned and waited, and the two of them disappeared through the heavy front door of the hotel.

They returned in less than ten seconds and climbed back into the van. "We gotta go back down to the village." Edna cackled, "They call it a village, not a western town. They said Bert has his office in a spot between the Trading Post and the Saloon. They call it the Jail—said it's a little joke Bert made about having to work such long hours."

The drive down the hill and past the tents took less than a minute. They parked in front of the saloon at the hitching post. Everyone got out.

The twins were still grousing about the "fancy" tents and the "ski lodge."

Marvin headed toward the skinny building with the bars painted on the window, but before he could step up onto the wooden walkway, a red-headed, freckle-faced whirlwind of a cowboy came flying out the door and pumped Marvin's hand up and down.

"You made it. Man, how long has it been since we saw each other? We were kids, maybe thirteen, fourteen? You still look just the same. You have Aunt Jean's eyes and her trademark underbite. I'd know you anywhere by seeing that jawline."

Marvin retrieved his hand and raised his eyebrows at his overly informative cousin. "Hi, Bert, good to see you too. Been a long time." He turned to the others. "These two ladies are Edna Gratzer and Gertie Larsen, and these gentlemen are Boyd and Floyd Osterman. Every one of us is from Texas, and we're pretty pumped about being up here in Colorado. Thanks for giving us a good deal so we could all afford to come."

"Well, cuz, the pleasure's all mine. As I said, we got new owners from back East, and they're putting a lot of pressure on us to build up the numbers here. We got our regulars who come every summer and the ski folks who do the same, but we got downtimes in the fall and spring. So, the board sent us some instructions straight from the owner to put out new advertising and offer some weekend fun that's out of our normal routine. It's different, but, hey, we'll give anything a try once, right?"

Edna's whole body went on alert. Could they trust this red-headed Howdy Doody? There'd been mention of costumes and photoshoots ... And he was downright rude to Marvin.

Marvin began to answer, but Bert forged on. "Let's get you guys and gals settled in your accommodations, and then, we'll have a little pow-wow about the schedule." He turned to Boyd and Floyd. "I put you two guys in tent number ten. It's at the end of the road, toward the stables and should be out of the way of the other guests. The folks love these glamping tents, you know ... glamor plus camping. There are two cots in that one, and it's not too far from the bathhouse."

Boyd turned to Floyd and muttered something that sounded like "sissy," but Marvin hurried into the conversation asking, "Where you got me?"

"I put you in tent eight with a guy from Kansas City. He seems like a nice, quiet guy, and I figured you'd be okay sharing with a total stranger." Bert laughed a big braying laugh and clapped Marvin on the shoulder.

"Now, you ladies get the champagne treatment. I put you two in the hotel in room nine overlooking the river. It's a really pretty view and has everything you'll need. You share the bathroom at the end of the hall, but we're booked light this weekend, so you should do fine. Go ahead and unpack, and let's meet at the Saloon in about thirty minutes. We can have a bite to eat and a beer while we plan things out."

The five travelers piled back into the van and headed for their homes away from home.

Edna clucked her tongue a couple of times and sighed. "I'm not sure I like the sound of Bert's 'out of the ordinary' and 'we'll try anything' stuff. What's he up to?"

Marvin drove back to the hotel and parked. "I don't know. I forgot how loud and obnoxious old Bert can be. He means well, but he kind of gets on a guy's nerves. Anyway, we'll get the schedule and lunch in half an hour. I could use that beer. You gals go ahead and get settled, and we'll come back up for you in a jiffy."

Edna and Gertie got out, hauled their suitcases from the back of the van, and headed for room nine.

"Remember when you smelled a rat on our Vegas trip, and we ended up at the MGM Too?" Edna opened the hotel door for Gertie and followed close behind. "Something tells me there may be a rat or two residing here at the beautiful Colorado Pines."

Everyone sat around the shiny, circular pine table. A large tray of sandwiches, bags of chips, and some oatmeal cookies sat in the middle of the table alongside pitchers of beer and red plastic glasses. Paper plate settings graced each spot.

"Don't think cowboys ate off paper plates," Boyd groused.

"Well, to be fair, they didn't get to drink beer often, either. Just when they left the herd and rode into town," Marvin said.

"Go ahead and dig into the food," Bert said. "Slim, our *cookie*, baked some cookies for you all." He stopped to chuckle at his joke. "I've copied the schedules for the whole weekend. Some of this came direct from headquarters, but I embellished it here and there 'cuz I know this place inside and out. Know what the people like and what'll make 'em

227

laugh. They all signed up for this weekend, so they have an idea of what's to come."

"What *is* to come?" Edna came right to the point.

"Hold yer horses, and we'll read through this whole schedule together. It'll be up to Marvin to make assignments as he knows each of you best. I got some props and stuff over to the Chuckwagon. There's a couple of rooms behind the kitchen where you all can change and get ready."

Edna narrowed her eyes. "Get ready for what?"

"Whoa! Hey, Marvin, is this little gal gonna do all the talkin', or am I gonna get a chance to go through the schedule?"

Edna gave Marvin a look that said something like *not a darn word* and then she turned the same scathing look on Bert. She eyed the stack of papers. "Give 'em here," she growled.

Bert dealt out the schedules around the table and waited a bit for everyone to scan them.

"Okay, let's begin with today. You all can enjoy your lunch, and then relax for a bit—maybe take a nap or whatever. But sometime this afternoon, everyone needs to get down to the stables and meet your horse and wrangler. You get your own horse for the weekend, and your wrangler knows them like the back of his hand. He'll show you how to saddle up and get you all set for your first ride whenever you find the time. I got you scheduled here and there, but you'll have plenty of time to ride."

The Posse perked up at the talk about horses and wranglers. Boyd and Floyd both began to talk at once. "Are they real cow ponies? Got any palominos?"

But Edna had read the heading for the weekend. *Woodstock Weekend: A Trip Back in Time.* "Wait a minute. What's this Woodstock Weekend stuff? This here is a dude ranch. What does a wild hippie get-together have to do with bein' a cowboy?

Bert looked at Edna with his head tilted downward and his eyes and eyebrows high. "We do cowboy all year long. The bosses want us to try something new, and that's what we're doin'. There's plenty of time for the normal stuff— riding, fishing, and river rafting, if you want. Got a campfire every night after the entertainment—there's no call for you all to get your dander up. Besides, you got a free ride for the weekend, and Marvin promised you'd help us get this photoshoot done. You'll have a ball—wait and see. So, let's run through this schedule ...

Edna tromped down the hotel hallway, muttering as she went. The ambiance of the tasteful cream-colored walls and plush forest green carpeting was lost on her. "Who does that guy think he is? Never did like runty little redheads. Reminds me of Mickey Rooney. And I don't like the way he talks to Marvin, either."

"Now Edna, we did agree to come here for free and do our part to help." Gertie struggled to keep up with her hot-headed friend.

They reached door number nine, and both came to an abrupt halt as a couple of aged flower children emerged from the bathroom at the end of the hallway. Fresh from their shower, their long, graying hair in ringlets, the man was resplendent in a tie-dyed shirt and she, in a sarong. The man wore a purple-flowered headband, and his hairy legs showed below the hip-length shirt. Both wore shell beads around their necks and large, contented smiles on their faces.

"Peace, sisters," the man said and made the sign with two fingers. His damp towel was bunched up in the other hand.

The woman smiled and said, "I hope you weren't waiting for the bathroom. We took a little longer than we planned." She grinned up at her lushly-bearded partner.

Gertie shifted from one foot to another, keeping her eyes above the man's waist level. "No, thanks, we're just getting settled. We had our lunch, and now we're going to unpack and rest before meeting our horses."

"That's cool," the man said. "We love all living creatures, don't we, Bessie?"

"We do," the woman said. "We volunteer often at the animal shelter when we're home."

"But we don't abide using animals for sport," the man continued. "We see that as intrusive on their freedom—a form of slavery, don't you agree?"

Edna narrowed her eyes and searched for a sharp retort, but Gertie opened their door and hustled her through it.

"Hope to see you two at dinner," the woman said and closed the door behind them.

"My, weren't they interesting?" Gertie said.

"Interesting isn't the word for it. And you didn't have to shove me through the door. I was only going to say something about horseback riding being an art."

"Well, I don't think they would agree. Anyway, I'm tired, and I'd like to take a nap before we go and meet our horses. I'm a little nervous about it."

"Okay. Let's rest and then head on down to the stables. Don't worry, they got folks to show us everything we need to know."

Their room was wildlife-themed in shades of greens and browns. Bear and elk heads decorated all the spreads, throws, and pillows.

Edna pulled off her boots and stretched out on her bed. "Gertie?" she said. "How come that guy wasn't wearing any pants?"

"I truly don't know. Perhaps it's a hippie style." She lay down with her fingers locked beneath her head.

Edna harrumphed. "Sometimes critters with four legs are more sensible than those with two." She closed her eyes for a siesta.

CHAPTER SIX

Marvin interrupted the girls' afternoon nap by calling an emergency meeting of the Posse. They gathered in Edna and Gertie's room with Edna perched on the edge of her bed and Gertie on the end of hers. The boys pulled folding chairs out of the closet to form a circle.

"Now, Edna," Marvin began, "I know a few things are bothering you, but let's take a little time and talk this out.'"

"It's not only Edna," Boyd spoke up. "Floyd and I are pretty darn disappointed by the turn of events too. We had our hearts all set on a real cowboy weekend, and it wasn't easy finding someone to feed and water the turkeys for us. We aren't real pleased to be *glomping* or whatever they call it."

"Now, we need to settle down and figure this out," Gertie said. "Marvin had no way of knowing about this Woodstock Weekend thing, and we *are* getting our accommodations and meals for free. I think we should go through the schedule again and volunteer for some of the activities. We should each try to take one thing that is, shall we say, a challenge, and do it for the good of the Posse."

Everyone stayed quiet for a long moment.

"Thanks, Gertie." Marvin sat with his legs wide apart and his head down. He looked up at each of the members of the group in turn. "I'm mighty sorry for the surprises here. I should have known Bert would come up with uncomfortable stuff. He always had a way of messing things up when we were kids."

Edna slapped her schedule with the back of her hand. "I'll be darned if I'm gonna volunteer for goat yoga. Maybe some of the lip syncs—in fact, I think Sonny and Cher might be kinda fun. Besides, I'd have a long, black wig on, and no one would know it's me anyway. You wanna do that one with me, Marvin?"

Gertie smiled kindly at her best friend. "That's a wonderful attitude, Edna. Who else?"

Boyd nudged Floyd. "I guess me and Floyd could do the goat yoga. We don't know anything about yoga, but we had some goats when we were kids." He nudged Floyd again to emphasize his pun. Floyd nudged him back a little harder than necessary.

Gertie perused her schedule. "I really can't see anything here that appeals to me." She studied the papers again.

"Well, since you were the one who went all peace, love, dove on us, why don't you take the Janis Joplin number?" Edna's face held a wicked grin.

"Janis who?"

"Oh, I don't know about that," Marvin said.

"No, Edna's right," Gertie agreed with a nod of her head. "Janis Joplin, yes, I remember. I have some notion of the kind of person she was. She was a Texas girl too. And like Edna said, we'll be in costume so no one will know it's me anyway. I can stand up there and pretend to sing one of her songs. Let's see. It says, 'Piece of My Heart'. Does anyone know how that one goes?"

"Okay, then." Marvin stood to signal the end of the pow-wow. "I sure appreciate all of you making the best of a bad situation. Hey, we might even have some fun with all this hippie stuff. Let's head on down to meet our horses."

Edna tromped down the trail to the stables, her fringed jacket flapping in the breeze. The rest of the Posse followed like ducks in a row.

"Okay, everybody," she said. "We got enough time before our rehearsal for tonight to meet our wrangler guy and get our horse assignments. Boy, howdy, this is more like it. I'm not gonna let this Woodstock nonsense get in the way of having a great time riding the range."

Boyd and Floyd, resplendent in their hats, boots, and new Levi shirts, wore mile-wide smiles as they approached the stable doors. "Right," Boyd said, "Me and Floyd are so excited we're about to bust."

Marvin and Gertie brought up the rear and were silent as church mice.

Edna peeked her head into the stable and let out one of her ear-splitting whistles. "Hey, anybody in here?"

A tall, skinny cowboy carrying a saddle met her face to face. "Ma'am, we don't like to make loud noises near the stalls—tends to startle the horses and get 'em all riled up. You folks here to meet your horses?"

"You bet," Edna said and added, "Sorry about the whistle."

"No problem. My name is Charlie, and I'm the head wrangler. Buddy is around somewhere. He and I take real good care of the horses, and Wanda here helps out when she's not helping Slim with the cooking."

A chunky, pink-cheeked, middle-aged woman in jeans and a leather vest and with her hair in two ponytails appeared from behind Charlie. She smiled at the Posse and waved a greeting with one hand while carrying a bucket of grain with the other. "I'm a little late with my chores today— hope you folks enjoy your weekend." And she proceeded to pour out measures of grain into troughs all along the stanchions.

Boyd's gaze followed her as she stopped at each stall. "Now that's a mighty fine-looking filly."

Floyd didn't respond. He too was watching the husky gal. "What's her name?"

Charlie grinned and answered. "That there is Wanda. She's kind of a Jill of all trades around here. Nice as they come, too."

Charlie turned to Edna, looked her up and down, and tipped his head toward the closest stall on the left. He dumped the saddle over a nearby railing. "Follow me, I got just the right guy for you." Edna moved along behind him and looked up.

"Meet Buck," Charlie said.

Thirty minutes later, all five Posse members were proud "owners" of steeds of various sizes, shapes, and colors.

"You folks come on back here tomorrow morning, and we'll do our saddle and tack lesson, then take a nice little practice ride through the meadow. Lots of wildflowers in bloom now, and the weather's supposed to be perfect."

Edna beamed at Charlie. "Thanks. I think Buck and I will get along fine. He's a handsome fella, isn't he?"

"Yup."

"Let's get on back to the Saloon. We gotta practice before dinner time. Man, this ranch air is making me hungry." Edna headed back up the trail and the rest fell into line.

"You know, I've always been afraid of horses," Gertie said. "But I feel better since I met Betsy. She seems nice and calm."

"I hate to say it, but I'm petrified of horses," Marvin said. "Had a bad experience as a little kid. One of those ponies that ride you around in circles bucked up and scared the daylights out of me, and I haven't been on the back of a horse since."

"Me and Floyd can't wait to get going tomorrow, but ..." Boyd kicked a dirt clod off the path. "We got them Kentucky Mountain horses though—kinda short and stubby."

Edna laughed. "Well, if they have four legs and a tail. I say they'll do fine. Come on, Bert wanted us there to practice at four."

A gentle breeze blew through the village. Marvin sniffed the air like a hound after a raccoon. "Buffalo burger night. Man, that smells good. Looks like they're serving off the back of the old chuckwagon instead of inside."

Edna and Marvin hurried to the front of the line and piled their plates high. "I wonder if this is actually buffalo or if they buy frozen meat patties from the store like the rest of us," Edna said.

"I don't know. Sure looks good anyway. I get so darned tired of my cooking at home I'll eat anything they got."

The twins hurried to join them. Their hair was damp, and they'd added bolo ties to their western shirts. "That rehearsal plumb wore us out, had to take showers to be presentable," Boyd said. "Haven't twisted my body into so many silly positions since I was a kid playing Twister at the church picnic."

Floyd nodded. "Yeah, I can't figure out how goat yoga ever came into being. Seems like a darn silly thing for folks to do."

Edna added a fat chocolate brownie to the edge of her plate and turned to head for a nearby table. "Hey, you boys got nothin' to complain about. You don't have to stand up in front of all these here folks and pretend to be a rock and roll singer, or folk singer or whatever they were. We're gonna look like darn fools up there."

Marvin grinned. "At least we'll be fat and happy fools. Nice work, Slim." He complimented the cook and followed Edna to the table.

Boyd, Floyd, and Gertie allowed some of the other guests to go ahead of them, then fell in line and dished up their plates.

"This potato salad looks wonderful," Gertie said as she spooned up a serving.

Boyd glanced down to the end of the table where Wanda stood pouring out cups of lemonade. "'Scuse me, I need something to drink," he said, and off he went.

Floyd watched him go. "Wish I had my brother's gumption. That there is a nice-lookin' woman." He sighed and headed over to join the others at the table.

Boyd returned, and the Posse sat together at a rustic-pine table. Everyone tucked in for a bit, and then, Marvin surveyed the crowd. "I'd say there's only about sixty folks here, tops. I guess that's why Bert is so nervous. I think this place can accommodate over three hundred when they're full."

Edna ate the last bite of her brownie and wiped her mouth with a napkin. "A small crowd is okay by me—fewer people to heckle us tonight. What time are we gonna get all costumed up? Do we have time for a snooze before we're on?"

Boyd nodded. "I bet we could. Maybe it's the Colorado air, but I'm sort of tuckered out too. Me and Floyd don't have to do our yoga thing until tomorrow morning, so we can sit back and cheer you on tonight."

Edna glanced at Boyd, ready to light into him if he was making fun of their ridiculous situation, but he met her gaze with all the innocence of a true Osterman brother, so she nodded and stood to return her dishes to the chuckwagon.

Floyd had tracked Wanda all through the meal. She was currently scraping and stacking dishes as folks brought them back to the chuckwagon. "I bet that little gal has to haul all those stacks of dishes back inside. They look awful heavy. I wonder if she needs help from an obliging cowboy." He hitched up his britches and sauntered over to offer his services.

Boyd shook his head. "Dang, he beat me to it. Never thought Floyd would work up the courage to talk to a pretty girl. And right in public too."

Marvin eyed Edna and Gertie. "You girls want a ride up to your place?"

Edna bent to touch her toes. "Nope, not for me. I think it's time you parked the van and we all started getting a little exercise after that heavy meal. I figured out a shortcut to the Lodge. Come on, Gertie, we can go the back way. This ranch reminds me of summer camp when I was a kid. Pretty soon the grounds will feel like the whole world to us."

Gertie hesitated. "I was thinking of going back inside to practice a wee bit more. I don't feel fully ready for the show tonight. Now that we know it's karaoke and not just a lip-sync, I feel like I should get the melody down a bit more."

Edna put one hand on her hip and beckoned with the other, "Aww, come on, none of us are ready. We got our lyric sheets—we just have to live through it. Let's go up to the room and rest for a bit and enjoy the view of the river. Hope I get to dangle a line in the water and catch myself a big Colorado trout."

"Okay, a walk will do me good, I guess." Gertie took a few quick steps to catch up with Edna. "See you boys in a bit."

Boyd removed the satchel with all his ranch clothes and necessities from his shoulder and dropped it unceremoniously on the floor of the tent. "Don't this beat all?" he said.

"Yeah," Floyd agreed in a grumpy tone.

"Least we have our own beds. Still feels way too girly," Boyd said.

"It's all this fancy-schmancy stuff in here." Floyd eyed the flounces around the bottom of the beds and the arrangement of dried flowers on an end table. "I was all set for a real cowboy bunkhouse and ... I don't know ... real he-man stuff. This is for rich guys pretending to camp. I got a mind to pack up and head home."

Boyd took off his cowboy hat and hung it on a nearby wrought-iron coat rack. "I feel the same way, but we gotta think of the rest of the Posse. Marvin got us this deal for free, and he has Bert to answer to. And the girls would be real disappointed if we did that."

Floyd kicked his bag under the bed and straight through the flounce. "I s'pose you're right. But it don't feel right. On the brighter side, we got our horses, and we get to ride. And the food is pretty good too. Better than we rustle up at home, anyhow."

Boyd grunted his agreement. "Dang, I was looking forward to this weekend, and now I gotta pretend to be roughing it." He sat down on the edge of his bed and pulled off his boots. "We gotta be back at the saloon at seven." He stood and threw back the down comforter and tried out the bed. "Feels good, even if it is for pansies."

Floyd grinned. "I think we got lucky with the goat yoga. I feel darn sorry for Marvin having to get up there in front of folks with a Sonny Bono wig on."

"You and me both, brother. You and me both."

CHAPTER SEVEN

The guests were glammed up in their versions of hippie attire and paraphernalia—beads galore and tie-dyed shirts, some flowing robes, flowers in their hair, and a few conspicuous 'roll-your-owns' sticking out of pockets.

The Saloon lights were dim, and folks had spread out comfortably at the tables. Conversation buzzed throughout the building, and the subtle clink of bottles and glasses underscored the casual air as old hippies swilled beer and sipped wine. The ranch had thoughtfully placed dishes of peanuts and pretzels at each table, and Wanda had been tapped to be bar girl for the evening.

The stage was no more than a couple of microphones and a portable speaker on a tripod. A CD player sat ready on a nearby table with Bert at the helm.

Boyd and Floyd sat together at a table near the front. Each had a beer in front of them and they tracked Wanda's movement like two dogs chasing a tennis ball. "Don't like to think of Wanda tending bar," Boyd said. "But I guess since she does all sorts of jobs here, it's not like working in a tavern."

Floyd nodded. "Yeah, she works darn hard here. She barely got the dishes from supper through the big old washer before it came time to do this. I bet she's tuckered out at the end of a day."

Marvin, Edna, and Gertie stood fidgeting near Bert's table, all three wearing pained expressions as if they'd like to bolt and run out the back door.

Bert fiddled with the CD player and seemed satisfied. "Okay, you guys go back and get ready, I'll entertain the crowd with a few jokes and things and then you're on. Sonny and Cher first, and then, we'll hit them with Janis. Don't worry about a thing. Most of these guys have been here drinking since dinner, and they aren't gonna be too particular about the entertainment. Just be sure to ham it up for the photographer. He's got to get some good shots of these Woodstock events to keep the brass happy."

Marvin led the way to the back room where all three hurriedly threw on their costumes, such as they were. "We could've found better stuff than this if we'd have known," Edna said as she pulled a ratty, long, black wig over her spikes and donned the frilly blouse and vest she'd been given. Marvin had a shorter black wig, baggy striped pants, and a blousy shirt with the front cut open to show a huge gold chain.

"Hey, I don't look too bad in this get-up. I might have to take it home and wear it around town. You look great, Edna. I like the black hair."

Meanwhile, Gertie had dropped a huge, flowered tunic over her clothing and added a bright-yellow, feather boa. She stood in front of a floor-length mirror and carefully placed the headband with feathers sprouting above it over her hair. As an added piece of theater, she'd been given an empty Southern Comfort bottle to hold in one hand, leaving the other open for the microphone.

"Mercy, I feel silly. Plus, I think Janis had a whole lot of frizzy hair, and they didn't even give me a wig to wear. I hope people don't recognize me."

Edna as Cher ran her fingers through her long, black tresses and said, "I think you look fabulous, darling. Where's that cheat sheet with the lyrics on it?"

"Welcome everyone, to our first Woodstock weekend at Colorado Pines," Bert's voice rang out over the microphone. "I'm told you always open with a joke, so here goes. Why does a chicken coop have two doors?" He paused. "Because if it had four doors, it would be a chicken sedan!"

A smattering of laughter and lots of coughing followed.

The three lined up at the door and waited for their cue.

"And now all you flower children will be thrilled to know we have some special guests tonight all the way from 1970. Get ready. Here they come ... Sonny and Cher!"

Marvin grabbed Edna's hand, and they lumbered out to Bert's side. Bert clapped Marvin on the shoulder and moved out of the way. Edna grabbed one microphone, and Marvin followed her lead. They looked out over the audience with nervous grins on their faces. Bert hit the button, and the music started.

Edna began swaying to the beat.

"Psst, Edna, hold the words where I can see 'em too."

She moved the lyrics closer to Marvin's eyes and put her arm around his waist to steady herself.

Marvin looked at her and gave a nod, and they both relaxed a bit. Then away they went.

Edna's deep alto voice melded nicely with Marvin's. They really got going on the 'I've got you, Babe' parts, pointing to each other and laughing. The audience showed their approval by joining in. All too soon the song was finished, and they left the stage area to whistles and hoots from the crowd.

Bert stood and clapped along with the audience. "Great job, guys," he said. And he had them take another bow before heading to join the twins at their table. Then he introduced the big finale. "And here, direct from The Fillmore West in San Francisco is Janis Joplin!"

Gertie teetered to the microphone, Southern Comfort bottle held tightly in her left hand and lyrics in her right. She stood, flummoxed, trying to figure out how to hold the microphone without a third hand. Finally, Bert walked over, took the bottle from her, and handed her the mic.

"And here she is, Janis Joplin, singing 'Piece of My Heart'." Bert faded away, pushed a couple of buttons, and a small spotlight hit Gertie in the eyes. The music blared.

Gertie stood there, frozen in place, eyes wide and vacant. Her mouth opened, but nothing came out. Bert hit a button and reset the CD. Gertie looked over at him and shook her head.

A short, heavy-set, love-child hippie circa 1972 marched up and stood beside Gertie. Her outfit wasn't far from Gertie's get-up, but her hair was more authentic. "Here, honey," she said in a gravelly voice. "Let me help you. I usta' sing this little number at the bars in North Beach back in the day. I got this song cold." She turned to Bert and said, "Hit it."

She proceeded to sing the socks off the song in soul-wrenching style, her eyes closed and feathers flowing as she moved.

Somewhere in the middle of the piece, Gertie seemed to awaken from a deep sleep. She shook her head and peered at her lyrics. Clutching them close to her chest, she found her place in the song and moved closer to the wailing woman. Her eyes lit up and took on a look of fierce determination. She put her arm around the woman's shoulder, raised her chin, and joined in on the chorus.

"Break it!" she shouted and followed along with the rest of the lyrics. Her sweet soprano tones were tiny in comparison to her partner, but she held her head high as she intoned them.

Someone in the audience hollered, "Atta girl!" and a murmur of approval ricocheted around the Saloon.

The two soul sisters did Janis proud.

The songstress from San Francisco ended in style with a screeching "Waaaaaaah."

Gertie pulled her feather boa from her neck and threw it into the crowd. They took a quick bow. The crowd jumped to their feet as one and cheered at the top of their lungs.

Marvin and Edna hustled to the front.

"Holy cow, Gertie," Edna said. "I didn't know you had it in you. That was fantastic."

"Did we do okay?" Gertie's cheeks were bright pink with excitement.

"You two sang it all right. You really sang it. And Bert will be happy to know that I saw the photographer snapping his fingers through the whole thing. Bert should be one happy rancher."

Marvin let out the big breath he'd been holding. "Okay, ladies, let's get these costumes off, and get some beers into us. Sure glad that's over."

The three hustled into the back room and returned in time to hear Bert announcing, "And that's it, folks. See you all at the campfire in half an hour.

Gertie collapsed into a chair and fanned herself with her hand. *What a night.*

The Posse hunkered down together on a log facing the huge cowboy campfire. Slim had been chosen to give a demonstration of making cowboy coffee and proceeded to give a longish lesson on how to fill the blue ceramic pot with fresh river water, warm it up, add fresh coffee grounds, and then bring the whole shebang to a rolling boil. He pulled the pot off the fire to let the grounds settle and proceeded to pass out matching blue-enamel cups to all who wanted a taste.

"I was hoping for s'mores" Edna groused. "Who cares about a cup of bitter old coffee with grounds floating around in it?"

Gertie raised her hand and took a cup from Slim. "Oh, they went to the trouble to show us how to do it, so I'll give it a taste."

"Guess you're still on a high from the Janis Joplin experience then?" Edna guffawed. "I can't believe that song came out of you."

Gertie fixed a withering look on her friend. "The Posse exists to hold one another up and protect. We do not humiliate or tear down."

"That's right, Edna," Marvin said. "Gertie was mighty brave to even try that particular song, and I couldn't have been prouder when she chimed in and gave it her best." He had positioned himself next to Edna on the end of the log.

Then in full cowboy regalia, Bert showed up with his guitar and began a rousing version of "Get Along Little Dogies."

The twins perked up and sang along, Floyd taking the high, melodious part.

Marvin took the opportunity to scoot a bit closer to Edna and put his arm around her.

Gertie sipped her cowboy coffee and hummed along.

The crowd grew quiet as the last song was sung. Bert carefully balanced his guitar against a log. He nodded to Slim who came forward and pulled a piece of paper from his back pocket. He unfolded it and stood ready.

Bert continued. "In true cowboy style, we here at the Pines like to end each evening with a genuine cowboy poem. This here's what Slim come up with for tonight."

Slim read out the poem loud and clear.

When day is done and evenin' comes to Colorado Pines,

Us cowpokes like to sip some Joe and dream of olden times.

Back when the saddle was our home, and the dogies were in our care,

Back when mustangs ran wild and free, breathing clean, mountain air.

We rode the range from dawn to dusk, with nary a mild complaint.

We worked the herd midst sun and dust, never knowin' the words, "I cain't."

We roped and branded, rescued the stranded, and rustled up our own grub.

Beans and bacon, biscuits, and Joe, to fill our bellies up.

And when the fire burned down to embers, we sang of this life we love.

The spurs and the saddles, the sagebrush and cattle, the brave, the true, the tough.

Then we bedded down under prairie skies and slept under stars and moon,

And thanked the Lord we'd lived that day, for a new one was dawnin' soon.

Slim took off his ten-gallon hat and took a deep bow to the applause of the crowd.

Bert popped up beside him. "Good night, everyone. See you bright and early for a big country breakfast and your first trail ride at the Colorado Pines."

The Posse roused themselves to say their goodnights and headed for their respective sleeping quarters.

Boyd clapped his brother on the back. "Boy, oh boy, that cowboy poetry gets right into a guy's heart, don't it?

Floyd shook his head in wonder. "You're right about that. Practically brought a tear to my eye."

Edna had sidled away from Marvin and raised her arms over her head as she let out a huge yawn. "I think I've done this day. I'm plum tuckered out as the cowboys say." She turned to Gertie. "Come on, let's hit the hay."

"You ladies want an escort to your room? Never know when a wolf or a coyote or whatever they got here might come your way." Marvin was trying hard for charming.

Edna answered, "Sure, why not. Guess we got breakfast at eight and then our first ride. You boys excited?"

Boyd and Floyd both nodded. "Yes, ma'am," Boyd said.

Floyd scanned the stragglers as they left the campfire and headed in all directions. "Haven't seen Wanda since we left the Saloon. Guess maybe she had to stay there and clean up."

"Good night, boys, see you in the morning," Edna said and struck out for the shortcut to the hotel.

Marvin and Gertie hurried to catch up.

Marvin trudged through the darkness to tent eight.

A tall, thin man with a receding hairline and a ponytail met him at the entrance. "Wayne Marshall," he said and stuck out his hand.

"Glad to meet you, Wayne. Looks like we're roomies for the weekend." Marvin tossed his backpack at the foot of the empty bed and removed three throw pillows from in front of the headboard. "Never slept in this fancy a bed even when Anna was alive, and we stayed in hotels. Don't think a guy needs a potted plant in his tent either."

Wayne retreated to his bed and stretched out with his hands behind his head. "Don't matter to me either way. I like the idea of hanging out with all these old hippie types and eating and drinking my fill. The grub here is great."

"My cousin, Bert, runs this place. Haven't seen him since we were both kids, and he sort of set this weekend up for me and my friends. The bad part is he wants us to help do all these workshops, and they are a royal pain in the ass." Marvin plopped down on his bed.

"Yeah, I can see that. I'm not going to any of them anyway. Got better things to do with my time. Hey, you need anything to help you relax?"

"What do you mean?"

"Well, let's say I got some stuff in case you feel uptight or, you know, you want to unwind a little while you're here."

"No, thanks. I don't do any of that. I have a beer or two now and then—that's enough for me."

"Okay, to each his own. I figured there'd be "kindred spirits" signed up for this particular weekend if you know what I mean." Wayne sat up and took off his work boots.

Marvin eyed his roomie. "I suppose there could be druggies in this batch of folks. They mostly look like they're ready for a rocking chair. Me included."

"Hey, is that gal you sat with at the campfire your girlfriend? There's something kinda sassy and cute about her."

"We're just friends for the time being. But I wouldn't like to think you'd offer her drugs. For one thing, she might punch your lights out."

"I'll take my chances. Besides I like my women to have some spunk."

Marvin eyed Wayne again. He opened and closed his mouth several times. Then he stepped toward the tent flaps which were tied to one side with long, fabric bows. "Gotta use the facilities," he said.

"Sure, I might be snoring when you get back."

"Right." Marvin stepped off the porch, shaking his head as he hiked toward the privy.

CHAPTER EIGHT

Bert's freckled face scrunched up as he gave out the bad news. "Sorry, Marvin, but that's the way it is. Charlie can only handle so many folks at a time on a trail ride, and he has four full sessions this morning. The twins are doing goat yoga anyhow, so you'll all have to get your first ride in tomorrow. Gotta serve the paying customers first, y' know."

"Dang it, Bert, you've got us so scheduled up with all this hippie nonsense we don't get to do any of the fun stuff. Look at this schedule—bead and macramé classes, crystal power lessons, Intro to I Ching for Pete's sake ... when do we get a chance to fish and hike and ride like the others?"

"Tomorrow. Sunday. Saturday is our busiest day, and it's the day our photographer wants to get most of his stuff for the new brochure and website. This is important, Marv. I'm sorry if it's not much fun for you guys today, but the ranch's bottom line is what we're talkin' about here."

Marvin shook his head and exited the fake jail. "I'm sorry, guys. I wanted this weekend to be something special for all of us, but ..." His voice trailed off, and his mouth turned down in defeat.

Bert wasn't giving an inch, and the Posse wasn't one bit happy. They stood by the hitching post, a miserable countenance on each face.

"I gave it my best shot, guys," Marvin told them, "but Bert won't budge."

Just then a pickup and trailer rolled into the Ranch and headed toward the stables. "Looks like your baby goats have arrived, fellas. Guess we have to make the best of a bad deal."

Boyd scowled, and Floyd did the same. "Gonna spend our whole morning with those critters climbing all over us. We're sure not gonna be telling anybody back home about this."

Edna cackled. "Aw, it's not so bad. Look, they're unloading them and putting them in that little pen. They're kinda cute. And I bet they don't weigh but a few pounds each. Kind of like doing yoga with Chihuahuas."

Gertie checked her schedule. "I'm off to the Chuckwagon in the north corner. It says I'm leading a beading project. I sure hope I can do it right. I'm not much of a craftsperson."

"Yeah, well I get the pleasure of doing the *Introduction to I Ching*. I don't even know what that is, but Bert says it's self-explanatory, and we read through the beginning of the book and talk about it. How about you, Marvin? What did they stick you with?"

Marvin dug his toe into the gravel at his feet. "I gotta help folks make some tie-dyed T-shirts over to the stables. Got about a million rubber bands, some tubs of dye, and white T-shirts. Guess it could be worse."

Gertie surveyed the Posse, her little circle of friends, and she smiled. "Hey, everyone, this isn't so bad. It's only this morning. The schedule doesn't have us doing anything this afternoon, and tonight they're showing a Woodstock video, so we're off the hook there too."

"Yeah, but we don't get to ride until tomorrow," Boyd said, and Floyd huffed in disgust.

Edna tossed her spiky head and planted her hands on her hips. "We'll see about that," she said as she tromped off to her I Ching class.

★★★

Boyd's forehead dripped with sweat as he struggled to bend his chubby body into the downward dog position. Bert had thoughtfully given the twins a chart of basic yoga poses, a CD of a yoga lesson complete with encouraging words to participants, and some exercise mats to supply the session. A motley assortment of old hippies was spread out in an empty, wooden-floored room attached to the barn while perky little goat babies meandered all around.

Some participants were in nirvana while others shared the twins' pain. The background music on the CD was Middle Eastern-sounding and meant, Boyd was sure, to help everyone relax as they twisted their bodies up like pretzels. Edna had been right. The kids were so light they barely registered on the folks twisting and turning into impossible positions as they skittered over and under bodies.

"That's right. Hold that pose and feel the negative energies melt away. Good. Now stretch up into a nice, tall mountain pose and ... hold." The butter-smooth voice of the yoga instructor on the recorded session droned on, and Boyd's red face got warmer as a kid dropped a few manure pellets on his back and neck. He shook them off and turned his head as far around as he could to try to get a glimpse of Floyd. But the recording went on to the warrior pose, and it took all his attention to stand and accomplish that maneuver without tipping over.

I feel like a darn fool. Worse than the eighth grade when Robby Johnson swirled my head in the boys' bathroom toilet. I'm done. And he lowered his arms, shook himself to be sure all the pellets were gone, smashed his Stetson on his head, and marched out of the room.

Floyd was right on his tail. "Hey, wait. I'm outta here too. Me and yoga are never gonna be friends. Let's go find Wanda and see if she needs some help with lunch."

The instructor's voice faded as the twins made their escape.

253

"Where are we going?" Gertie followed closely behind Edna as they left their room at the Lodge. "That barbecue lunch was delicious. Nothing like the one we had back home in that stinky restaurant."

"We're gonna have some fun, my friend." Edna walked with purpose, her head held high.

"I was all set to relax on our little deck over the river and read my memoir. It really is a pretty setting, isn't it?"

"Yup, the setting is great. But I came for some action, not for listening to some ancient Chinese guy spout his philosophy or mooning over some person's stale old life story."

Gertie recognized that tone of voice. Her friend was on a mission. Edna struck off down the back trail, arms pumping and a dangerous bounce to her step.

"Well, you don't need to be so huffy. I spent the morning chasing beads all over the place trying to turn them into necklaces." Gertie struggled to keep up.

Edna took a turn off the trail and headed for the stables.

"What are we doing here?" Gertie asked. "We can't ride until tomorrow morning. Charlie's gone to town and ... Now, wait a minute, Edna, you aren't going to try to ride without anyone's help, are you? We don't have a single clue how to put on the saddles, let alone ride by ourselves." Gertie's voice had risen in pitch with each word.

Edna stared her down. "How hard can it be to throw a saddle on and cinch it up? And besides, I used to ride Uncle Louie's horses, and he said I was—"

"A natural, I know." Gertie moved closer to Edna and stood her ground. "But that was ages ago when you were a kid. We could break something doing this now."

"I don't intend to break a thing. I'm gonna get on old Buck and take it nice and slow. You can get on Betsy if you want—I'll leave it up to you, but I'm not gonna sit around here like an old lady."

Gertie quieted, seeming to weigh her decision. "I don't suppose it will do any good to remind you we *are* old ladies?" But she relented. She knew when she was beaten. "Actually, I think Betsy will be fine. She's gentle and not too tall. But Buck is huge. How are you even going to get up on him?"

"Not to worry. I have a plan. But let's get inside and make sure the coast is clear first." Edna stepped into the dark of the stable and stood quietly until her eyes adjusted. "Seems pretty quiet. I wonder how we know which saddle goes on which horse?" The girls set to work.

"Man, I never knew a saddle and bridle had so many little buckles." Edna wiped a drop of sweat from her forehead. She sat perched on top of a fence railing and eye to eye with Buck. "Do you want me to cinch up Betsy's saddle a little tighter? Takes some strength, doesn't it?"

Gertie carefully looped Betsy's ears through the bridle and stepped back to survey her work. "I think we're fine. Now I call that a job well-done. Really, it's common sense. Everything needs to be buckled into place so we can guide the horses where we want them to go."

"Okay, let's get going. Yeehaw! This is the reason we came." Edna threw her leg over Buck's back and settled herself. Buck stood still, flicking flies away with his ears. Gertie managed to climb aboard Betsy, and there they sat, two cowgirls astride their trusty steeds. They gathered up their reins and clopped out the back door of the stable to a nice, flat meadow. The trail was wide, and they rode side by side.

"See? I told you." Edna was in her glory. "Now when we get back, I'll have to find another fence to climb down. Let's head out toward those trees over there and follow the trail for a bit. Man, I wish I knew how to gallop. But even a nice walk makes me feel like a real horsewoman."

The sun shone pleasantly, and birds chirped in the bushes while hawks floated high overhead. The scent of mown hay from a nearby field lay heavily in the air.

Gertie leaned forward to pat Betsy's neck and sat up again, tall in the saddle. "It feels like being on a boat, kind of bouncy and side to side. I've decided to relax and enjoy this even though we're going to be in a lot of trouble if we get caught."

"Aw, we won't get caught, and if we do, we'll plead ignorance. After all, they did assign us our horses. They're ours for the weekend."

Gertie surveyed the scenery. "My, this is a beautiful place. Don't you wonder what it looked like a hundred years ago when Indians ran around here?"

Edna closed her eyes as if imagining. "Hmm, yup. I would have loved to live back then and be close to the land and all. I wish I could get Buck to pick up the pace a little. We're barely moving, plus I got an appointment with Marvin to go fishing at three o'clock."

"I've been meaning to say something about Marvin. I noticed he had his arm around you at the campfire last night. I'd hate for him to get his feelings hurt if he likes you, and you aren't inclined to return the favor."

Edna shook her head. "Nah, old Marvin and me are good friends—we understand each other. We're both kinda tough, and we're both lonely. But I'm looking for a lot more fire than Marvin can spark." Buck moved off the trail and began to munch on the tall grasses. Edna reined him back onto the trail.

"It would be detrimental to the Posse if there were misunderstandings. And isn't it cute the way the twins have taken to Wanda?"

"Yeah, but the same goes for them. They could get their feelings hurt too. What a world we live in, my friend. There seems to be heartbreak lurking around every corner."

Gertie sighed and lowered her head.

"Aw, sorry, Gertie." Edna slapped one hand on her leg. "Dang, I didn't mean to bring up that rat, Grayson.

"It's okay. The cruise is a distant memory now. And I believe we must find the good and cling to it. After all, we formed the Posse onboard that cruise. And now we're best of friends. The good far outweighed the bad once I got over my little escapade." She nodded once to cement her belief. "Look at these wildflowers and the beauty of the pine trees."

"Yeah," Edna said, "You're right. Life only gets ugly when people are involved."

Gertie reined Betsy to a halt while she let that bit of wisdom settle. "I think we should be getting back."

Edna nodded. "Okay, we aren't gonna get much action from these nags, I guess. I suppose they tame 'em down to make sure no one gets hurt."

Edna pulled Buck back from nibbling on a nearby bush and turned him toward the stables. He snorted and raised his head, his flanks quivering. "Whoa, there," she said, "Let's not get too excited, Old Man." He reared up and snorted and took off hell-bent down the trail.

Edna grabbed onto the saddle horn with both hands. "Whoa, slow down now, oh my ..." She stopped talking and hung on for dear life. Buck broke into a gallop and covered territory at breakneck speed.

Betsy increased her speed too, but at a much more manageable pace. She and Gertie trotted along behind. "Edna!" Gertie shouted. "Be careful of the trees!"

Buck barreled along close to some scrubby pines, and Edna had to duck as well as grasp the reins and saddle horn. By this time, the saddle had worked its way loose and leaned precariously to the right side of Buck with Edna's spiky head and body listing right along with it. Her right arm flailed through the air.

By the time the girls reached the barn, Edna clung to Buck by a thread, her saddle some forty-five degrees off his back. She managed to get him wedged up against the first fence railing she found and steadied herself as she dismounted.

Gertie trotted up beside her as she stood shaking in her boots. "My word, Edna, are you okay?" Gertie reined Betsy into her stall, dismounted, and hurried back to see about her impulsive friend.

A voice boomed from the front of the barn. "All right, you two. Front and center. Now!" Charlie had both hands on his hips and a frown the size of Texas on his face. "You two ladies broke our cardinal rule. No one goes out alone and especially without a practice ride."

He walked over to Edna and took Buck's reins out of her hands. "I'll put Buck away. You two skedaddle out of here, and I don't want to see you back. You're grounded from the horses for the rest of your time here. These are valuable animals, and they can be dangerous too if we don't follow the right procedures. I'll let Bert know what happened, and I'm right disappointed in the both of you."

Edna looked Charlie in the eye, fire snapping from her eyes.

Gertie looked at her feet. Edna appeared to be on the verge of some sassy retort, but Gertie gave her a quick shove, and they hurried out of the barn.

"Well, crapola." Edna slapped at her jeans to remove some of the dust. "Busted," she said.

"Yes, we are." Gertie sighed and followed Edna up the path away from Buck and Betsy.

Edna stomped her boots in the mud and gravel as she made her way to the river's edge. The late afternoon sun shone on the surface of the water, ripples swirling and rushing downstream. She could see Marvin knee-deep in the water with a pole in his hands.

"Hey, Marvin, I'm finally here. Sorry, I'm late," she hollered. Marvin half-turned without moving his feet, which were clad with rubbery hip-waders. He waved and motioned her to come closer as he made his way carefully back to shore.

"Where's the worms? I better get going or it's gonna be dinner time before I catch anything."

Marvin struggled out of the water, moving in slow motion, and dripping. "It would be a sacrilege to fish with worms on a beautiful current like this. You gotta use a fly and cast your line out just so, to let the water do the fishing for you."

Marvin busied himself setting up a pole for Edna. He chose a bright red fly with black feathers and secured it to the end of the line. "Have you ever tried fly fishing before? It's a bit tricky."

"Nope, me and my Uncle Louie always fished in the lake. With worms. We got some nice trout that way too."

"Well, there's nice trout in this river, but they haven't been biting so far. Fish generally feed early in the morning or at dusk. The idea is to make them think they're biting into a big, fat insect that landed on the water. You gotta flick your wrist and send the line way out there so the current can take it."

"Okay, that doesn't sound too hard. Let me try." Edna grabbed the end of her pole and waved it up and down to get the feel of it.

"Careful. These poles and lures cost a fortune. Don't want to get hung up in the brush around here." Marvin reached out to steady the pole, but Edna jerked it away. The line went behind her and, sure enough, caught in the bushes.

"Drat." She tromped back to untangle her line. The lure was easy to spot, and she had it freed with a few quick jerks on the line.

Marvin took a deep breath and tried again. "Now, Edna, you gotta listen to me. If you keep being so rough with the

259

gear, we're gonna have to pay for repairs back at the shop. I rented all this stuff, and it don't come cheap. Now there's an art to this whole thing. Watch me once and see what you need to do."

Edna gave Marvin the stink eye, but she secured the fly, reeled in the line so it wouldn't drag on the ground, and moved back beside Marvin. "Go ahead, I'm watching," she said.

Marvin moved to the side a few steps, pulled his arm back smoothly, snapped the line with it, and then sailed the line out to mid-stream with a whoosh. The fly settled down nicely and traveled with the current for a good distance before he brought it back. "See? Like that. If you do it right, the water does the work, and the fish get a meal of fly a la hook."

"Okay, let me practice a few times," Edna said and retrieved her pole from Marvin's hand.

"Reel it in nice and smooth. That's right. Get it all taut and then you'll let out a nice length to cast onto the water." Marvin moved in close and reached as if to place his hand on her pole again.

Edna froze. "Listen, Marvin, are you gonna micromanage every bit of this fishing time? If so, I think I'd rather go back to my room and take a nap. I already ran into one stubborn-as-a-mule man this afternoon. I don't need another one." Her eyes squinted as she talked, and she shook her head for emphasis as she spoke.

Marvin took a deep breath and tried again. "What's the matter with you? I'm only trying to help you get started right. Fly fishing isn't like dumping your line into a lake. There's an art to it. You gotta learn to cast with finesse."

Edna dropped the pole on the ground. "Well, mister professional fisherman, you can finesse this." She shook her fist at him to underscore her displeasure, turned, and stomped back up the incline to the trail leading back to the hotel.

"Dang it, Edna. Why do you have to be so headstrong? I hope you didn't break any of that gear." But he was talking to a retreating figure. He yelled a parting shot. "If you broke anything, you have to pay for it!"

Edna kept walking.

A tall, skinny guy in denim joined the Posse as they dug into the dinner of chuckwagon stew and fry bread.

"Hey, everyone," Marvin said, "this here is Wayne. He's my glampmate."

Everyone looked over at Wayne.

"Hi," Wayne said with a nod. "Glad to meet you. This ranch is perfect, isn't it? I mean we got all the beauty of the great outdoors and all the weed we can smoke along with it. I thought I'd died and gone to heaven when I saw the brochure advertising a 70s hippie heyday."

Edna eyed the man. "Just so you know, we all came to enjoy a real dude ranch complete with horseback riding. We're not interested in all that hippie stuff."

"To each his own," Wayne replied as he took a big bite of stew. "We can agree on how great the food is though, can't we?" He grinned at Edna as he chewed.

"Yeah, I guess."

Marvin spoke up. "Wayne comes from a little town right near Berkeley, California, in the East Bay. That right, Wayne?"

"Yup, El Cerrito. Didn't make it to Woodstock back in the day, but me and my girlfriend at the time made it out to Altamont. Man, that was a scene. Hell's Angels all over the place and people as far as the eye could see."

Gertie smiled sweetly at Marvin's roommate. "It would be lovely to hear about it sometime. I always wondered how it would feel to be in a crowd that large with beautiful music all around."

"The music was great, and we could hear it, but the stage was so far away from our little patch of grass we couldn't see a thing. Still fun though."

Edna scowled. "Doesn't seem like much of a concert if you couldn't even see the stage. Besides I heard people got killed that day—the scene turned deadly."

"Yeah, things happened. Lots of drinking and drugs. Three people died, and I think maybe a baby was born there. But you know there were hundreds of thousands of people, and we didn't see any of that. A few Hell's Angels went through the crowd and took whatever they wanted. They grabbed a bottle of wine from some people next to us, and no one asked for it back. Anyhow, we enjoyed a nice, little picnic with psychedelic amenities and some great music in the background. You don't forget things like that."

The twins' eyes had gotten large and round. They didn't say a word.

"We get to watch the Woodstock video tonight," Marvin chimed in, changing the topic. "Might be fun to see all these old hippies reminisce about the days of their youth. Maybe some of them were there."

"Probably were," Wayne said. "You know what they say, 'Old hippies never die; they just go to pot.'"

"Never heard that," Marvin said. "Think I'll take a walk before the campfire." And he took his leave.

The Woodstock video ended and was followed by a smoky fire and some cowboy songs. Everyone was ready for a good, long night's sleep.

The twins headed off to their glamp site, and Edna led the rest of the posse up the back trail, arms pumping at her sides. She came to an abrupt halt. "Whoa."

Gertie and Marvin caught up with her.

"Hey, you lit out like a bat out of Hell. What's the hurry?" Marvin huffed as he spoke.

"Shh, look up there, over by the trees." Edna pointed to several people huddled together under some pine trees further up the hill and well away from the campfire crowd.

Gertie spoke softly, "It looks like some of the folks from the campfire. Maybe they're friends and—"

"Holy cow. Look, they're up to something. One of them exchanged some money for a little package."

"Now Edna, don't go jumping to wild conclusions. They might be sharing cigarettes or trading phone numbers and addresses. You don't know it's something illegal." Marvin's tone begged for reason.

"Uh-oh, I think they heard us." Edna took a few steps back, but the three had turned toward them.

Edna, Gertie, and Marvin gawked at the men, but they quickly disappeared into the pines. Next thing they knew, the spot was empty.

"Did we imagine those guys or what? I'm pretty sure one of them was your buddy, Wayne. He wore that paisley shirt with the Nehru collar." Edna tromped up the hill to the exact spot where the exchange occurred.

Marvin and Gertie followed.

"See? You can see a footprint right there in the dirt." Edna surveyed the area looking for any clues to what those men had been doing but found nothing. "Do you think we should go and get Bert?"

"Aw, come on, Edna. I'm beat and want to get back to my little glamp site for a good night's sleep. If you want, I can ask Wayne if that was him. He has as much right to be here as we do. Let's get you two up to your hotel and call it a night.

The three finished their hike in silence.

CHAPTER NINE

Gertie wiped the last of the cold cream from her face and then fussed with the shades at their bedroom window, making sure they would keep the morning light at bay. She'd returned from a soothing shower to clear away the smell of that night's campfire.

"Shall I turn out the light?" she asked.

"Sure, I'm one step from climbing into bed. Go ahead." Edna plopped down on the edge of her bed as Gertie turned off the lights.

"I've actually enjoyed the campfires," Gertie said as she made her way to her bed. "I didn't expect to. I thought they would be ... I don't know ... sort of like grade B cowboy movies. But they are quite moving, especially the poems at the end. They're admittedly schmaltzy, but they have a sort of melancholy quiet to them too."

"Mm," Edna said.

"What are you thinking about? You seem miles away."

"I'm letting my mind deal with the question you asked earlier. You know, about Marvin. I'm not sure I know how I feel about him anymore. At first, I couldn't stand him. Then he sort of mellowed, and now he's ... well, he's nice and sweet. It's making me nervous."

Edna turned on her side to face her friend. "We had a spat this afternoon when I tried to fly fish. Got myself all in a tizzy when he tried to give me instructions, and I had to apologize at dinner."

"Oh?"

"Yeah, and the thing is, he was real nice about it. Didn't make me feel guilty or lecture me like other men would. He said, 'Apology accepted,' and patted me on the shoulder. Made me feel about two feet tall."

Gertie fluffed her pillow and settled her head. "I like Marvin—no pretenses with him. He's an honest man and a lonely one too."

"We all know that. He can't stop talking about Anna. Makes a person feel like he's stuck in the past and maybe not ready for a new relationship."

"Oh, I don't know. I still talk about Donald because he's the only husband I had. But that doesn't mean I'm never going to move forward. I think if a nice man came along, I'd be ready to try again."

"That's just it. I had one strong, if a bit boring, marriage, and then got sucked into a mess and ended up being left for a young, blonde airhead. It really did a number on my confidence with guys. I know I talk big about cowboys and such, but Gertie, I'm afraid of trusting anyone again."

"Yes, I can see that. After Grayson turned out to be a con man, I've had to rethink my ability to make good choices when it comes to men." Gertie sighed and lay her head on the pillow.

"Looks like we're both in the same boat. So far, Marvin is sticking to me like glue. He doesn't say anything remotely romantic, but I can feel it coming. By now, he has to know how I am—sort of rough around the edges."

Gertie yawned. "Let's be careful, you and I. Men can be a lot of trouble."

"Ain't it the truth?" Edna said, "Good night, Gertie."

The two friends settled down in their beds and all was quiet.

"Psst. Hey, Gertie. Before I forget to tell you, I was real proud of you last night when you sang that song." Edna roused up in bed.

"Thanks, I surprised myself."

"Kinda reminds me of when we were kids, and you got the part in the high-school play. I never thought you'd do something so brave."

Gertie was quiet for a bit. "No, I wasn't the kind to get up in front of others. The fact is, I had to stay after school to finish a chemistry lab assignment, and as I was leaving, someone said, 'There's an audition across the hall.' We wandered into the audition room, were given a handout, and before I knew what was happening, I read for a part. I didn't think anything of it until later in the week. Sure enough, I'd been given one of the supporting roles. I was an avid reader back then, and I guess I knew how to make the words sound like I was saying them."

"Fate. That's what it was." Edna spoke with authority. "Gertie, you sealed your place in the high-school pecking order when you did that part. I was so happy for you. I can't remember much about the play now, but the kids said you were good—they admired your talent."

"Yes, it was a turning point for me. Before that, I was a little mouse in a big cage, and I needed you to make me feel safe. After, I relaxed, and it felt good. And the funny part is I actually loved doing the part."

Gertie scrambled out of bed and got a drink of water at the sink. She turned, glass in hand, and said, "You get a special closeness when you work with people on a performance. I can't quite describe it, but I've missed that sort of camaraderie." She put the glass back on the counter and climbed back into bed.

"Yeah, guess the church ladies and the garden club women don't fit the bill."

"Yes, I do have friends in those groups. It's only that when you rehearse and work intensely for several months, you feel part of something bigger. And even though it's scary to perform in front of an audience, it's invigorating too." She stopped and smiled to herself. "I guess that's what happened last night on a smaller scale. I felt the freedom to let go and give it all I had. It felt right."

Edna clapped her hands in mock applause. "Good for you. We all need to let go and enjoy life a little more. The gal who sang with you was pretty good too. There are some interesting folks here this weekend. Guess the Woodstock theme still has a strong pull on hippies grown old."

"I guess so." Gertie's voice diminished as she burrowed into her pillow. "'Night."

"Goodnight." Edna pulled the covers up to her chin. "I'm glad we're friends, Gertie."

Breakfast consisted of piles and piles of flapjacks with all the bacon, sausage, and ham a person could load on their plate.

"Man, this weekend is evaporating on us fast," Marvin said around a huge mouthful of flapjacks. "Feels like we just got here, and it's Sunday already."

Boyd slurped his coffee. "I know. Me and Floyd finally got to ride our horses, and now we only get one more ride before we go home. Hope we get to do more than trail ride today. We want to gallop or at least trot, don't we, Floyd?"

"Sure do. Hey, I'm gonna help Wanda with the dishes again. That girl works too darn hard."

"I'll help too," Boyd chimed in.

Edna winked at Gertie. "Don't suppose you boys are interested in more than dishes, are you?"

Floyd lifted his chin with a defiant look on his chubby face. "What if we are? Wanda is about the nicest girl we've ever met."

"Now, don't you let Edna tease you," Gertie broke in. "She's upset we both got banned from the stables. We aren't allowed to ride anymore after yesterday's escapades. I'm looking forward to a nice, quiet afternoon of reading. I'm going to sink into the plush chair on our deck overlooking the river."

"Phooey. I'm not sure what I'm gonna do to fill up the time. I dang sure don't want to do anymore I Ching or beads or—"

Bert rushed up to Marvin, slapped him on the shoulder, and said, "Meet me at the jail. Pronto." Then he turned and practically ran back up the village road.

"I wonder what's got his dander up." Marvin wiped his mouth with his napkin and piled up his dishes. "Sure hope we don't have more hippie assignments. I want to get another bit of fishing in if I can."

The Posse stood from the table to bus their dishes, and Marvin headed up the road to find out what bee had gotten into Bert's bonnet.

Bert met Marvin at the door to the Jail and hustled him inside. He hurried around his desk, sat, and motioned for Marvin to do the same. His forehead was all scrunched up.

"What's this about? You look like steam could pour out your ears." Marvin said.

"We got trouble. That big-mouth roommate of yours, Wayne, started bragging about doing drugs—back in the day and right up to the present. Wanda overheard him say he's made out pretty good with sales here this weekend. She reported it to her husband, Clay, who happens to be the deputy sheriff around here. He's a jerk too and would like nothing better than to put a feather in his hat with a big drug bust. Wanda says he's comin' up here later today along with several of his cronies, and they're gonna raid the place. Just what we need. It's gonna hit the local papers, and we're gonna be in deep doo-doo." Bert was red in the face after his frantic speech.

Marvin's jaw dropped. "You serious? He did sort of offer me drugs, but I thought he was talking about weed. That's legal, and pretty much all these hippie folks have some. Is it worse than that?"

"Wanda says he has some pills called Oxy he's hawking to anyone interested."

"Dang. He doesn't seem like the most upstanding citizen around. I think me and the Posse better hightail it out of here. I hate to leave you in a bind, but there's nothing we can do, and I don't want my friends to get frisked or booked, or whatever's gonna happen here."

"Yeah, I was gonna suggest you pack up and skedaddle. Wanda gave me a heads up because she's fond of those twin cowboys of yours—doesn't want them in any trouble. I don't think much will happen in the long run. Old Clay will make a big fuss, and probably get photos for the local rag, and then he'll arrest Wayne if he can find any evidence. I have half a mind to go over there and warn him, but I don't want to find my butt in jail."

"I'm sorry, Bert. I know this weekend was important to you. But look on the bright side. You'll get some free publicity, and maybe even the big wigs back East will see the benefit of it. If you invite hippies, you're gonna get drugs, sex, and rock and roll—part of the package."

Bert's scowl grew bigger, and the wrinkles on his forehead deeper. "Go on, get out of here and pack up. Wanda says Clay will show later this afternoon, so you should have time to make your escape before then. Sorry to ruin the rest of your time here."

"That's okay. I'm sorry for your trouble too."

Marvin stood, shook hands with his cousin, and headed out to warn the Posse.

Edna perched on the edge of her bed. "Marvin, what's this all about? You got me real nervous."

Gertie's head bobbed up and down. "I agree. Tell us what's wrong. Is anyone sick?"

"Naw, nothing like that. Let's wait until Boyd and Floyd get here. I told 'em to meet us here as soon as possible but to pack up first. I'm afraid they're still in a daze overhearing Wanda is married to the sheriff and has five kids."

Gertie tsked. "Now that must have been a big disappointment to them. They both seemed to have a crush on her."

Marvin had been pacing, but now he took the chair from the little desk area of the room and sat on it. He hung his head until it almost reached his knees. "This is sure one big mess."

There came a timid little rap on the door, and Edna hollered, "Come in!"

Boyd and Floyd, both of their faces flushed, came through the door, hauling their baggage behind them.

Gertie motioned for them to sit on her bed.

They stowed their bags by the door and sat.

Marvin lifted his head and shook it. "I should've known when Bert was involved nothing would go right." He leveled his gaze at each Posse member and spilled the beans.

"The sheriff got wind of some goings-on here that could get his big, fat face in the local papers. Seems my roommate sold pills to some of the hippie types here for the weekend. Bert is plain beside himself with worry. He might lose his job over this. Although, I don't know what he could have done."

Marvin looked over at Edna and said, "You were probably right the other night when you saw those guys in the middle of the trees. They probably *were* doing a deal. Sorry, I pooh-poohed your idea."

Edna gave Marvin a quick smile to encourage him. "Oh, that's all right. But what's next?"

"We got to get packed up and head on out of here ASAP. Bert said Wanda convinced her husband to give us time to leave before the fireworks begin."

Boyd and Floyd looked like death warmed over. Boyd spoke up.

"Me and Floyd are heartsick about Wanda. We both thought she was about the best thing we'd ever run into. And you know we aren't the kind of guys who take to girls so quick, normally. Why didn't she tell us she was married and had a string of kids? We both made right fools of ourselves falling all over her." He scuffed his cowboy boots back and forth over the carpet as if trying to remove some dog poo from the soles.

Gertie stood near the sink and reached out to pat the closest twin on the shoulder. "You boys have nothing to be sorry about. Wanda *is* a sweet, hard-working girl, and you couldn't have known she's already taken. She's a friendly girl and didn't realize you two could get your feelings hurt."

"Yeah, no way you could have known she has a string of kids a mile long," Edna added her two cents worth.

Marvin intervened. "Hey, we can talk about all of this on the way home?" He looked at his watch. "We got a little over an hour to pack and head out of this place. Bert's fit to be tied, and I want to leave without getting in his way again."

He whistled a low whistle. "Never thought this weekend would go sideways as it has. Hippie stuff, drug busts. Sorry I got the Posse involved. All I envisioned was horseback riding, a little stream fishing, and nice, comfortable campfires. I'm sorry."

Edna stood and fished her suitcase out from under the bed. "Aw, don't take it all on yourself. We *did* have some nice campfires. Gertie and I snuck in a horseback ride, and we had some mighty fine meals. And, hey, we got to perform in front of a whole bunch of over-the-hill hippies and become near celebrities. What's to be sorry about?" She rolled her clothes and crammed them and other belongings into her suitcase.

Marvin ran his hand over his hair. "Okay, I'll grab my stuff and be back in ten or fifteen minutes. You boys bring your bags down right now and stow them in the van. Looks like we'll miss lunch, but we can stop after we make our getaway."

Marvin and the boys left.

"Holy cow," Edna said. "A real drug bust. I'd sure like to stick around and see it for myself, but I suppose Marvin's not up to that kind of adventure."

Gertie laid her suitcase on her bed and opened it. "I should think not. I don't know about you, but I'm not ready for a night in a jail cell. They might round up everyone here and haul them all off."

"No. I bet they don't have more than one or two jail cells in a Podunk place like this," Edna said. "They'll grab that guy Marvin bunks with and maybe a few others who bought the stuff if they can even prove it happened. I bet everyone goes scot-free tomorrow. Too bad for Bert though. He hoped this weekend would build the business, and now they'll get a bunch of bad press."

Gertie looked thoughtful, her head tipped and one hand on her hip. "You know, as crazy as things are today, this might turn out to be a boost for Colorado Pines. People will hear the story and remember the name. They say everything turns out for the best, and maybe bad press today will turn into good publicity in the future."

She pulled her garments out of the closet and folded them carefully as she packed her bag.

"Get a move on, Gertie. You can deal with the wrinkles in your clothes when we get home. We need to get out of Dodge if we want to avoid the hoosgow." Edna grabbed her suitcase and her jacket and headed out the door.

CHAPTER TEN

Marvin drove cautiously through the Village but put his foot down on the pedal once they reached the highway. They hadn't gone half a mile when they saw the Sheriff's car heading toward them at breakneck speed. His siren blared and the lights on top of the vehicle flashed. A dusty pickup followed closely behind.

"Looks like we got out in the nick of time," Edna said. "Dang, it would have been kinda fun to see how they do it. I wonder if they'll round up everyone in one place and then lower the boom?"

"I don't care how they do it, I'm just glad we're heading in the opposite direction." Gertie's voice sounded tired and a bit grumpy.

Boyd leaned forward from his seat in the back and said, "I can't believe Wanda ratted to her husband. 'Course drugs are bad, but still, she should want the ranch to do good, and poor Bert is gonna take the blame for this."

Floyd nodded and said, "Yeah, and I still wonder why she never told us she was married. That girl was about the most perfect woman I've ever set eyes on." He paused and squinted. "But she would've caused trouble between me and you, Boyd. We couldn't both have her unless ..." He considered a moment. "... unless she had a twin. We never asked her about that, or a sister at least. Guess now we'll never know."

Gertie grinned at the interchange. "You boys. We'll have to get you on a dating site when we get home."

"That's a great idea." Edna perked up and started listing all the benefits of online dating. "You fill out your information so the folks on the site can get to know you, and you can weed out the losers. You can see what they look like before you meet them—you can say what you're looking for—"

"Sounds a lot like what we did for the Singles cruise, don't it? And we all know how that turned out." Boyd leaned back in his seat. "I'm gonna take a nap."

"That's a good idea. We got to drive a while before we hit any restaurants. Looks like lunch will be late." Marvin sounded glum too. "And just so everyone knows, I feel bad about this whole thing. Guess *free* was too good to be true."

Edna patted his shoulder. "Don't worry about a thing. We'll chalk this up to another adventure for the Posse. I mean, how many folks get to channel Sonny and Cher these days?"

"Or escape a drug bust?" Gertie added. She rifled through the bag at her feet. "I think I'll read a bit of my memoir. I never did get a chance to relax and read by the river."

Edna yawned. "Sounds like about as much fun as watching paint dry." And she closed her eyes for a snooze too.

Marvin had the radio turned to country, and George Strait was begging his girl to run home from Dallas. The entire Posse slept except for him, and he was trying to figure out if the knot in his stomach was from guilt or hunger.

Edna roused and let a slow smile spread over her face at the sweet strains of the song. "Oh, man. George, what a guy. Now there's a *real* cowboy, not like that skinny runt of a wrangler back at the ranch."

Marvin grunted in response and pulled off the road into a strip mall that offered both a fast- food joint and a family diner. He waited for the Posse to wake up.

"Where are we? I could eat a horse." Edna stretched and bumped into Gertie in the process. Gertie's glasses were still on, and her book lay open in her lap.

"Guess I fell asleep," she said.

"Yeah, your book must have been riveting."

Gertie opened her mouth to argue, but the twins beat her to it. "Let's get out and eat," Boyd said.

"Yeah, I'm starving," Floyd added. "You girls gotta get out before we can move."

"Okay, hold your horses," Edna said and opened the side door. She looked at the two food options. "I vote for the diner. We can use the restrooms, and we can eat something besides a burger if we want."

They all tramped into the diner and found a nice corner booth with ample elbow room. The girls hurried off to the bathrooms while the guys ordered water all around.

Marvin read through the menu. "Everything sounds good. Think I'll get a chili burger. It should stick to my ribs until we get home."

Boyd looked up from his menu. "Thought we'd be staying at the Bide a Wee again. That was a right nice place, and we could enjoy one more campfire before heading back to feeding turkeys."

"I thought about it but figured you all were tired of this trip after all the trouble. Let's see what the girls think."

Edna and Gertie returned and slid into their places in the booth. "Hope the food is nicer than the johns in this dump." Edna grabbed a menu and began to read.

"I'm quite hungry," Gertie said. "I think I'll have a French dip sandwich with fries. I'll have to get back on a healthier regime when we get home."

"Speaking of that …" Marvin eyed the girls and continued, "Me and the twins were wondering if you want to drive all the way home tonight or stop at the Bide a Wee again. I know it'll cost more money, but … what do you think?"

Gertie returned her menu to the spot behind the salt and pepper. "I enjoyed the Bide a Wee. I'd like to stop there again if they have vacancies. Maybe we'd need to call them. What about you, Edna?"

"I'm game for staying there. We'd be overtired by the time we got back to Marvin's, and then we'd have another hour and a half to get home. I vote we stop if there's room."

Marvin nodded. "Okay, it's settled. I'll call right after we eat."

The Posse sat around a crackling fire while strains of "Red River Valley" faded into the evening calm. Only the five of them had enjoyed the setting, plus the guy with the guitar, who said his 'good nights' and disappeared into the office.

"That was lovely," Gertie spoke in a hushed tone. "Music has a peaceful effect on me. Makes me believe human beings can be better than we usually are."

Marvin leaned a bit closer to Edna. "Me too. I'm not one to play music when I'm home. Maybe I should start. Give me something to think about when I'm bored."

Edna stretched and made to get up, but Gertie stopped her. "Before we call it a night, I think we should take some time to process our weekend at the ranch. We're all a bit disappointed, I know, but let's try to think of five good things that happened, one from each of us. We need to be thankful for something every day, so I'll begin. "I loved our horseback ride and the beauty of the countryside along the river. I'll remember that after we get home."

The rest of the Posse took some time to think.

Finally, Boyd spoke up. "I guess I'm glad I met Wanda. It's good to know there's nice, kind women in the world, even if she was taken."

"Yup," Floyd added. "Wanda was the main thing for me besides the good grub. She works hard and doesn't complain, and she takes time to talk with folks. I appreciated that."

Marvin had let his arm settle around Edna's waist and gave her a squeeze. "I'm kinda glad we had Posse time again. When we left the cruise, I wasn't sure I'd ever hear from all of you again. I was real glad when I got the round-robin. So, thanks for the time together, even if we did have to run for our lives."

Everyone laughed, and Edna gathered her thoughts. "You all know I wanted to experience real ranch life. I wanted to ride like the rodeo gals and find a nice, tall cowboy and all of that. But I'll tell you what made my weekend—Gertie belting out the Janis Joplin song in front of all those people. I laugh out loud every time I think of it, and it takes me back to our high-school days when Gertie learned to stand up for herself—come out of her shell. That's what I'm gonna remember."

Gertie let that sink in for a bit. Then she said, "I do have my moments." And she smiled sweetly at each Posse member in turn.

"Well, time to turn in," Boyd said, and Floyd stood too.

Gertie said her goodnights and turned to wait for Edna, but Edna was listening to Marvin whisper something in her ear. She headed to her room alone. The twins ambled off too, leaving Edna and Marvin by the fire.

Marvin shuffled his feet around and sighed a time or two. "It's near impossible to find a time to talk to you—just the two of us."

"Yeah, well the Posse sticks close to each other. I like that." Edna suspected what was coming, and she tried to keep the tone light.

"Dang it, Edna, you know I'm no good at this. I always say the wrong thing. But we got some sort of close there at the campfire at the ranch, and you didn't act like I got the plague. You sort of cozied up too."

Edna took her time answering. "It felt nice. You know, to have someone sitting close and an arm around my shoulder. I don't want you to read anything into that."

Marvin sat quietly, staring at his shoes. "We both know what it's like to be alone. And sometimes it stinks. In fact, most of the time it stinks. I talk too much about Anna, but she was my whole life for all those years, and now I rattle around in the house all alone, and sometimes I want to scream just to hear a sound."

"Yeah. It's why I get out and about most of the time. Can't stand to sit in the apartment by myself." Edna snuck a peek at Marvin and saw the grim look on his face. "But hey, you and me, we can be good friends. Despite my big talk about finding a man, I'm not ready to jump into anything yet. Maybe never. That rat of a second husband of mine left me feeling like yesterday's leftovers. Don't think I'll ever get over it."

Marvin nodded. "I'm sorry that happened to you. You deserve better."

"Thanks." Edna reached out and patted his shoulder. "You're a good friend, Marvin. Can we leave it at that for now?"

He smiled a wistful, little smile. "Good friends don't grow on trees. Sure, I guess I can settle for that for now."

"And you can call and talk any time, you know. And maybe we could get together once in a while and have dinner or something. It's not far if we both drive halfway." Edna stopped to think before finishing. "It wouldn't be a date, exactly, but it would be nice to spend time with someone. It would be something to look forward to when the nights get long." She looked to see how Marvin reacted to this offer.

"That sounds nice. To be honest, I don't know if I'm ready to jump into a real love thing either, but I hate being alone. Maybe we can be alone together ... if you know what I mean." He grinned at her.

"All righty then. We got a deal. Good friends and maybe once a month get-togethers." Edna jumped up and put out her hand for a handshake.

"Aw, for goodness' sake, Edna. This deserves better than a handshake." And he grabbed her and squeezed her once before she could reply.

EPILOGUE

Edna grabbed her phone and found Gertie in her favorites. She dialed. "Hey, Gertie. How you doin' this morning? Did ya get some sleep? I did, I conked out as soon as my head hit the pillow."

Gertie's voice came back faint and scratchy. "I slept well, but I could have slept longer if you hadn't called so early."

"Oh, sorry. I guess it *is* only 7:00. Anyhow, do you want to meet up for coffee later? Maybe give us both time to unpack first. Hey, we did it again, girlfriend. We had ourselves a great, big, fat adventure."

"We certainly did. I'm not sure my heart can take many more of these little adventures of yours."

"Aw, you had a good time, and you know it. It's not every day a person gets to channel Janis Joplin then escape just ahead of a drug bust."

Gertie laughed. "You're right, I suppose. And before we get too far away from the details of the trip, what's the news with you and Marvin?"

"Nothing, really. We just decided since we're both lonely at times and both free as birds, we'll get together—maybe once a month and have dinner or something. No big deal."

Gertie paused before answering. "That sounds nice, and I think it is a big deal. Even though you and Marvin had a little trouble at the beginning, he's a good man. And good men aren't easy to find, as we both know."

"Yeah, you're right," Edna admitted. "Okay, see you about 10:30 at the Coffee Clatch?"

"Sounds good. And, thanks, Edna for getting me out and about. I think I'm becoming a little bolder with each trip. We did have a good time at the Ranch, didn't we?"

Edna's mouth widened into a huge smile. "That we did, my friend. That we did.

About the Author

[Insert Pic]

Jan Pierce, MEd, is a retired teacher and reading specialist. She also holds a certificate in Pastoral Care to Women. She began writing in 2007 and is a member of Oregon Christian Writers and Willamette Writers.

Jan writes devotional material, parenting and grandparenting articles and loves to send her favorite ladies, Edna and Gertie, on wacky adventures.

She resides in the beautiful Pacific Northwest with her husband of fifty-five years. Jan loves the ocean, reading, playing tennis and gardening. She is extremely partial to her two children, their spouses, and her four grandsons.

Jan says, "In all of my writing, I strive to both inform and encourage. I want my writing to reflect the goodness to be found in each day. Edna and Gertie are good for each other, and ... they make us laugh."

ABOUT THE AUTHOR

Jan Pierce, MEd, is a retired teacher and reading specialist. She also holds a certificate in Pastoral Care to Women. She began writing in 2007 and is a member of Oregon Christian Writers and Willamette Writers.

Jan writes devotional material, parenting and grandparenting articles and loves to send her favorite ladies, Edna and Gertie, on wacky adventures.

She resides in the beautiful Pacific Northwest with her husband of fifty-five years. Jan loves the ocean, reading, playing tennis and gardening. She is extremely partial to her two children, their spouses, and her four grandsons.

Jan says, "In all of my writing, I strive to both inform and encourage. I want my writing to reflect the goodness to be found in each day. Edna and Gertie are good for each other, and ... they make us laugh."

Made in United States
Orlando, FL
05 July 2022

19450602R00163